Praise for Ward Just and

AN UNFINISHED SEASON

"Ward Just has established himself as one of the most accomplished and admirable American writers of his time. With *An Unfinished Season,* he puts an exclamation point on that . . . On all counts a splendid piece of work: leisurely in pace and meditative in tone, as is much of Just's writing, but also emotionally freighted, witty and sophisticated, and powerfully evocative . . . It seems to me that Just has never been so observant as he is here, and that his prose has never been so layered and rich . . . A beautiful, wise book."
— *Washington Post Book World*

"Stunning." — *USA Today*

"In the pantheon of expert fictional observers of the Western political scene, Ward Just is both the most American and arguably the least recognized. Perhaps this is because his vision of the people who run the world on our behalf is, for all their conventionality, the most profoundly subtle and, in its insight, the most radical."
— *Los Angeles Times Book Review*

"A moving and beautiful reminiscence of a time of great change."
— *Christian Science Monitor*

"Rich . . . tightly wrought . . . one of Just's finest novels."
— *Seattle Times*

"[Just writes] with the same fascination for the levers of political power that Scott Fitzgerald had for wealth."
— *San Diego Union-Tribune*

"Just's most trenchant read to date." — *Village Voice*

"[Just's] writing is old-fashioned in the finest sense — graceful, articulate, full." — *The Economist*

"Ward Just is one of the country's finest novelists." — *Baltimore Sun*

"Every Chicagoan understands how fractured and stratified the city is, but only the best writers can articulate it as well as Just does here . . . another reminder that Just quietly resides among the A-list of living writers . . . In its intelligence and range, *An Unfinished Season* proves itself fit for the city's canon." — *Chicago Sun-Times*

BOOKS BY WARD JUST

An
UNFINISHED
SEASON

WARD JUST

A MARINER BOOK

HOUGHTON MIFFLIN COMPANY

BOSTON · NEW YORK

For Sarah

---

and for two friends of fifty years,

Bunny Carney Heuer and

Ann Terry Pincus

First Mariner Books edition 2005

Copyright © 2004 by Ward Just

All rights reserved

For information about permission to reproduce selections
from this book, write to Permissions, Houghton Mifflin Company,
215 Park Avenue South, New York, New York 10003.

Visit our Web site: www.houghtonmifflinbooks.com.

Library of Congress Cataloging-in-Publication Data is available.

ISBN 0-618-56828-X (PBK.)
ISBN 0-618-03669-5

Printed in the United States of America

MP 10 9 8 7 6 5 4 3 2 1

Book design by Melissa Lotfy

An excerpt from this book appeared in *Five Points*.

QUARTERDAY

1

T HE WINTER of the year my father carried a gun for his
own protection was the coldest on record in Chicago.
The winter went on and on, blizzard following blizzard,
each day gray with a fierce arctic wind. The canyons of the Loop
were deserted, empty as any wasteland, the lake an unquiet pile
of ice beyond. Trains failed, water pipes cracked, all northern
Illinois was locked in, the air as brittle as a razorblade. The
newspaper story that had everyone talking was the account of a
young colored woman found frozen solid in an alley on the
South Side and taken at once to the city morgue, where an alert
doctor discovered the faintest of heartbeats. She was revived,
thawed as you would thaw a frozen piece of meat, and in the
course of the subsequent examination was found to have so
much gin in her veins that—"Jeez, it was like she had swallowed
antifreeze," the doctor said. Religious leaders, ignoring the lurid details in the papers, declared her survival a miracle. She
was a young woman touched by the hand of the son of God. Jesus had visited Chicago and saved the humblest and most desti-
tute of his creatures, praise the Lord.

Happened all the time when I was a boy, my father said.

Some poor bastard wandered away, got lost, passed out,
froze to death.

Happened to our neighbor. They didn't find him for a week.

We didn't have morgues out here. And the doctor was twenty miles away.

My father was born on a farm on the prairie north of Chicago and insisted that this winter was nothing compared to the winters he had endured as a boy, interminable winters when the snow reached to the eaves of the roof; and when the western wind from the plains blew away the snow, the icicles remained, icicles as thick as your arm. My father had an imaginative memory stacked with stories and often different versions of the same story. One time he had the wind howling like wolves and another time wolves howling like the wind. When he told his stories, my mother always rolled her eyes and winked at me. We lived in his family's homestead, except now it had nine large rooms instead of six small ones, and where the barn had stood, an emerald lawn with oval flower beds and a great oak so broad two men could not reach their arms around it. The house was on the grounds of a newly minted golf club in a township that was unincorporated but known informally as Quarterday, meaning that in the previous century it took a quarter of a day to reach Half Day, itself half a day's ride to Chicago. Tell someone from the North Shore that you lived in Quarterday and you got a condescending smile because to the suburban gentry it was nowheresville, a common flatland of family farms and a few estates and the newly minted golf club, a crossroads with a drugstore, a market, and a gas station, the unfashionable western point of a triangle whose eastern points were Lake Forest and Winnetka. What do people do out there anyhow? What do they see in it? The suburban gentry associated Quarterday with one-room schoolhouses, pheasant shooting in the cornfields, hayrides in the moonlight, and the annual agricultural fair. Something unsettled about it, a place that never developed. There were rumors of gambling in the roadhouse down the highway from the club, the roadhouse owned and operated by Italian interests from Chicago.

The sixth green of the golf course was visible from our terrace. Between the terrace and the fairway was a shallow pond shaped like an eyelid and fringed with high-crowned sycamore trees,

4

and among the trees swaybacked metal chairs. That was where my father went each evening when he returned home from work, duckwalking in his skates, his long stick over his shoulder, huge in pads and decades-old leather gloves, a worn green jersey (the number 33 still distinct on the back), and a black wool balaclava. He had installed arc lights in the trees so that the pond was brilliantly lit, the cage with its floppy net at one end. My father stood quietly a moment, breathing deeply, his breath pluming in the frigid air. Most nights the ice was covered by an inch or more of snow, which he cleared with a wide-bladed shovel, skating patiently from the edges of the eyelid to the center until the surface was clear. Then he opened the small duffel he carried and scattered half a dozen pucks on the ice, using a sidearm motion as if he were skipping stones over water. And then he would step gingerly onto the ice and begin to skate in earnest, long powerful strokes around the pond, tapping the stick on the ice to some mysterious rhythm. Then he would rotate and skate backward, his elbows close to his body, his knees churning. He looked as indestructible as a truck. After a few minutes of warm-up, he would execute a sweeping curve and take the puck up the ice, nudging it gently as if it were an eggshell, swiveling left and right, his head high, and at the last moment fire the puck into the net. He rarely took a slap shot. Slap shots hinted at desperation and he believed in patience and thorough preparation. Due diligence, he called it. It was easy to imagine the defensemen he eluded, confused opponents scrambling to check him or steal the puck. My father did not stop until all six pucks were in the net and at that time he took one, two, three victory laps, skating as fast as he could around the perimeter of the pond, his stick held high above his head, hearing the tick-tick-tick of the stick striking the bare branches of the sycamores. I imagine he was remembering his days at Dartmouth College, captain of the almost-undefeated hockey team in his senior year. He was fifty now, his hair thinning and his waistline spreading, nearsighted behind wire-rimmed glasses. On the ice, he looked twenty years younger. I watched all this from my desk in my second-floor bedroom, schoolbooks piled around me, my father's athletic skill a momentary distraction from European history, art appreciation, and Spanish. Everyone said we looked alike, but I didn't believe it. The photograph on my desk showed an outdoorsman, a few years older than I am now, burly in a Dartmouth letter sweater. I am taller than he is, and thin, an indoor man. When they say I look like him, they mean our mannerisms are similar, the way we walk, our gestures, and our voices.

From the pond my father could see the lane that meandered around the club grounds. There was little traffic in January, most of our neighbors in the South somewhere, Florida or one of the Caribbean islands. When my father saw a car's headlights, his pace would slow and he would follow the lights until they were lost to view; and if the car hesitated for any reason, he would move to the shadows of the pond, out of the bright lights and into the sycamore grove, where he would wait in one of the swaybacked metal chairs, the duffel beside him out of sight. He removed his gloves and placed them beside the duffel while he waited. When the car disappeared, my father would emerge from the shadows and resume his practice, puck after puck fired into the net, and then the victory laps, ending always in a defiant spray of ice when he came to a full stop. After an hour of this, the arc lights blinked twice, my mother's signal that she was preparing cocktails. Practice was over. Time to come in. Time to shower and say hello to the family. I knew she had been watching him from the French doors that opened onto the terrace from the den, trim in slacks and a sweater, an ascot at her throat; of course she was worried, and I imagined her hand moving in a tentative wave, though she knew he could not see her, so complete was his concentration. He always took two final laps, and when he removed the balaclava you noticed his damp hair and the sweat on his forehead, his face flushed, smiling broadly—and as he stood, his chest heaving in the bath of bright lights, you could almost hear the applause. When he took a last reluctant look around, I knew he was remembering himself as a boy on the same pond, those interminable winters when the icicles were as thick as your arm, vibrating from the howls of the wolves on the prairie. The prairie swept away in low undulating swells like a great inland ocean, the soil unimaginably rich, everything else inhospitable. The horizon line was out of reach. And then it seemed overnight Chicago's sprawl defeated the farmland. Roads replaced wagon tracks. The golf course arrived. My father stood on the ice, shimmying on his skates, looking at the fairway in the darkness, remembering that a barn once stood there stark against the empty sky and beyond it cornfields for miles and miles. In such a landscape a human being was diminished. You knew your place.

Then he fetched his duffel and duckwalked back into the house, where minutes later I heard the rattle of ice cubes and a companionable round of laughter before their voices lowered and I knew he was telling my mother about the events of his day, how it began and how it ended and everything in between. How things had gone at the office, and when the crisis would be over.

It was not over in the spring. The weather changed. The pond's ice melted in late March and I was no longer able to watch my father skate. I missed the evening interlude, looking up from my books, watching him step onto the ice, his spirits visibly rising in the frigid air, arms high above his head, his speed increasing with each lap, skating in a zone of absolute privacy. I watched most carefully when he saw a car's headlights and moved into the shadows, lowering himself into one of the swaybacked chairs, his hand bare on the crimson duffel at his feet. That was where he kept the gun, a long-barreled Colt .32, the identical model favored by gangsters in B movies, a sinister accessory along with a fedora and a trenchcoat. The revolver was a gift from his friend Tom Felsen, the county sheriff. Tom Felsen had an arsenal in his office at the courthouse, firearms that had been used in the commission of crimes. The long-barreled Colt was a murder weapon, exhibit A in a case that involved a poker game, a quart of whiskey, and an unmarried woman. The sheriff and my father had been best friends in grade school and hell-raisers together in high school and each had been an usher at the other's wedding, though they no longer saw one another "socially," as my mother said. They had taken different paths in life, beginning when my father went away to college in the East and his classmate stayed home. Tom and his wife lived quietly in one of the new subdivisions out near Mundelein, their life together circumscribed by the complexities of county law enforcement and Tom's political ambitions; he wanted to run for the state legislature and needed my father's financial backing. In any case, the Felsens did not belong to the country club, the center of my parents' social life. My father and Tom Felsen spoke on the telephone almost every day, and two or three nights a week the sheriff insisted on escorting my father home from work, meeting him at the office and following him to the club entrance but no farther.

PRIVATE CLUB
MEMBERS AND GUESTS
HOMEOWNERS ONLY

My father always motioned for Tom to come along and have a drink but he never did. He dipped his lights once, gave a little whine of his siren, and was gone.

Deprived of his ice hockey, my father arrived home a little later each evening, his arrival announced by two short toots on the horn of his Oldsmobile. He put his overcoat and the duffel in the coat closet and joined my mother for their evening drink, now more often two drinks; and their conversation ended when I entered the room. I felt like the walk-on who had wandered onto a stage set from the wings, the actors momentarily at a loss, in their surprise and confusion forgetting their lines—until one or the other smiled or laughed falsely, suddenly remembering the cue. How was my homework coming along? Did you finish your history paper, the one you worked on all last weekend? What was the grade?

That's good, Wils.

That's very good.

But I wish you didn't spend all your life with books.

There's more to life than homework.

Book-smart's one thing. Nothing wrong with book-smart. But books only take you so far when you're in a jam.

After this interval my mother would comment on the events of her day, a trip to the hairdresser's and a call from her father (they spoke nearly every day), an invitation to dinner on the weekend, harmless gossip concerning the so-and-sos who wanted *very badly* to join the club, but perhaps not this year. There were so many new members now it was hard to keep them straight, their names and the names of their children, and what he did. Where do they come from anyhow?

My mother sat on the davenport and my father in the leather chair, the one with the reading lamp and the footstool, a Munnings sporting print on the wall behind him, the phonograph playing softly, usually Benny Goodman or Eddy Duchin. My father was irritable most nights and his irritability increased with the second cocktail, overflowing when I entered the room. He was disappointed in my refusal to participate in team sports, football in the fall, ice hockey in the winter, and baseball in the spring. He believed in team sports, so important in building lasting friendships. Team play was what made America the great country that it was, cooperation and teamwork, teamwork and team spirit, a common effort leading always to success. You played as a team for the team, a philosophy that endured for a lifetime. You couldn't run a business without teamwork, focusing always on *product*. Do you want to be a loner your whole life? Teamwork built character. Wars were won on the playing fields of youth, he said; and when I replied that the expression was English and the word was "Eton" and it hadn't helped them much in World War One—my history instructor had assigned an essay on Siegfried Sassoon's *Memoirs of an Infantry Officer* and I was caught up with the futility of life in the trenches of the Somme, a melancholy hopelessness that was attractive to a nineteen-year-old living on the grounds of a golf club north of Chicago—my father told me not to get fresh with *him*, that I didn't know the score and would never know the score without knowing teamwork. Teamwork and team spirit and hard knocks that led to lasting friendships and success in the world generally.

And as I recall, he said, the English won the war.

Not according to Sassoon, I muttered, not quite loud enough for him to hear.

With the help of Pershing and the Americans, my father added. God damn Europeans never could've done it alone.

My mother said mildly, Now, Teddy, that's harsh. Everyone

9

has to find their own way. Not everyone—and here she smiled fractionally as Eddy Duchin ran off a silky riff—has a taste for the locker room, as you do. Wils is a fine student. Can't we let it go at that? It's not his fault—

It's not good to be a loner, my father said.

Wils was out for *a year*, my mother said. Hard knocks enough for anyone, she said slyly, nodding at me. I had had a mysterious illness in the eighth grade, diagnosed first as scarlet fever, then as pneumonia. Finally the doctors admitted they didn't know what it was but that I probably wouldn't die of it. Meanwhile, I was bedridden with a high fever and hallucinations that accompanied the fever. My legs ached. I lost weight and lay for days in a kind of dreamless torpor. From my hospital window I watched the crowns of the trees change color, the leaves brittling, vanishing one by one; and then they were gone. I was uncomfortably aware of my own body, my skin slack, the muscles made of putty. I had the idea that my body was betraying me, and that I was divided against myself. During the worst of it my parents would appear at my bedside, their faces huge and indistinct; they would murmur something and go away. They stood in the doorway with the doctor, talking in whispers, and my mother would cover her eyes and go into the corridor while my father and the doctor talked man-to-man, the doctor's hand on my father's shoulder while he made his explanations. I was in the hospital for six weeks, then quarantined at home in bed for four months. I devoted myself to books and jazz music on the phonograph, except in the afternoon when I listened to soap opera on the radio, the backstage wife and the woman who was married to the richest and most handsome lord in England, though these romantic deep-voiced men rarely made an appearance. The backstage wife and the lord's lady led turbulent emotional lives in which housework did not figure, so there was time to solve the many misunderstandings that plagued the household. Illness was often present and toward dusk it was with relief that I turned to *Terry and the Pirates* and the other thrillers. I discovered that no one wanted to be around a sick person, and not only for fear of contagion. Something medieval about it, an evil spirit that could leap from one body to another without warning. When the quarantine was lifted, my friends would come to visit and never knew what to say to me except that I was different somehow, and hard to reach. What was it like in the hospital? What do they do to you there? We lived in different worlds. I began to think of my sick year as a vanished year, and the next year my friends were in the ninth grade and I was a year behind. I had learned that I did not mind being by myself, even if my self was divided. My hearing became acute, the smallest sound or the whisper of a conversation audible to me as I lay in my bed. My father thought my contentment unnatural, and let me know it.

Loners lose, he said.

Teddy, my mother said, her voice rising an octave.

A father can speak his mind to his own son, he said.

Wils was *sick*, my mother said again.

And now he's well, my father said.

When she retired to the kitchen to see about dinner, my father turned to the evening news. This was the month Hollywood personalities were testifying before the House Committee on Un-American Activities, Communist influence in the entertainment industry. The enemy within, it was called. Quarterday was on the margins of effective television reception from Chicago, so the picture was erratic, the screen mottled with visual static, "snow," so that Chairman Velde and his committee appeared as phantoms. The witness was a phantom, too, an actor unknown to me but very well known to the prewar American Communist underground; he had since left the party but was happy to name colleagues he had seen at meetings. The quality of the sound began to fail, the hearing suddenly a flickering pantomime; and then Chairman Velde's gavel crashed and the screen went black for a moment. My father nursed his drink while he listened to the news and then, in a gesture of reconciliation, asked me if I wanted a beer. I drank a glass of Pabst while he sat hunched in his leather chair, his eyes half shut, watching the pantomime. The line of muscles in his jaw worked to and fro, and all the while he was muttering, mostly to himself but partly to me, "Bastards . . . lowlifes." Artists, they called themselves, but they had no loyalties, not to their art, not to their

11

country, not even to each other. They called themselves intellectuals but they'd sell their mothers for a dime and a film credit. Listen to them, he said, they talk like politicians, up one side and down the other. They did not have respect for a committee of the Congress going about its lawful business. It was alien influence, an unwholesome, un-American influence. The country was in a hell of a mess, altogether better off if both coasts were amputated and allowed to drift away, the East in the direction of Soviet Russia and the West to Red China, allowing the heartland to manage its own affairs.

Then I wouldn't be in the fix I'm in, my father said.

At dinner that night I asked my father if Tom Felsen intended to run for the legislature this election or wait for the next. And if he ran, would he make a good candidate? Tom's sound, my father replied. A small-government man, all for a balanced budget and lower taxes, a practical approach to things. Whether he's a good campaigner, we'll have to wait and see. Probably it won't matter because he knows where the bodies are buried. Obviously he has the sheriff's department behind him, so he begins with a solid base. Deputies know how to get out the vote. That's why they're deputies, he added with a smile. But he's a good friend. I'll support him.

He's been a good friend to you, my mother said.

He's gone above and beyond the call. Tom's staunch. He's the man to have on our side.

Loyal, my mother said.

You don't want him on your wrong side.

Why not? I asked.

My father paused before answering, and when he did he lowered his voice as if he feared being overheard. Tom can be— rough, he said. Tom's no-nonsense. Tom flies into the boards with his stick high.

My mother raised her eyebrows and looked at me. She said, Your father says that Tom Felsen keeps the lid on.

He nodded. There's an unsavory element here, like everywhere else. Tom keeps things in check. He's broken the rules, that's for sure.

Rules? I said.

Whatever do you mean? my mother asked.

My father had grown expansive, enjoying the story. He pushed his chair back from the table and grinned as one does when disclosing an unsettling secret. He said, Tom knows their plans. The how and the when and the where. And when my mother looked at him strangely, my father steepled his fingers and looked across the table to the wall opposite, a hunting scene from the eighteenth century, supercilious Frenchmen in plumed hats accompanied by wolfhounds, chasing a stag through a country park, the scene repeated every few yards around the room. The glass chandelier cast little broken shards of light; and at the kitchen door, the Frenchmen, the wolf-hounds, and the stag vanished.

He listens in to them, my father said at last.

Listens in?

We can talk about it later, he said.

There's cake in the kitchen, my mother said to me.

Cut a slice for me, too, my father said with a bemused smile. He continued to stare at the French dandies on horseback, waiting while I rose from the table and retreated to the kitchen, where he mistakenly believed I was out of earshot.

Tom's tapped their phones, he said.

Oh, dear, my mother said.

So he listens in. And shares the information.

With you, she said.

With me, he replied. I think he has some help. Someone at the FBI owes him a favor. He's listening to them day and night, two deputies on the phones full-time. Calls between the national headquarters and the local here. Pretty rough stuff, what they say to each other. My father paused there and lowered his voice. If I could find a way to split them, to make our boys see that the national's just a bunch of left-wing troublemakers, don't have their best interests at heart, well, then, this strike would be over in a week. My father paused again and I imagined him staring across the table at the Frenchmen on their high-stepping horses and wondering what they were doing in his dining room. He said, The national sees my business as a test case. Win here, they win everywhere. They're dug in for the duration. As long as it takes. They're cocky as hell. They think I'll throw in the towel, just give them whatever they damn want on a silver platter, same's Roosevelt did at Yalta. That bastard Hiss. Same thing exactly. So it'll go on for a while.

I returned with two plates of cake.

My father said, Did you hear any of that?

Some, I said. Not much.

Forget what you heard.

I heard you say it'll go on for a while.

It will, he said. How long's hard to say. As long as it takes. As long as they have their strike fund. And if their morale doesn't crack. You know the secret weapon, when you're management and there's a strike? It's the women. Mama goes a few months pinching pennies for groceries, the old man hanging around the house drinking beer and bitching because the kids're crying and there's dirty laundry everywhere and he's gone most evenings to a union meeting and comes back smelling of more beer. Drives the women crazy, their husbands underfoot all day long. So they'll settle eventually. They'll settle because their wives'll make them settle.

I couldn't stand you around the house all day long, my mother said.

No chance of that, my father said. I'll never retire. And when you own the company, you don't go on strike.

I said tentatively, Are you worried?

He moved his head, neither yes nor no. He was picking at a slice of chocolate cake, edging it around the plate as if it were a hockey puck, apparently thinking through the answer to my question. Then he looked up suddenly, rising from the table and striding into the den, where he stood rigidly at the French doors leading to the terrace. He was looking across the terrace to the pond and the fairway beyond the pond and the green, rising in the moonlight. I thought I saw something, he said. Something moving. He flicked the switch that illuminated the arc lights in the trees surrounding the pond. Then he switched them off and darkness returned.

He said, You can't be too careful.

Maybe when this is over we can take a trip, my mother said.

No one wins a strike, my father said.

A second honeymoon, my mother went on. She had a dreamy look, staring fondly at my father. The Caribbean, Havana. One of the boats that leaves from New Orleans. We could spend a day or two in New Orleans, dinner at Antoine's—

That's what gets lost sight of, my father said.

—and then a week in Havana. We could go from Havana to Curaçao. Dancing every night with an orchestra, black tie. Teddy, it would be such fun. Get away from this for a while. It's been such a long time for us, a vacation.

All that production lost, you never make it up. Wages lost, revenues lost because your customers don't think they can depend on you to deliver. Rumors everywhere, none of them to your advantage. Teddy Ravan's bust, his firm's down the drain, you can't count on Teddy. So your customers begin to trade with the competition, and your competition is only too happy to oblige. It's business after all. The business has to go somewhere. These idiots talk about class solidarity but there is no class solidarity, on my side or their side, either. And you and the people who work for you are divided, suddenly on opposite sides of the ring, gloves off, no referee. Loyalty vanishes, and men you've known for years, you know the names of their wives and their children, they turn their backs because they see you as their enemy. The atmosphere's poisoned, and some mornings you just hate to go to work. The bad blood can last for a generation.

Will you think about it? my mother asked.

Some business you lose, never comes back. And some days you just wish to hell you'd never gotten into it.

The vacation? she said.

Just give it to them on a silver platter. Here, take the damned business, you run it, you think you're so smart.

I'd like it so much—

I'm sorry, what did you say? my father said.

To go away, just us two. You remember Havana, our honeymoon, the fun we had on the boat, we met that couple from Kansas City and played bridge in the afternoon and dined at the captain's table and then, our last day in Havana, we all went shopping together and you bought me the antique cigarette box.

It wasn't antique, my father said with a smile.

I want to go back, my mother said.

We'll see, my father replied.

I'll go *by myself* then, my mother said, but we both knew, my father and I, that she never would.

So much was out of sight, between the lines, a narrative vanishing like the Frenchmen on horseback where the wallpaper met the doorway. What remained was the last inch of feather on the Frenchman's hat. At nineteen you are bored witless by the family stories, the Havana honeymoon story and the others, varied according to the point being made and the response that was expected. Then suddenly, without notice, you learned how the world worked, Tom Felsen tapping telephones with the assistance of the FBI, a favor given for a favor received, Tom "rough" in his determination to keep the lid on, owing to the unsavory elements, present in Quarterday along with everywhere else; so he flew into the boards with his stick high, a good man to have on your side—and somehow all this had to do with my father's business and the strike. My father's misprision was breathtaking and he must have had some idea himself along those lines because when the specifics were announced, I had been banished to the kitchen. But I did not fail to notice my father implicitly comparing himself to Winston Churchill, heroically struggling to hold the line at Yalta while Franklin Roosevelt absentmindedly gave away half of Europe to the tyrant Stalin, thanks to that bastard Hiss. Naturally the presumption of it was comical; even at nineteen I found it comical. I was less amused at his martyred just-give-it-to-them-on-a-silver-platter conclusion; that was unworthy of him. Yet I knew without a doubt that my father had a hard-won understanding of how the world worked—and chose to dispense this knowledge with circumspection, a worldly Croesus distributing his wealth a dime at a time.

My father was preoccupied all that winter and spring, mostly silent at the dinner table, and later alone with a book until well into the evening. I watched him worry and he seemed to age before my eyes, settling into the peevish funk of an old man. I was watching him in order to learn what it was to be a man, with a man's burdens, how to behave in adversity. I assumed this meant acting from the center of yourself, discovering your own natural motion and in this discovery learning just how far apart it was from the world's natural motion, and how estranged you were likely to be. Would you and the world be on speaking terms? I knew that as a family we were on the outside of things, separated from each other and from the wider world, so mysterious and out of reach. At nineteen you inhabit a multitude of personalities, trying them on like hats, Siegfried Sassoon and Jake Barnes and Bogart and the great tactician Odysseus and Fats Waller and the bon vivant in chemistry class, all of them observed by the nurse in the nerves ward and Lady Brett and Ingrid Bergman and Calypso and Billie Holiday and the blond girl who bounced on the trampoline in the gym after school. Your father is the shadow of these multiple personalities, physically up close, his spirit far, far away. What animated *him* at nineteen? What lurid fiction has he made of his own early memories? Surely more than icicles as thick as your arm and the wind howling like wolves. Yet when my father said, "Sometimes you wish to hell you'd never gotten into it," he sounded as if he meant life itself.

At nineteen you dread the occasion of courage in the way the Catholic Church dreads the occasion of sin, and when the moment came it helped if you had an idea of how the world worked. What it valued and what it threw away. How much you could get away with. You knew that the gods—perverse, malignant, cunning, capricious—were perched in the trees like vultures, eager to pick apart the virtuous and the wicked alike. Even at nineteen you knew there were occasions of high complexity, come and gone in an instant; and that there was a choice to be made and you made it or didn't make it or made the wrong one, a consequence of the hat you wore that day. The films, the books, and my father hinted at the wider world, soon to be at hand, though perhaps not this year.

I had no idea what was in store—what goods were on the shelves and what birds were crowding the trees. Surely they would differ from my father's. Meanwhile, I tried to coax life itself in the way that Fats Waller coaxed a blue note from his piano never looking at his hands.

2

MY FATHER was five feet ten inches tall and wide at the chest, built like a stevedore with the unhurried stride of a farmer. He never looked entirely comfortable in city clothes. He never wore a hat. His heavy Goya face looked as if it belonged on an alcalde or other unsympathetic municipal official. My mother was quite beautiful, tall and slender as a fashion model. They made a striking couple, her eyes green against a luminous complexion, his two points of the blackest ink, wide-set in a weatherbeaten face. My father's bearing—you could almost say his "standing"—reinforced his ominous physical appearance. He was attractive to women because it looked as if he could handle himself and anyone else, and because he seemed to withhold so much. Women suspected, correctly, that he had a sentimental streak, something my mother had discovered years before on their honeymoon trip to Havana.

He had bought her a close-fitting ebony cigarette box decorated with a seventeenth-century Italian street scene etched in silver, Giacomo della Porta's palazzo for Prince Chigi in Piazza Colonna, Rome. The loving way he handled it made her think that he had actually bought it for himself, though, truth to tell, seventeenth-century Italian street scenes were not in his repertoire of interests, so far as she knew them. When she asked him about it, my father smiled and said he loved the tiny figures, the cavaliers in their flared jackets, the fountain, and the formality of the palazzo itself, five stories of princely living, each horizontal row of windows of a different size and shape so that it seemed to him that five separate floors had been laid one on top of the other like a stack of books on a bedside table. He thought it represented a world unto itself, all other worlds out of sight and out of mind, and so much to imagine of the interior of the princely stories, the bedrooms and the reception rooms, the dining rooms with their glittering chandeliers, the chandeliers no doubt as brittle as the conversations that went on beneath them.

And also, the box was beautifully constructed, airtight it seemed.

It feels good in your hand, he said, and went on to speculate what such a valuable object was doing in a nondescript shop on the Calle Obispo in Havana. He imagined it the last heirloom in the estate of an impoverished aristocrat, perhaps a descendant of Prince Chigi himself, exiled by a vengeful pope to the humid and undisciplined Caribbean, sea of hated English pirates. My mother listened to this aria with mounting exasperation and said at last, But you must have it for your desk at the office—and realized at once that she had offended him.

It's for you, he replied stiffly and then amended—a tactful amendment, for he had noticed her dismay—for *us,* for our bedroom or the cocktail table in the den, somewhere we can see it every day and remember Havana, our honeymoon. She was grateful for his diplomacy and said, Of course, what a good idea. With women generally, my father was courtly and always managed to ask questions that intrigued them. Do you ever wish you had been born in a different century, in a country different from our own? Could you ever have married an Italian from Italy and gone there to live, changing your citizenship, speaking Italian? My mother would watch his performance and roll her eyes, but she liked it exceedingly when she overheard a friend say, Doesn't Teddy Ravan have the most wonderful smile? Yes, my mother thought, and the more effective because he used it so seldom.

In a room full of people, your eyes went to him at once because of his actorly quality of stillness, his face immobile as iron. Of course people knew that our house had been his family's homestead and that his father had been a farmer but beyond that his early life was a mystery; not interesting, he said on the rare occasions he was asked, rising with the roosters and retiring with the hens. He seldom spoke of his childhood except for the unspecified adventures with Tom Felsen and the endless winters, the wind, and the wolves—fictitious wolves, I later discovered, wolves having disappeared from the northern Illinois prairie before he was born. However, the west wind was constant. I had the feeling that he and his father were at odds and I was not surprised, unable to imagine my father submitting to any authority except, conceivably, his mother's authority. Then, many years later, I discovered a book in his library, a birthday present many years before, my father to his father: "To the best dad a guy ever had." This was not his voice at all, and I imagined him hesitating over the inscription, finally writing swiftly in what I am certain was a flood of emotion. But what do I know of this? The childhood of our parents is forever inscrutable, the cave within the cave of our own. The light's too dim, the dancing shadows unreliable, fundamentally unstable, even the impromptu photographs and private letters somehow contrived. These years might as well have occurred in the sixteenth century, the salient facts etched on a cigarette box and sold at auction, the box moving from hand to hand, continent to continent, like Hammett's Maltese falcon. I was very young when my grandfather died, though I remember the flowers, the crowded church, the closed casket, and my father entirely composed and reading the eulogy in a gruff voice, his body rigid, a slight flutter of his hands the only show of emotion.

My father was trained as a lawyer. He got to Dartmouth on a scholarship endowed by an industrialist from Lake Forest. He got to law school the same way, and returned naturally to Illinois to practice. His father-in-law was eager for him to join a New York firm and offered to open the usual doors but my father turned him down without a thought; yet whenever he was irritated by some aspect of his business life he always said, I should have gone the hell to New York when I had the chance. "New York" in our family was code for the greener grass, the pot at the end of the rainbow, or the successful inside straight, though as a concept it brought only sarcasm from my disappointed mother. There was *no chance in this world* that your father would have gone to live in New York or any other foreign city; he's Illinois bred and born, and does not feel safe anywhere else. Illinois is his native soil, the prairie and the cornfields and the waving fields of grain and the wolves and so forth and so on, and Chicago. So it was inevitable, my mother said, that he would join a small Chicago firm, not one of the established La Salle Street concerns, but a grittier firm on the Far North Side whose founding partners were a retired circuit-court judge and his nephew, a former assistant state's attorney. Uncle and nephew practiced political law and hired my father to do other work, outside work that did not involve representations to City Hall, the City Council, the county Board of Supervisors, and the tax assessor's office. My father claimed that the Hollywood Avenue offices of Greenslat & Greenslat were a microclimate of Chicago justice, and in them he learned how the weather worked, how the rain was made, and how the rain was paid for, and which crops flourished and which didn't and why. Chicago was a lawyer's paradise.

Not a wife's paradise, my mother said.

The city was dirty. Not a tree. We lived a mile from the lake. I had time on my hands. God, I was lonely. Your father told me to be patient, that when we had a stake we would move to Quarterday, renovate his family's house, begin a family of our own. My father offered to help but Teddy didn't want his help. So we remained in Chicago for five years, saving what we could, your father dreaming of Quarterday. And then Andy came riding to our rescue.

Early in his practice, my father was retained by the owner of a suburban printing business, routine corporate work that included union negotiations. Andres Carillo had a knack for infuriating labor unions, and there were three of them at his plant in the western lakes region. My father excelled at labor law and eventually Andy Carillo asked him to join his board of directors, and then to give up private practice altogether and work full-time as general manager and counsel to the corporation. These discussions took place on Friday afternoons at the Arlington Park racetrack, where Andy had a box. My father was also a dedicated horseplayer, so he was happy to meet his client each Friday at noon, a fine lunch at the Post and Paddock and then the races, all the while talking business and horses. He always had a tip on a horse from Judge Greenslat; and later in his life my father loved to reminisce about his afternoons at the track, the smell of the turf, the excitement when the horses broke from the gate, everyone rising, fists in the air, an animal roar from the grandstand. Andy Carillo was a widower and childless and gave my father to understand that he would inherit the business "in due course," meaning upon Andy's death or retirement.

You're like a son to me, Andy told my father.

You're the reason this business is as successful as it is. You've kept the taxes low and the unions down.

And I like the way you bet, Andy went on. Study the field, study the odds, study the track, and go with your findings. Screw the hunches.

My father knew he was not a natural lawyer. He was too impatient, often tactless, and perhaps not clever enough. A sly business, he called the law, a business without *product*. The lawyer gave the client advice and the client made money on the advice while the lawyer received a retainer. He hated the expression "on retainer," as if he were someone's manservant. Of course the Greenslats always seemed to be part of whatever legal hocus-pocus they were engaged in, part of the deal, part of the profits—"the whole shoeshine," as Judge Greenslat said. But the judge's sort of law was not my father's sort of law, so he would always be "on retainer" and driving Chevrolets while the judge and his nephew drove Cadillacs.

I've been expecting this, can't say I haven't, the judge said when my father told him of Andy Carillo's offer. I suppose it wouldn't do any good if I offered you a piece of our action. Small piece, but still a piece.

My father shook his head, smiling because he liked the

judge, whom everyone called Butch. They were sitting in a tavern around the corner from the office.

I want to run my own show, my father said.

I'll help you with the contract, if you like.

We have a handshake, my father said.

Teddy, Teddy, Teddy—a handshake isn't worth batshit.

I know more about his business than he does, my father said.

You want money, don't you, Teddy?

I didn't think I did but it turns out that I do.

I like money, too. But I've always known that. How come you just figured it out?

My father remembered Butch Greenslat's eyes sliding away to watch the waitress bend at the waist to say something to one of the customers, her skirt riding above her knees, and her giving a little backward glance to their table, and Butch smiling, entirely engrossed. Butch had forgotten his own question, but my father answered it anyway. Because the way the world's going, you're not going to be able to do without it. If you don't have it, they'll walk all over you.

But always, Butch said, still watching the waitress, someone has more.

Oh, sure, my father said. But there are fewer of them.

So my father was quick to agree to Andy Carillo's proposal and Carillo Printing became Carillo & Ravan Printing, and when the old man had a stroke at the outbreak of the war, he was as good as his word, retiring to an apartment in Fort Lauderdale, returning only for the quarterly meetings of the board of directors. My father became chairman and president. He said he liked the noise of the presses and the smell of the ink and paper, the heavy stock he used for his stationery line. This was hard, dirty, and dangerous work. My father had dozens of small scars on his hands from splashes of hot lead and two broken toes when one of the heavy iron turtles ran over his foot. He had no use for white-collar chairmen who did not know the details of the business they were in. Clean-desk chairmen who sat in suites of offices guarded by secretaries. Chairmen who didn't like to get their hands dirty—and in fact he was delighted when he returned to his third-floor office with his white shirt streaked black with ink, evidence of a day's work. My father thought of his men as collateral members of his family and each Christmas everyone got a bonus, the sum calculated by a mysterious formula known only to him. Not every bonus was the same and so there was resentment, and when one day the foreman asked him about it, my father whirled and snarled, None of your business.

It's my money, my father said. I'll decide the bonus.

The foreman did not flinch. Clyde said, If that's the way you want it, Ted. But the men—

That's the way I want it, my father said. It's my business. Not their business.

I'll tell them that, Clyde said.

Tell them any god damned thing you want, my father said.

They won't like it, the foreman said. And bonuses aren't the only grievance. There's overtime and vacation time and the pension. We're not making progress at the table. And the contract expires end of the month. You're not around as much as you used to be. We were more comfortable when you were at the table in person, he said with an attempt at a smile.

I'm around as much as I need to be. My offer's fair and the men know it.

The men don't see it that way, Clyde said. They see themselves falling behind. And the national, they don't see it that way either.

Your national's in Philadelphia. What the fuck does Philadelphia know about conditions in Illinois? What does Philadelphia know about my business?

More than you think, Ted.

Your national wants a strike. Doesn't want a settlement, fair to both sides. Your national likes unrest, the more unrest the better. Put it to an honest vote, secret ballot. And when the ballots are counted, let's be certain neutral parties are present to verify the tally. I don't trust your bosses in Philadelphia. I don't like their politics. I don't like their threats.

I'll see they get the message, the foreman said.

That was the conversation as my father replayed it to my mother that night, my mother sitting on the davenport, her legs curled up beside her, reaching for the cigarette box and running her fingernail across the chased silver before lighting a Pall Mall and blowing a perfect smoke ring, her eyes focused on a Havana of the middle distance. My father, pacing in front of the fireplace, continued to complain about outsiders interfering with his business.

What's gotten into my men?

Teddy, my mother said. *Tranquilo.* You'll have a heart attack.

Bastards, he said. He thought he had gotten too close to them, too familiar, remembering the names of their wives and children, caring for them like members of his own family. And then he said something about making changes on the floor, and if it was outsiders they wanted, he had some outsiders of his own.

What outsiders, Teddy?

Strikebreakers, he said.

Scabs, I said.

We call them strikebreakers, my father said evenly.

Please, my mother said wearily. Enough. Stop it.

Strikebreakers, my father said again.

My mother threw down her cigarette and left the room, rushing upstairs, an act that surprised my father and me. The dishes were left undone.

When the weather turned at last, each evening around ten I put aside my schoolbooks, threw on a sweater, and slipped out of the house. I made my way in the darkness to the pond, sat in one of the swaybacked chairs, and smoked one cigarette after another, thinking of the life I would lead once I was free of Quarterday and my father, and when a girl would figure in this new life. September seemed years off and I did not know what to expect at the University of Chicago, except girls were present and they were said to be uninhibited. The older brother of a friend of mine was actually living with a girl in an apartment near the Midway, an unheard-of arrangement. They shared the rent along with the double bed in the center of the living room. They entertained guests from the bed. They spent whole weekends in the bed, eating Chinese takeout between bouts of love-

26

making. She was a political science major from Milwaukee, dark-eyed, long-legged, a devout socialist and admitted existentialist. Of course they were headed for trouble with that sort of behavior, the parents understandably furious—why couldn't Walter have gone to Yale like everyone else? But before I could muse on the possibilities of long-legged existentialists I had to get through graduation, the party season on the North Shore, and a summer job that began in June. I rocked in the chair and looked at the sky, thinking about the long-legged girl as I identified the Dippers, Orion's belt, the five stars of Cassiopeia, and the two Bears. One thing I would do when I was away for good, out of college and into a man's life, was to see the Southern Cross from shipboard; and just then the Southern Cross was as remote as the unknown girl, though I was still wondering what it would be like to have a double bed in the living room and entertain from it, everyone loose and good-humored, not giving a damn about anything. Probably that was the secret, a casualness of approach. It had worked so well for me in the past, an attitude about as casual as the organization of the heavens, except who was to say that the heavens weren't casual, the consequence of a cosmic roll of the dice. Einstein didn't think so, but what did Einstein know? Einstein was an optimist. So you were attracted to a girl and set about coordinating an approach and halfway into the waltz you watched her eyes glaze and commence to peek over your shoulder, searching for a way out. You were false to the ground, about as persuasive as a clamorous radio jingle. It was not possible for one second to forget yourself and step into the life of another. It had never worked, not with the girl in the ninth grade, not with the girl in the tenth, nor the trampoline star later on. Naturalness was as elusive as smoke—so vivid one moment, vanished the next—and so you remained in your own bed alone, waiting for something magical to happen, as surely it would, tomorrow or the next day. The Midwest was so fertile, so enormous, the horizon line stretched to the limits of the known world. But there was no space to breathe.

Away in the southern sky I could see the reflection of the lights of Chicago, a pulsing orangy glow, the throb of the future. On brilliant nights the Milky Way seemed almost close enough to touch, spread out like a great glittering banquet, though never pristine owing to the lights of the metropolis that nibbled the rim of the heavens. You had to turn your back to the city to get a chaste view of the stars—my father's thought on those occasions when he felt crowded by Chicago's muscle. He believed Chicago was a separate and hostile nation. Chicago was where you went for a loan when times were hard, and Chicago in turn looked east, where the muscle was bought and paid for. My father grew up believing that Illinois was a colony of some greater, more prodigious society to which he did not have access. This feared society was controlled by secretive personalities in New York, Philadelphia, Boston, and London. They owned the banks, the railways, the steelworks, and the oil. They owned the electricity you needed to turn on a radio; and they owned the radio. These were the people who had nominated Eisenhower at the criminal convention in Chicago, summer of 'fifty-two, stealing delegates from poor Bob Taft, Mr. Republican, who had earned the nomination fair and square but refused to wheel and deal. No honor among them, the moneymen from the East, malefactors of great wealth. Who said that? Theodore Roosevelt, the good Roosevelt, the rough-riding Republican Roosevelt said it; and his appalling cousin, the bad Roosevelt, the socialist Roosevelt, expanded the definition to include any hard-working businessman trying to make ends meet in a tough economy. Some poor bastard owns a gas station or a shoe store, he's a malefactor of great wealth. Meanwhile, the millionaires got away with murder.

Well, I had said, now you've got Eisenhower.

We'll see about Eisenhower, my father said. Good man, I guess, but I don't trust generals. He's an improvement over Truman. And a damn sight better than Adlai.

I would have voted for Adlai, I said.

Of course you would, my father said, barking a laugh. When was the last time you filed an income tax return?

That was the world I sought to escape, for a double bed in the living room of an apartment off the Midway on the South Side of Chicago, and if I could find a dark-eyed, long-legged girl to share it with me, I would not care if she was a Republican, a Teen for Taft, even. I shivered in the chill, looking at the constellations and Chicago's sulfurous glow on the southern horizon, wishing to God I was five years older and out of Quarterday, out of college and out of the Midwest, freely sailing the oceans under the Southern Cross. I stood and walked to the edge of the fairway and flipped my cigarette in the direction of the green on Six—and out of the evening mist came a herd of deer, a buck and three does and their fawns, gliding lightly up the rise of the fairway, the does leading the way, moving their heads like turtles. They made no sound as they glided along, high-haunched, the fawns pausing to graze a little. The buck turned his heavy head to look directly at me and then back again; and in a heartbeat they were gone, vaulting into the mist where they vanished for good. I stared at the place where they had been, shaking a cigarette from the pack and trying to light it. But my fingers would not work properly. I waited a minute or more for the herd to reappear but they were gone.

We lived in a political house that season, nightly communicants at the evening news. The mess in Springfield, the mess in Washington, subversion in Hollywood, corruption in Chicago, stalemate in Korea, unrest generally. My mother was a ghost at the table, patiently knitting while the news was read by a sad-eyed middle-aged man with a baritone voice and a reassuring manner. Once, when he devoted a sentence to a strike at my father's plant, my father looked up, startled; but the sentence came and went in an instant.

Did you hear that?
No, Teddy. What was it?
He mentioned the strike.
Your strike?
My strike, my father said.
What did he say?
That there was trouble at Carillo & Ravan.
I'll be damned, my father went on, pleased but trying not to show it.
My mother rarely spoke during the news, though often she

would look questioningly at my father, who offered his own commentary on the events of the day. He believed things were out of control, by which he meant directed by unseen hands. He knew that something had changed with the winning of the war and the unquiet peace that followed. He knew this from conversations with his friends at the club, and listening to the men on the floor talking about their new Ford coupe or the Johnson outboard they had their eye on, and the washing machine their wives were after them to buy. Commotion was in the air, both grievance and a new sense of destination. The whole nation had won the war and the whole nation was entitled to share in the victory. My father looked into the eyes of this new face and saw something of himself; but still he would not yield.

His situation had changed. By the early 1950s, Carillo & Ravan had greatly increased revenues and had branched out from stationery and business forms to company reports and catalogues. My father quite suddenly discovered he was rich, and when friends approached him about forming a real estate syndicate, he agreed at once. Syndicates were the new thing. Downstate Illinois was underbuilt and the banks had money to lend. The moment he reached out (as he said) into real estate was the moment his life changed. The printing business occupied less of his time, and his shirts were free of ink. He no longer talked so much about "the business" as he began to spend as much time on the financing of a subdivision in Pekin as he did in the backshop of his printing business. It was strange at first, my father said, very strange that a partnership in northern Illinois could have a profound effect on the economy of central Illinois, and then it didn't seem strange at all but logical and natural.

He laughed and said, The colonized have become the colonizers.

Little fish eating littler fish. Scraps enough for everyone.

And the profits are phenomenal.

The labor negotiations were conducted by the general manager, my father "saving himself," as he put it, for the climactic round. A strike deadline was set and postponed when new proposals were laid on the table. Still, my father stayed away. He ignored the stubbornness of the union and failed to detect the determination of the men to share in the new prosperity. When the strike came, he was unprepared. He felt betrayed, as if he were the object of a coup d'état. It had never happened before, collective bargaining always a kind of dumb show of exaggerated gestures; and then they settled for a two-and-a-half-percent wage increase. My father, on business in Pekin, heard the news by telephone. His general manager was convinced the Communists were behind the strike. Carillo & Ravan had an important government contract and surely this was an effort to embarrass the Eisenhower administration, compromise it in its valiant Cold War struggle. The leadership of the union was suspected of having links—that was the word, "links"—to the American Communist Party, Comrade Earl Browder's party, the party that everyone knew was a puppet of the Kremlin in Moscow, Browder a frequent visitor to the Soviet Union, and always under the personal surveillance of J. Edgar Hoover's most trusted assistants. When word came of the tyrant Stalin's death, Earl Browder wept bitter tears. The union leadership had refused to sign non-Communist affidavits as the government demanded that it do pursuant to the Taft-Hartley Act, the law of the land—and were they not therefore in contempt and unworthy of public support? That was the verdict of the local newspaper, and the first time I ever saw the words "pursuant" and "affidavit" in print.

The strike began when the printers downed tools and threw up a picket line manned by their rowdiest members. Windows were smashed and employees harassed and when my father brought in his strikebreakers—men every bit as rough as the men they replaced—the death threats began, first in the form of crude anonymous letters to my father at his office, and then obscenely to the house, terrifying my mother and infuriating my father. By then, my father's good friend Sheriff Tom Felsen had suggested he arm himself for his own protection, and gave him the long-barreled Colt .32, a box of ammunition, and the crimson duffel.

My mother wanted him to give in, settle the strike or sell the business, so we could live in peace. She was afraid to answer the telephone. She was afraid to work in her garden or meet friends for lunch. You should show some consideration for your family, she said.

It was late April. We were at dinner, my father picking at his food and saying very little. He was at his usual place at the head of the table, looking through the den to the French doors that led to the terrace.

I hate it, she said.

You can't give in to them, my father replied.

Why not? she said.

For one thing, they're Communists.

I don't care who they are, my mother said.

They're trying to destroy me, he said with sudden passion. Destroy me, destroy my business. They hate our way of life.

Why are the Communists interested in a little printing plant in Illinois? What interest do they have in your stationery? Answer me that.

Not so little, Jo. We grossed three-five last year.

You know what I mean, she said.

But my father looked away, irritated, poking at his pork chop, then murmuring something about his strikebreakers, tough men, good workers when they weren't drinking. Some of them had been threatened also and were carrying firearms provided by the sheriff's office. Strikebreakers cost more when they had to arm themselves, sort of like combat pay in the army. He said, It's just a hell of a mess for everyone.

You don't need it, she said.

I don't want anyone to get hurt. But god damn it, if they push me —

Teddy, *you don't need it.*

Need what? said my father.

Don't be obtuse, my mother said. Your business. You have other interests, your investments downstate. You're doing fine without Carillo & Ravan, so you could sell it and give someone else the headache. Let someone else fight the Communists.

I don't like sarcasm, Jo.

I can't bear another of those telephone calls, my mother said, more softly. That voice, the breathing —

32

I said, What did he say exactly?

Keep out of this, my father said, and abruptly the room was so silent you could hear the clock tick.

It was a woman this time, my mother said.

A woman? my father said.

Vile language, my mother said. And, she continued but did not finish her thought.

And what? my father said.

She mentioned Wils, my mother said curtly.

What did she say? I said.

My mother shook her head. She would add nothing further.

A threat? my father said.

What do you think, Teddy? Do you think she wished him health and happiness? She said if you weren't careful Wils would end up *in a ditch*. There was more but I will not repeat it.

There was a note of triumph to my mother's voice, a note I had never heard. She had the look of a card player with a pat hand. Whatever it was, I was at that moment on my father's side, and taking obvious pleasure from my sudden notoriety. I was an object of Communist treachery no less than my father and his business, or the entertainment industry. What had Sassoon called such heroics? A mention in dispatches.

We will talk about this later, my father said quietly, but I knew he was alarmed at what he had heard. He glanced at me briefly and offered a hopeful wink.

We certainly will, my mother said.

That's enough, my father said.

I'll give you chapter and verse, my mother said.

I said, that's *enough*, my father replied sharply, more sharply than I had ever heard him speak to my mother. He returned to his pork chop, his eyes inward, his thoughts apparently far away.

You've become a different person, my mother said after a moment. I feel I hardly know you. I can't get your attention. You won't talk. You're so—inflexible. We never go anywhere. We never see our friends. They ask us to dinner and I tell them, No, Teddy's out of town. Teddy's working late. Teddy has a meeting. Teddy's here, Teddy's there. I never know when he'll be home. Because of the strike at the plant. Because of the threats. We had the trip to Havana planned and then you called it off, because of the strike at the plant. Answer me this. What's the use of being successful if you can't enjoy the success? I'm *frightened,* Teddy.

My father sighed and did not reply. But then he smiled, looked up, and said, New York. We should have gone to New York.

Don't start that, my mother said, suddenly very angry.

Dad was making a joke, I said.

She did not look at me or give any sign of having heard what I said. She continued to sit, staring straight ahead, her hands in her lap. I realized then that she was near tears, her face flushed and her lips trembling. She said at last, I'm frightened all the time. There was a strange car this morning, drove past the house once and again from the other direction, back and forth, two men in the front seat, I couldn't see their faces. They drove so slowly. One of them wore a hat. And this afternoon, the telephone call . . .

My father rose at once and went to her, his hands on her shoulders and his chin touching her hair. He said something I couldn't hear, but whatever it was, she shook her head in response.

Yes, he said. Believe me.

How can I? she said. How can I when strange men drive by on an ordinary afternoon and I know they mean us harm? I don't have a way of coping, Teddy. How am I supposed to behave? You tell me.

He was looking up now, staring at the wallpaper, the Frenchmen in their plumed hats and flared jackets and the stag high-stepping through the tangled forest, dimly lit by the chandelier over the dining room table.

Trust me, he said, and my mother smiled bleakly. He said, I guess this is the modern world and we're going to have to live with it, insecurity. Everything was different before the war. My business, Quarterday. Different time, a prewar time, everyone pulling together. Teamwork meant something. She raised her eyes to look at my father, an expression of perfect bafflement on her face. I believe this, he said. You can only have one boss of an outfit.

I suppose so, she said doubtfully, but—

We have to stick together, he said as he moved his hands in slow circles over her shoulders. And then he brightened and playfully tapped her water glass with a spoon, as if he were about to make a toast. I want to tell you a story. Funny thing happened at the office this morning.

—there were *two men*, Teddy.

I know, my father began, and then started because the telephone rang.

I'll get it, I said.

Let it ring, my father said.

I don't mind, I said.

Let it ring, he ordered, and so it rang, one ring after another, each seeming louder than the one before. My father gave my mother a final caress and returned to his chair and the pork chop cold on his plate. We three sat in silence and listened to the telephone ring.

It might be them, my mother said.

My father reclined in his chair, grinning. He said, Let me tell you the story. Salesman came in with samples of silk, beautiful stuff, beautiful weight and texture, like parchment except it was supple. Silk paper for wedding announcements, party invitations, debutante parties and the like. I listened to his pitch and said no thanks, not even when the strike is over. He was a charming character, born in Persia. He had a suitcase with him. The suitcase was on wheels; it must have been three feet across. He said he wanted to show me something, so he opened the suitcase and took out a shallow basket. The basket looked like the hats Chinese coolies wear. He removed the lid and invited me to have a look. And there were the silkworms, scores of them no bigger than your thumb, resting on mulberry leaves. They were blurred and I thought for a moment there was something wrong with my eyesight, and when I looked closely I saw they were moving, all of them, minute movements among the mulberry leaves. As if they were shuddering, like a heartbeat. And all the time they were moving they were making silk. What you thought was still was not still at all but—seething. I thought of that time when Wils was so sick, unconscious for days on end, yet when you put your hand to his forehead you felt this tremendous heat. I knew that he would be all right. And the times I had watched you, Jo, sound asleep like a statue, not moving a muscle. But inside your head you were dreaming. And I could not see that at all.

He said in a voice not his own, It was the damnedest thing. And then the Persian went away, taking the silkworms with him. They were for demonstration purposes only.

I never dream, my mother said.

Everyone dreams, my father said.

I had a fever, I said. How did you know I would be all right?

I knew, he said.

We were silent again, listening to the telephone.

Or the colored girl, my father said. The girl they found in the alley, full of gin. A pulse so faint they needed a stethoscope to find it. What do you suppose happened to her? The paper never said. Where did she go? Where is she now? My father paused, lost in thought. He said, The Persian insisted they'd love it on the North Shore. Winnetka ladies just died for silk. My silk invitations would be hotter than Ford station wagons. But I couldn't see it. Certainly not now, with the situation. So I wished the Persian good luck and sent him on his way. My father sat quietly a moment, staring at the ceiling. He said, I would love to've taken a shot at it and I probably would have, before. But you need craftsmen for that sort of job. Strikebreakers are not craftsmen, they're mercenaries. The men they replaced, my men, those men are sharpshooters. They could make a calling card out of a bat's wing. Took pride in their work. These new men, I need them but they're not quality men. They're strikebreakers, that's what they do for a living.

I said, Where did you find them?

My father smiled and replied, Judge Greenslat. Butch Greenslat can find you anything. He has a friend in Indiana, specializes in hard-to-get journeymen for businessmen who need them, maybe they've done some time in Joliet or Folsom, but they like travel and the combat pay. Men trying to find their feet. Butch finds them the feet, and takes a fee.

Jailbirds, I said.

Some, my father said. Not all.

I said, I want to meet one.

My father waved his hand, end of conversation.

You never told me that, my mother said.

I didn't want to worry you. Besides, I don't want to talk about the strikebreakers. I just wanted to tell you about those critters nesting in the mulberry leaves, damnedest thing.

My mother had turned away, her chin in her hand, listening to the telephone.

It could be Tom Felsen, she said.

Could be, my father said without enthusiasm.

With news, my mother said.

My father did not reply, but turned to me instead. Do you want to play a round, late Saturday? We could get in nine holes before dark.

It's forty degrees, my mother threw in. You'll freeze to death.

I'd like that, I said. My father almost never asked me to play golf. He had a regular foursome, three overweight businessmen who loved the game but could not play it.

Golf, my mother said, her voice harsh against the ringing telephone. You ought to try thinking about your family, making us safe. Why can't you *end this?*

My father was not listening.

God *damn* it, he said then, rising from his chair. He threw his napkin on the table and strode to the den. The phone was on a table next to the French doors that opened onto the terrace. I suppose it had rung thirty times and when he picked up the receiver and put it to his ear, the abrupt silence was so thick you could feel it gather. My mother watched with her hand covering her mouth so that when we saw the window glass shatter and heard the explosion her scream was muffled until her hand fell away and her voice rose in the high notes of a clarinet. My father stood rigid as a tree, then fell into his hockey crouch, his fists in front of his face. When he dropped the receiver, it broke apart on the parquet floor. I could see the blood on his hands and arms, his shirtsleeve torn as if someone had sliced it with a knife. My mother half rose from her chair and remained there, bent at the waist, clutching the pearls at her throat. We felt the cold night breeze pushing in from the shattered window and smelled the sweet odor of new-grown spring grass. And still my father did not move, except to raise his hand, a command for us to remain where we were. He did not speak but I could hear his breathing. I was watching him, horrified at the blood on his hands, frightened, naturally, but resolved to act as a man should act, as he would wish me to act at this moment when our tranquillity was destroyed, everything familiar vanished in an instant. I waited for another gunshot or for one of them to appear at the window, and then I remembered the duffel in the coat closet, useless. I waited for my father's signal, any signal—and in some back chamber of my mind I saw him as the skipper of a vessel struck by a terrible and unexpected storm, one that he could not turn from even as it overwhelmed him. This was the violence of the outside world, and he was responsible for it and responsible for us and I prayed he would not fail as I knew my mother expected him to do. And still he did not speak, remaining in his hockey crouch, his head moving this way and that. Considering this, all in a split second, I knew I was traveling from one realm to another, crossing the line that divided youth and maturity, and that this moment had tremendous weight and that I would refer to it often and that later on it would have more than one meaning.

Then I was standing at the French doors without any clear memory of how I had got there or what I would do now. I could hear my father's breathing and wondered then if the invaders were still outside, their business unfinished. I looked left and right but could see nothing through the ragged hole in the window glass, the grassy breeze in my face and the sound of the explosion in my ears and all around me. The terrace no longer looked familiar. My father said something I could not hear, and then I noticed it had begun to rain, a soft drizzle that became a downpour as I watched, a ragged line of lightning straight ahead, rainwater flying through the window and puddling on the floor. Beyond the fairway and the green, I thought I saw headlights but I could not be certain, the rain descending in sheets and thunder crashing in the distance.

From the dining room my mother gave a little strangled cry

and my father lowered his hand, wiping blood on his shirt. When I turned, I saw he was white as ash and his eyes were unfocused, his forehead slick with sweat and his shoulders sagging. I did not know how many times he had been hit but he looked as if he might collapse at any moment. His arm leaked blood but he paid no attention to it. When my mother reached his side he seemed not to notice, his bloody arm automatically around her waist and his eyes far away. I thought he would break down and I held my breath; and then I saw the expression on my mother's face, a confusion of concern and helpless fury and a kind of grim satisfaction that her warnings had come true. Her family was not safe and her husband was responsible. When I reached for my father and took his hand, as one would the hand of a blind man, he turned slowly to me and spoke in an unnatural voice.

Son, he said. Go next door. Call Tom Felsen. Tell him to come here.

The hospital, my mother said.

Will you do that, son?

Yes, I said.

You're shot, my mother said.

I'm not shot, he said. I'm cut.

We could all have been killed, she said.

Flying glass, he said.

We could all have been killed, she said in her clarinet voice.

Call Tom now, my father said to me.

You're bleeding, my mother said.

He raised his arm to look at his wounds, the ones on his forearm, and then he noticed his hand, blood rising from his fingers. A shard of glass was lodged in the skin at the base of his thumb, and as we watched he deftly plucked it out, looked at it, and dropped it on the floor where he ground it under his heel. The lips of the wound gaped white and red. When he looked at it with his slow smile, I smiled with him; and he looked at me and winked.

We'll go now, my mother said. You must have your hand seen to.

It wasn't gunshot, my father said. They weren't armed except for that, he said, pointing to the brick at his feet. They threw a brick through the window when I answered the telephone. I never should have done it. They were waiting for me to do it. Watching me through the window—that was their signal. He turned to my mother, standing impatiently at his side. They're just cuts, nothing more. I don't need a doctor. I need a Band-Aid. It's not a question of anyone being shot, Jo.

It's raining, he added.

Your arms are cut, my mother said.

Yes, they are, my father said, and reached down to pick up the brick, hefting it in his hand. He said, I never believed they'd do something like this. Never believed it in the world. Tom warned me—

What do you think? my mother demanded. They'd do anything given half a chance, the threats they've made. Why did you think they wouldn't act? *They told you they would.* My God, Teddy.

Threats are one thing, my father said. Acts are something else.

Have it your way, my mother said. Don't ask me to believe it.

When did it start to rain? my father asked in his normal voice. He was trying to return things to normal, to our family dinner before the telephone began to ring; and then I realized how far from normal our family had become, my mother frightened by cars in the road and threatening telephone calls, my father carrying a gun and worried about the Communists and the future of his business, and I—I, so far on the margins of the family, a spectator only, trying to read between the lines and discovering that the spaces were infinite but that one thing was certainly true, my father and mother loved each other and cared about each other, and then from the moment the brick crashed through the window I knew that was an illusion and the space between them was infinite, too.

I'll be in the car, she said. Unless you want Wils to drive you.

Tom Felsen first, my father said, nodding at me and moving to the sideboard where he poured a glassful of scotch. When he raised the glass to his mouth, his hand was steady as a metronome, but when he bent to sip, something went awry and the whiskey splashed on his shirtfront.

Tell Tom to get here pronto, he said, his hand now locked at his side, and then he thought to ask the question that must have been on his mind all along. Are you both all right?

They never caught the brick thrower, though the sheriff suspected it was Clyde, the foreman, bitter that the strike had gone on for so long, bitter at the strikebreakers, bitter that he could not afford medical attention for one of his children. When the telephone calls didn't work, he thought he'd try something dramatic, calculating that my father would yield and settle the strike. Clyde thought you'd be scared shitless, the sheriff said to my father. He thought you'd cave, Teddy; but he doesn't know you like I do. When he heard the name, my father was shaken. He and Clyde had worked together for fifteen years, ever since Clyde arrived as an eighteen-year-old apprentice. You're sure? my father asked the sheriff, and Tom Felsen tapped his ear and smiled.

Clyde left the morning after. He's downstate now, with the wife and kids.

We're keeping an eye on him.

My father had trouble believing. What had he done to provoke such an attack, so carefully planned, so potentially lethal. He had never thought of himself as one who collected enemies. He came to accept my mother's prophetic words. Why did you think they wouldn't act? *They told you they would.* Unnerved, my father came to believe that enemies were part of every life and there was nothing to be done about them except to remain alert and take nothing for granted, reserving to yourself the right of self-defense. He did not inform my mother of the sheriff's suspicions; there was enough between them already without adding yet another irritant, this one so deeply troubling.

Your mother can't take much more, he said to me one night. So not a word to her about this.

I'm afraid, he went on. I'm afraid I haven't handled this situation very well. I'm going to have to make it up to her. I underestimated the threat, what they were capable of. I just never believed it would go this far. Never in a million years. I got careless, Wils. I neglected things.

People don't understand about a business, he continued

thoughtfully. You have a loyalty to it because it's yours. It's a living thing, it's not inanimate, only bricks and mortar and numbers. Even a balance sheet is alive when you know how to read it. You have a duty to protect the business and you can't walk away from the duty, any more than you can walk away from your family. Business is healthy, you play with it. Business is sick, you look after it. Course, it's not what it was. Some things were said, can't be unsaid. I did some things, too, that I wish I hadn't done. And I have to make it up with your mother.

Take her to Havana, I said. I can look after things here.

You can't look after the business, Wils.

I meant the house, I said.

Anyone can look after a house, he said gruffly.

No charges were ever filed against Clyde and the threatening telephone calls ceased, but that is not to say that in our family a ringing telephone did not cause anxiety, that year and for many years to come. The strike continued through the spring and the early summer and then petered out—"the exhaustion factor," according to my father, by which he meant the anger and frustration of the strikers' wives. Naturally he was happy to see it end, though he acknowledged the terms were similar to what he could have had at the beginning; and he repeated his glum assessment that no one ever won a strike. He gave up his real estate partnership—he seemed to see it as frivolous when measured against his responsibility toward his business—and now he spent all his time at the office, though less time in the backshop. The Linotypes and presses lost their allure, and he was irritated at the ink smeared on his shirts, a damn nuisance.

Now and again he received notes of encouragement from friends, businessmen who had labor troubles of their own, and these cheered him—though where were these friends when he needed them? Profits were down, and he complained now that he worked twice as hard to make half as much money. He never looked on his business in the same way, with affection and pride in the company's growth. He said he felt he was mopping up after a war, clearing out pockets of resistance and caring for the refugees. There were frequent small acts of sabotage that interfered with production. The work force was sullen, men calling

42

in sick with dubious ailments. Each evening at five the plant was empty, no matter what work remained to be done. The strikebreakers drifted away, back to wherever they had come from, awaiting fresh assignments. My father said that in some cracked way he almost envied them; there was something to be said for mercenary work, here today, gone tomorrow, but always a paycheck at the end of the week.

My father came home early, too, and refused to speak of his business at the dinner table, preferring instead to make tentative vacation plans with my mother or to chat with me about my entrance into college in September, repeating his assurances that it was all right with him if I didn't go to Dartmouth but, Jesus, why did I have to choose the University of Chicago, the hotbed of American socialism. I agreed with him that it was a hotbed, all right, and when I found out where the hotbed was, I'd let him know. He spoke to my mother about improvements to the house and grounds, about which he had developed a sudden enthusiasm. She was pleased at his interest and announced she had a number of ideas but first she wanted to hire a landscape architect. There was so much to do because they'd let things slide for so long, and he agreed, they certainly had, though it was also true that they'd come a long way.

Remember what we started with, Jo. Two rooms, one of them the size of an ashtray.

Don't remind me, my mother said. We'll see what we can do with this place when we put our minds to it. Now that we don't have to worry so much. That's true, isn't it, Teddy? We don't have to worry anymore?

My father nodded pleasantly but did not answer the question.

The death threats ceased but he continued to carry the long-barreled Colt in the crimson duffel, eventually paying no more attention to it than if it were an umbrella.

3

THAT LONG SEASON I lived in a morbid condition of continual anticipation, always with an eye on the clock: tomorrow, the weekend, the summer, the university following the summer, the working life following the university. No moment seemed complete or satisfying in itself, only a forced step on the way to somewhere else. I was fixed on a fabulous point in the middle distance; and I could not define it, except that whatever it was, I would not find it tomorrow or the day after. And would I know it when I saw it? On weekends I would drive to Chicago to listen to jazz, old music from New Orleans. I walked through the door of the jazz club on Bryn Mawr and I belonged, losing myself inside the music and between sets talking to whoever was at my elbow, the advertising man and his girlfriend or the airline pilot and his young wife or the graduate student from Loyola, the talk impersonal, sports or the latest municipal scandal or the new Ford line, or the fashionable foursome in black tie sitting at the table in the corner. And at midnight I would drive back to Quarterday, the music alive inside my head.

Weekdays I marked time at the day school, half an hour's drive from my house. I had few friends because of the age difference and my own dissatisfied state of mind. By befriending my classmates I would regress one year, a year too hard won to forfeit. Many of the students were transfers from eastern prep schools, boys who had had disciplinary problems; a few had flunked out. Their brusque manners set them apart from the local boys like me. They met the world eye-to-eye with a sneer and a fart (as one of them said), believing themselves infinitely superior to the day school they had been exiled to, aristocrats obliged to make do in the company of yeomen. Of course the girls found them attractive, men of the world who didn't give a damn about anything except the day's pleasure. Nothing would stand in their way except their parents, guardians of the family money; and it went without saying that their disgraceful behavior in the East meant a short leash in the Midwest. These boys were objects of curiosity, not least from the instructors. Tell me, what's Hotchkiss really like? How do the masters live? Do they have dormitory apartments or houses of their own? I understood after a while that even the instructors wanted to migrate east, trading up, Hotchkiss or Choate or Deerfield a settled perch at the top of the tree. Who wanted to spend his life at a struggling day school north of Chicago? Everyone, it seemed, wanted to be moving on to somewhere else. Meanwhile, I had *Memoirs of an Infantry Officer,* the romance of the trenches of the Somme.

In May my mother went back east to visit her parents. It had been a year since she had seen them, and her father was not well. She stayed two weeks and then announced she would be a while longer, owing to her father's second stroke. He was bedridden and needed assistance around the clock but was improving every day. She and my father had many long conversations in the evening, my father's voice a low rumble punctuated by long silences during which I heard ice cubes rattle into his glass. He was sitting in his leather chair in the den, his voice all but inaudible to me, bent over homework in my room upstairs, and finally the sharp click of the receiver when he replaced it in the cradle. Later, during my evening walkabout, I looked in through the French doors and saw him sitting in his chair, disconsolate, a closed book in his lap.

My mother returned for my graduation in June but left

again the next day. A week later my father flew to New York, where he had reserved a suite at the Waldorf and arranged for theater tickets and dinner at "21" and a carriage ride in Central Park at midnight, when he would present her with a gold bracelet from Marshall Field's. But he returned a day ahead of schedule, explaining cryptically that Yalta was no place to decide the future of the world.

We needed a neutral venue.

We should have gone to Havana when she wanted to, he said to me.

While my mother was in the East, my father and I played golf regularly on the weekends and joked about "batching it," a disheveled locker-room life in which women did not figure. We existed on a diet of sirloin steaks, baked potatoes, caesar salad, and chocolate ice cream, and after dinner we played pinochle. Alone together, we grew close, much closer than when my mother was with us. I discovered I hardly knew him at all, and of course I was surprised that there was anything to know. I never understood much of what my parents said to each other because I was not aware of the private language of married people, a tongue I came to believe was invented to keep outsiders at a distance, like a military code in wartime. My mother's things were all around us, the pictures she owned and her grandfather's set of the Harvard Classics, and the objects that dressed up the coffee table and the mantel over the fireplace in the den. These things reminded us of her every day. But she herself was absent and seemed to slip from us, a photograph fading in the sun. When she called on the telephone, I described to her the golf matches and the evening diet and the pinochle and how well we were getting on, my father and I— though we both missed her and hoped she would return soon. Things weren't the same without her. Dad and I have long talks every night and he's teaching me things—

What things? she asked.

Things, I said. Things that men have to know, I added, and when she did not reply I knew I had blundered. I had said too much without saying enough, and when I asked if she wanted to speak to "him," she said she couldn't, someone was at the door, and rang off without another word.

46

My father told me a good deal about his business and much else besides during the hour of drinks before dinner, when he was in a reflective state of mind. I had the idea that he was telling me things he had never told anyone. He said we were in an enviable zone of trust and I did not know how rare that was, so we should enjoy ourselves while the trust lasted. He taught me how to read a balance sheet, more complicated than it looked at first glance, assets and liabilities not always obvious; often they were fungible (and he was careful to define the word), and assigned with an eye always on the taxman and the shareholders. He resolved to teach me how to drink well, drinking well being a skill like anything else, playing the piano or coming out of a fairway sand trap with a five iron. Sloppy drunks were a menace, and none more menacing than teenage drunks, a menace to themselves and everyone around them. Clichés, he called them. Nothing more trustworthy than a young man who can hold his liquor and be seen to hold his liquor. That way, my father said, you gained the respect of older men. That counted for something. That was the world we lived in, like it or not. He smiled and said in a voice not his own, Never cheat at golf; never get rough with women.

You get a reputation for being sound. You have standing.

This voice that was not his own puzzled me. Sarcasm lay beneath its skin.

They won't worry when you take out their daughters, he went on. And you'll have the respect of your own cohort. He paused then, his thought unfinished. He was worried that I did not have a close circle of friends, and disconcerted that I seemed to enjoy the company of older people. But he left the thought hanging.

Girls like it, he said suddenly. You'll seem older to them. Experienced. Discreet. Capable. Up to the mark.

Up to the mark, I repeated in a reasonable imitation of his borrowed voice.

Yes, he said, smiling broadly now. That's the ticket.

Sounds boring, I said.

It does have that disadvantage, he said, rising and stepping to the sideboard, pouring a finger of whiskey. But you can live with it, he said, his back to me as he dropped ice cubes into his glass. He was silent a moment. I envy you your summer. I never had one like it. It's only a few weeks now, the dances begin. How many invitations do you have?

About twenty-five so far, I said.

Twenty-five, he repeated, staring at the ceiling, cradling his scotch in both hands. You'll need a new tux—

Mother calls it a dinner jacket, I said.

Does she? Well, you'll need a new one for your summer season, and remember to get it cleaned now and then. And don't forget what your mother told you. Always dance with the deb and the deb's mother and shake hands with her father and say How do you do, sir, and generally kiss ass up and down the receiving line. I laughed but my father did not laugh with me, absorbed as he was with the shadows on the ceiling.

He said softly, It is not boring, Wils. Experience and discretion will make you seem to them just the slightest bit dangerous, not a man who'll say anything that comes to mind, and it's my guess that dangerous is what you are. You go your own way, that's for damned sure. Women like danger, my father said and cocked his eyebrow. Let me put that another way. Women like to be around a dangerous man, perhaps a man who seems in his nature to be not entirely reliable. Not entirely predictable in his emotions or anything else. Because, he said, taking a thoughtful sip of whiskey; and he said no more.

Because what? I asked after a moment.

Because women like excitement, too, same as the rest of us.

I said something noncommittal because I did not believe he said what he meant; he had something else in mind but was not ready to disclose it.

Loyalty also, he added, and when he said it the word had the weight of the world. And then he went to the heart of the matter: You have to exercise some control over yourself or someone else will do it for you.

Women, I said, catching on at last, though my father's sidelong glance suggested otherwise. After a moment he said, Women are among them.

My father had many theories about women, older women and younger women, loose women and modest women, girls he

48

had grown up with and dated, and how things changed when he went away to Dartmouth and the wider world of Hanover, New Hampshire. He freely admitted his experience was limited, yet when he arrived in Hanover he discovered a strait-laced attitude at odds with the earthier climate of Quarterday.

You would have thought it would be the reverse, but it wasn't.

Quarterday was Sodom and Gomorrah compared to Hanover.

And believe me, not much was happening in Quarterday.

But at least we knew what girls looked like. And they knew what we looked like, too.

Well, there were the town girls. Girls out for some fun.

I'd forgotten about them.

I didn't know them. My roommate did.

Those girls were too much like the girls I'd grown up with.

He grew apart from his childhood friends, those who had stayed home and gone to work on the farm or in one of the shops or become teachers or policemen, like Tom Felsen. My father's vocabulary changed, the slang he used and the jokes he laughed at. He came home for Christmas wearing a long green scarf and whistling Gershwin tunes. "Lady Be Good" was a favorite. He had taken up the drums and was playing in his fraternity's jazz band. His second night home he went to a party and got into a scuffle with a boy he had known for years, and after that his Quarterday friends avoided him, except the girl he had known since grade school who sought him out to ask him about college life. What do you learn? Is it fun? What is there about it that can change a person so? And is it worthwhile? My father felt he was living in two worlds at once, the adult world of Hanover and the childhood world of Quarterday, and these worlds did not fit. The first year he was away, my father had dreams at night, homesick dreams of the prairie teeming with skaters in strange hats speaking exotic tongues. The prairie went on forever, a monotonous tableland with not a house or a tree in sight. When he awakened from these dreams he went at once to his desk and began reading where he'd left off, making notes as he went, as if they were sentences of atonement. He

49

thought of forfeiting his scholarship and returning home for good, though his experience at Christmas was not encouraging. He felt he had abandoned his family and friends and only later did it occur to my father that the reverse could as easily be said; he thought of these friends as leftovers and hated himself for thinking it but knew also that he was not the first American to betray his origins, moving on. When he tentatively mentioned his fears to his parents, his mother said she would love him no matter what he did or who he became, but perhaps it was a good idea to return home for a semester and take stock. His father listened impatiently and stated that if he forfeited the scholarship he was not welcome in "my house." You started it, now you finish it. Harsh words from the best dad a guy ever had.

Then hockey came along and in the spring his roommate suggested they spend the summer in Maine as sailing instructors, his family had a house there with a cottage they could live in and sailing was a cinch, anyone could learn to sail; and Teddy Ravan said yes, why not, so he spent that summer in Maine and the subsequent summers as well and that was where he met Jo Wilson, a freshman at Pembroke, whose family summered in the neighboring village. It took a while for my father to understand a society that summered in one state and wintered in another, but he was always quick so he caught on soon enough, as he had caught on to hockey, jazz, sailing, the stammer in the dramas of Eugene O'Neill, and the urban architecture of the Italian Renaissance. He was especially successful with older people, mature for his age, serious-minded, good at games, altogether winning.

Doesn't that Ravan boy have the most beautiful manners?

Where is he from again?

What does his father do, actually?

That long-ago summer, my father acknowledged, he and my mother were at odds, bitter arguments that would spring from nowhere. The importance of "background" in the life of a family. The beauty of a triple pass approaching the crease of a hockey rink, game on the line. He was unable to identify the sources of these arguments that arrived from nowhere, so emotionally complex; and much later he came to understand that they were not complex at all but simple. He and my mother did not believe in the same things. They were equipped with different measuring sticks as to the people they admired and the qualities they valued. My father believed this was the direct result of the differences of family background and the values of the region they each grew up in. My father believed that you arrived in the world unencumbered and my mother did not; encumbrances were what you were given and not allowed to surrender. Encumbrance was my mother's word for personality. Yet the mutual attraction, the force of nature, was so strong they knew they belonged together whatever their differences of taste and outlook.

Her family had a place on the Connecticut shore, the gray-green waters of Long Island Sound glittering in the distance. The morning light was crystalline. On bright days the light was so sharp it hurt your eyes. It had the quality of platinum, as opposed to the dull iron of the Midwest. My father, standing on a sand dune at Westport, called it the edge-of-the-continent light, an eastern doomsday light without interference until you reached Portugal; and when he mentioned this to his girlfriend Jo she looked at him with a slow smile and said, Well, yessss, except Long Island would get in the way, wouldn't it?

And you're looking at Venezuela, actually.

My father thought the East was crowded, a land of small-holdings, too settled, too complacent and sure of itself, so different from Illinois that it might as well have been France, he said, pointing across the dinner table to the wallpaper, the dandies in their plumed hats. In the East you did not know your place. You thought you could get away with anything.

The Wilsons loved their house, its age especially, three hundred years old and counting, the stone walls, the stone foundation and the walk-in fireplace, a flintlock and powder horn from the Revolution above the mantel, Audubon prints left and right, Mr. Wilson's own watercolors on the wall opposite. The house was situated on a rocky outcropping, five acres of land surrounded by other five-acre parcels, each with its centuries-old house and a stone wall, and where the property met the road a swale, which Jo's mother called a ha-ha. The garden, however, was the jardin des plantes and beside it a five-sided folie. They had a housekeeper, too, an ancient Chinese who ran things. Jo never knew where she came from, only that she showed up one evening with Jo's father and had been with the family ever since; her father said the woman had been in trouble, and he got her out of the trouble in return for her services. Remarkable creature, rarely spoke and seemed to be everywhere at once, gliding in and out of rooms like a ghost. She was definitely part of the family, called Ling, not her real name, a made-up name. She and Jo were especially close and whenever Jo was sick Ling would arrive in her room with a mysterious Chinese potion dissolved in tea; and the ailment, whatever it was, would vanish.

Everyone called Jo's father "Squire," Squire Wilson, Esq. He was a maritime lawyer at one of the small, very old Wall Street firms, founded before the Civil War, representing shippers and the owners of ships and the leasing syndicates and the insurance firms, often all four at the same time. Squire thought maritime law a cut above any other branch of law. Being a maritime lawyer gave one standing, like coming over on the *Mayflower* or having the Hapsburg lip.

My father said, Squire thought the law of the god damned sea was holy writ, and maritime lawyers the crème de la crème. He let you know it was lucrative, too. And he had the little Hinckley sloop to prove it.

He called the sloop *Marine Tort*.

An awful snob, my father said.

Ravan? Where does that name come from?

Hungary, I said, choosing the first nation that came to mind.

It doesn't sound Hungarian, Squire said.

Maybe Swiss, I said. I'll ask my uncle Laszlo.

And he thought I was an Indian from the West, some Potawatomi come to seize his daughter by force and take her back to the tepee. But he couldn't ignore what was in front of his eyes so he suggested instead that we settle in Westport or Cos Cob, one of those places, so we'd be nearby and come to lunch every Sunday, deviled eggs and cold roast beef after a pitcher of martinis. But I could never live in Connecticut, my father said, or any place near Connecticut, and I have to say Jo saw the logic to that. She saw the logic and at the same time she saw the hilarity, her husband-to-be and her father at daggers drawn—her phrase, daggers drawn. She and her mother laughed about it but they didn't give up. Jo never gives up easily. Can't you give way just a little? Would it cost you so much? She wondered if we couldn't compromise on New Jersey or Westchester County or some place near Boston, and I said I didn't think so; we needed a thousand miles between us, her father and me. I think it was perversity that caused me to join up with Butch Greenslat and his nephew because I knew what he'd say when I called to give him the good news, an associate in the law offices of Greenslat & Greenslat.

Jew firm, isn't it?

They do political work, I said.

Of course they would, Squire said.

It's big business in Chicago, I said.

Dirty business, he said.

Everyone has the right to counsel, I said with the gravity of an attorney from the ACLU.

Mixed up with Capone's people, are they?

They're fixers, I said. They can fix anything. Elections, grand jury indictments, traffic tickets, probate irregularities, municipal taxes, a construction contract. They're Chicagoans through and through. Chicagoland thrives on the broad backs of Greenslat & Greenslat and now I'll be thriving with them and before too long it'll be Greenslat, Greenslat & Ravan, and on that day I'll be buying Jo a powder-blue Cadillac, a mink coat, and an apartment in Miami Beach. And then I sat back and listened to him go on the boil.

Squire? I said when he finished his Jew rant. We can throw some business your way. Does the law of the sea extend as far as the inland lakes—Michigan, for example? Because if it does, we've had some suspicious yacht fires . . .

Jo was their only child, my father said. The Wilsons were a close family and there were a hell of a lot of them, aunts and uncles, cousins, stepcousins. I think there was even a stepgrandmother somewhere. I could never keep them straight, scattered all over the country but mostly in New York and New England. So when your mother insisted on naming you Wilson, I was in no position to object. Do you like the sound, Wilson Ravan?

I haven't thought much about it, I lied. The truth was, I tried out new names all the time. At the jazz club, I sometimes introduced myself as Bill. Another time I tried Eddie, but Eddie didn't fit.

I said, Where does the name Ravan come from?

Damned if I know, my father said. I was never much for family trees. Middle Europe somewhere, I suppose.

By then we had finished dinner and retreated to the den, where I was shuffling the cards for pinochle. My father was content to listen to the fall of the cards while he pulled on his cigar and leafed through phonograph records, discarding Duchin in favor of his favorites: Sidney Bechet, Fred Astaire singing George Gershwin, Art Hodes at the Blue Note, and Georg Brunis. We played cards for an hour or more, not talking much, a companionable game with neither of us winning big. Art Hodes had yielded to Fred Astaire and now we were listening to Georg Brunis, whose band was permanently in session at the jazz club on Bryn Mawr, the one called the Eleven-Eleven, my haunt on the weekends.

He plays in Chicago, my father said.

Does he?

Some joint on the Far North Side. We should go some night.

That would be great, I said.

Ever been there? he said.

Not that I can remember, I said.

That's strange, my father said. I found this the other day. Next to the phonograph, he added, and handed me an Eleven-Eleven Club matchbook.

Maybe I've been there once or twice, I said.

And I'll bet you didn't use your real name, either, he said.

I looked into his eyes, two black marbles, and decided not to answer. Where I went and the name I went under were none of his business. So we sat across the table from each other in silence, and it was then I noticed the stubble on his jaw and the

54

smudge of ink on his shirt pocket. He continued to move the cards listlessly from one hand to the other, his knuckles huge and skinned as if he had been in a fistfight. At last he put the cards on the table and sat back, staring at the ceiling.

You're not a very good liar.

Sorry, I said, and put the matchbook on the table.

The room was filled with Brunis's music and I wondered if he was manipulating the slide with his foot, as he had been known to do; the jazzman as comedian. I was thinking also about a new tuxedo with a shawl collar and wondering if my father would allow me to buy it at Brooks, along with a vest and two lightweight shirts and a pair of dancing pumps; probably not-very-good liars would have to settle for Field's. I had wanted to ask him if he would let me borrow his silver flask for the car later, after the dance. But now was not the time, nor tomorrow or the day after. My father had resumed shuffling cards. I took that as a sign that the crisis had past, though he remained mute and the expression on his face was not encouraging.

When the telephone rang, I knew it was my mother, and when I looked at my father across the table—do you want to pick up, or shall I?—he shook his head and I answered.

Squire's gone, she said brokenly.

Oh, I said, and my voice caught. The hum of the telephone wire seemed unnaturally loud. Gosh, I'm so sorry.

Oh, Wils—

Mom, I began.

He passed away this afternoon, she said.

This is terrible, I said, let me get Dad. My father was staring at me from the card table. He was still shuffling cards and listening to the music but I knew he had heard what I said and what it meant. I put my hand over the receiver and mouthed, Grandpa's dead.

We thought he was rallying, she went on. He ate a good lunch and then we put him down for a nap and he never woke up. He just slept away. My mother was openly crying now and her next words were disconnected, her thoughts coming in random order. He'd lost so much weight you'd hardly know him. We called the ambulance but the crew could do nothing. He was gone. They said he didn't suffer and I'm sure they're right. He was seventy-nine and he'd had a good life, but still. It was too soon for him. Me, too, and Grandma. I made him iced tea because that was what he said he wanted, a summer drink, to be reminded of summer in Connecticut and sailing *Marine Tort* on the Sound. He talked about *you*, Wils, what a fine boy you were and how proud he was. He talked about all the great things in store, and asked me if I thought you'd choose a career in law. I said I didn't know but I'd ask. So I'm asking. He'd be so pleased. I happen to know he left you his law books, all his books relating to the law of the sea. Piracy. Salvage. I don't know what-all, but he said his maritime library was the finest in New England.

She paused then and said, Is that music you're listening to? I suppose it's your father's music. Her voice trailed off and I thought she had hung up but then I heard her say something to her mother and she was crying again.

Dad's right here, I said. My father had turned down the volume of the phonograph and was standing at the sideboard pouring a scotch, his face expressionless. He motioned impatiently for me to give him the telephone, as if I were the one prolonging the conversation.

The funeral is Friday, she said.

Yes, I said.

Have your father make the reservations. The Twentieth Century Limited would be best and I'll pick you up at Grand Central.

I will, I said. He's right here—

I wanted a private funeral, family only, but Mother insisted and wouldn't give way. Squire had so many friends, his bridge friends, his boating friends, tennis friends, and his law partners. Never was a man with so many friends. It doesn't seem fair. But you know Grandma. Always thinking of others. Poor Daddy, she said, and her voice broke again. She went on to describe the funeral arrangements, the location of the church and the Episcopal minister who would conduct the service, the selection of music and the eulogists. She said, Mother wondered if we should speak briefly, she and I, but I didn't think so. I don't think I could do it and she couldn't, either. And he'll be well taken care of by his partners and his boating friends and the other friends. Men always know what to say, the *mot juste*. That sort of thing comes naturally to men. Everyone offered, it was hard for us to choose . . .

My father had opened the French doors and now stood looking across the lawn to the fairway. The moon was full, the fairway bathed in bright, thin light, a kind of glow. Beyond the fairway was a shallow sand trap and above the sand trap an undulating green with its limp flag. All this was visible in the moonlight. My father stood smoking his cigar and sipping scotch. When he stepped outside I thought he was walking away but he returned at once, bending to look at the repairs to the mullions broken when the brick flew through the window months before. He was bent in his hockey crouch and I knew he was remembering that evening, when so much changed in our family. Now he moved his foot over the scar in the parquet where he had ground the shard of glass that had torn his thumb; and I thought I saw a smile. The night air was still and the smoke from his cigar rose straight up, and when he turned to look at me, giving a little weary gesture, I saw the look of dismay on his face; and then he turned and pitched the cigar through the open doors.

Did he turn off the phonograph? my mother asked. I can't hear the music.

Yes, he did, I said.

We were playing pinochle, I went on. And listening to music.

Are you getting on all right, Wils?

It's awful news about Grandpa—

I mean generally, she said. You and your father.

Yes, I said. Of course. We're fine.

What were you doing when I called?

Playing pinochle. Listening to the music.

Your father and I used to play all the time, she said.

I remember, I said.

After a little silence, she said, All right. Put your father on.

I went out onto the terrace to give them some privacy. I could hear the rise and fall of my father's voice and an occasional phrase: so sorry . . . great guy . . . be missed . . . terrible shock . . . Of course I heard also hypocrisy, though his tone of voice seemed in no way insincere. Forgivable hypocrisy, I thought, intended to give comfort; and I hope my mother thought the same and understood that there were moments when a line had to be drawn between past and present; both sides of that line seemed to me blurred as I stood in the darkness, the bright lights of the den casting long shadows. Things were quiet now and I heard my father's voice again, this time a monotone, and I knew my mother was crying and that my father's words had not brought consolation. Certainly this was a moment when anyone would accept the hand of sympathy, a form of apology, even as you understood that what was done could not be undone, nor forgotten. It would be hard for my mother to be generous. I tried to imagine my grandfather dead but could not; and now I wondered how we would manage the funeral, the vast differences between us. Hypocrisy was difficult face to face. My father was not good at hiding his emotions and I knew my mother would see through him, and he would know it and try harder, and fail more completely. I began to understand that their separation—never acknowledged between us, nor to friends, my mother merely in the East to help her mother care for her father—might be permanent. They would never reconcile. She would remain in Connecticut and my father and I in Quarterday.

I listened to him conclude the conversation in monosyllables, his voice soft and polite, the voice he used when reserving a table at a restaurant. When my father hung up at last, I returned from the terrace to find him with his hands plunged in his pants pockets, staring bleakly at the scar in the parquet.

She's so sad, I said, and tears came to my eyes.

Yes, he said, his hand suddenly on my shoulder. It was a shock.

We have to help her, I said.

We'll do our best, he said. She needs you.

Both of us, I said.

She said I never loved Squire, my father said. And that's what comes between us. And now it's too late to make it right.

Well, I began, and said nothing further.

Something's broken that can't be fixed, your mother said.

It'll be all right, I said.

No, it won't, my father said.

She'll understand. It will take some time, and when she has time to think, she'll understand.

I don't think she will, my father said. She thinks I'm responsible for his death.

She's in shock, I said.

Probably, he said.

It's understandable, I said. People say things all the time that they don't mean, when they've had a shock. I thought of my mother and grandmother alone in the Connecticut house, deciding somehow that my father was responsible for Squire's death. I understood then that I did not know her at all; and my father and I had grown so close that she was on the outside. Talking to her on the telephone was like talking to a stranger and I did not know how that had come about.

My father sighed. She thinks Squire would be alive today if we hadn't had all those arguments. If I hadn't baited him. Unmercifully, she said. If I had agreed to live in the East. If I had gone to work on Wall Street. His high blood pressure, the stroke. Wouldn't've happened if I'd shown the slightest understanding of him and the life he led and how close they were, he and your mother. But I never accepted her family, she said. So she suffered and Squire suffered most of all because I had been—the word she used was "obtuse."

She couldn't mean that, I said.

But she does. Every word. She said I did not know the meaning of family because my own parents were so—mediocre, she said. Apparently my mother did not know the meaning of love. Mediocre as she was. He lifted his hands and let them fall, a gesture I had never seen before from him. I knew that he had been deeply wounded, his voice so soft it was almost a whisper.

Are you going to the funeral? I asked.

He looked at me angrily and said, Of course. And you are, too.

Mom's broken up, I said. We have to help.

Her heart's broken, my father agreed.

She needs us, I said.

Yes, she does.

To get her through this.

The death of a parent—

Yes, I said.

I never liked him, my father said.

I did, I said loyally.

You didn't know him, my father said.

That's not fair, I said, my voice rising.

Tell me something, Wils. At the jazz club. What's your alias?

None of your business, I said.

What do you call yourself? Sassoon? Adlai Stevenson?

I call myself whatever I feel like calling myself, I said. It's me, my life. I'll choose the name I want—

But my father had already turned his back and was walking out of the room, upstairs to bed.

4

M Y MOTHER stayed on in Connecticut after the funeral to help her mother with the estate. She said her
mother could not cope with the details of probate
and there were all Squire's things to dispose of, his clothes and
his wristwatch and cuff links and other personal items, his golf
clubs and collection of ships' models. She came home to Quarterday just as the party season on the North Shore was beginning. We met at Union Station and went to the Blackstone for
lunch. She looked frail and seemed distracted, insisting on sitting in the back seat of the car as if to emphasize her separation
from my father and me. She admitted she had hardly any energy and had been seeing a doctor for her nerves, a comment
to which my father did not respond. She was silent then, resting
her head on the seatback, looking indifferently out the window
at the shoppers crowding the sidewalks of the Loop.

The restaurant was noisy so my father handed the maitre d' a
bill and asked for a quiet table in the corner. None was available
so we settled for one in the middle of the room next to an as-
sembly of aldermen who were complaining loudly about the administration in Washington, ignorant fat-cat Republican businessmen who didn't know their ass from third base, and a
recession was coming on as it always did when Republicans
were in charge, and their answer to it was to screw the working-

man—that, too, a favorite Republican trick. My father moved closer to my mother, draping a protective arm over the back of her chair. He glared at the aldermen, who glared back but turned down the volume.

At lunch my mother asked questions about the parties I would attend, which debs were the most popular, and whether there were any I particularly liked. She said sternly, I want you to behave yourself, Wils. No monkeyshines. Wils is going to be a great success, my father said without explanation, except for the look that passed between us. I told her that my father and I had gone to Brooks to buy a dinner jacket and vest and dancing shoes. The kind with bows, my father said. My mother smiled and reminisced about debutante parties in her youth, at yacht clubs and golf clubs here and there in Connecticut and hotels in Manhattan and one especially splendid dinner dance in Old Westbury on Long Island, Claude Thornhill's orchestra. Of course the dances were not as opulent as they are today, especially on the North Shore. I guess those people feel they have something to prove, she said. Still, in the East the orchestras were always top-notch, and everyone danced until dawn that time in Old Westbury.

I met your father later that summer, she said to me, but I had three or four serious beaux before he came along. Oh, but it was fun, she said, dancing until all hours. It was a mating dance, she went on. We were all looking for husbands. And the boys were looking for wives, but not just then. College came first and wives came next. You'll remember this summer your whole life, Wils, so have fun. Remember to dance with the deb and the deb's mother, and say hello to her father and thank him for the party.

They cost a fortune, you know.

Especially the way they do them on the North Shore.

She said to my father, How many are we going to?

He said, Six, I think. The Bowdens and the Kendricks. The McManaways. That couple who go steeplechasing in England—

The Wickersons.

Yes, the Wickersons. They have twins so it should be quite a show. There are others, I don't remember the names. Friends of yours.

Oh, good, she said. I want to see Wils on the dance floor.

I taught him how to waltz, my father said.

You don't know how to waltz, my mother said.

I learned, he said.

My mother cheered up as lunch progressed, telling stories of her father, amusing stories that made my father and me laugh. There had been quite a to-do over the will, an exacting document that ran to more than fifty pages, much of it written in arcane maritime language. Squire's estate was large, larger than she or her mother expected, heavy in municipal bonds and New York real estate. She said I was getting the law books, goldtooled and calf-bound. Squire had mentioned my father also, bequeathing him a silver picture frame (with a photo of Squire himself in a blue blazer and yachting cap at the helm of *Marine Tort*) and a privately printed volume detailing the Wilson family tree, eight generations of towheads traced back to a crofter's hut in Scotland. At that, my mother raised her eyebrows and my father grinned gamely. She drank a manhattan and said she was glad to be home at last; she had stayed away longer than she intended. I've missed you both, she said. My father and I replied in unison, We're glad to have you back, and then it was her turn to smile gamely.

My mother set about redecorating the house, as if she wanted to remove all evidence of the former environment. Before long, her mother's housekeeper Ling arrived from Connecticut to help her. They rearranged furniture and the pictures on the walls, paying particular attention to the location of mirrors and the affinity of primary colors, yellow for one room, red for another, all according to some formula of Ling's. The old beige davenport was re-covered in yellow silk. My father arrived home one night to find his favorite chair turned ninety degrees, facing not the terrace but the fireplace. The Oriental rug in front of the fireplace had been removed and a white shag substituted. The French doors were gone, replaced by a glass slider; and its view was no longer of the sixth fairway and the sand trap and the raised green beyond but of a fat blue spruce, newly planted and flanked by stone birdbaths. She had added a ha-ha between the spruce and the fairway.

My father did not question any of these changes, except to

idly inquire whether there was some guiding principle behind them. Harmony, my mother said. Feng shui, Ling explained, to which my father nodded and pressed no further. He missed his view of the fairway, as he missed the Oriental carpet and the scar in the parquet, the scar having been sanded down and the parquet retouched. About as successful as a toupee, my father muttered to me one night. But he held to his view that a woman had the right to decorate her house as she saw fit, and it was true that my mother seemed content. Her fatigue had vanished and she was cheerful in the evenings, according to my father. He mildly objected when she removed an Edward Hopper etching of a steam engine and replaced it with a watercolor of Squire's sloop. But he admitted that the watercolor was attractive and the only thing he had against it was that it had been painted by Squire. In due course, Ling returned to Connecticut, having given my mother detailed instructions on how to maintain feng shui.

My mother and father struggled through that summer and by the end of it had reached an accommodation, making do in the way that older people did. My mother made new plans for a screened-in porch and a swimming pool, all arranged according to the principles of feng shui as she understood them. Our house had become a different house, its ambiance muted and unfamiliar, its furnishings such that you wanted to move around it on tiptoe, as Ling had done. It was no longer the place where you could play Georg Brunis, or Fred Astaire singing Gershwin, while you dealt the cards for a companionable round of pinochle.

By then I was preoccupied with my own life, my summer job at one of the newspapers downtown, and my strenuous after-hours carousing. The summer had turned out better than I ever imagined, and I realized soon enough that I was inhabiting three parallel worlds: the newspaper, the parties, and the house in Quarterday. Each day was a fabulous journey to the unknown, Stanley to the Congo or Lewis and Clark to the American West, yet when I arrived home there was little that was familiar. London and St. Louis were changed utterly, the

Houses of Parliament disappeared, the Mississippi a pitiful creek. The teller of tales needs a well-worn chair when he describes his adventures, for an adventure always implies a return for the settling of accounts. I found narrative difficult in these new surroundings. One night I came home late from a party, keyed up after the long drive from Winnetka, and found an antique oval mirror in the foyer and an armoire next to the mirror and an ornate Chinese chair next to the armoire, and reckoned I had somehow entered the wrong house, except the red duffel was resting on the chair. I wandered onto the terrace to find my father sitting alone in the moonlight, a nightcap in his hand. He asked me to join him and after a moment of frank appraisal—he was looking at me to assure himself that I was steady on my feet, no menace to him or to others—he disclosed that he had agreed to drain the pond and cut down the sycamores.

Your mother wants a gazebo, he said. She calls it a teahouse.

You can't give up your hockey, I said. That's crazy. Who needs a teahouse?

He looked at me sharply and replied that it wasn't crazy. The teahouse would be a fine addition on warm summer evenings. He added that his arthritic knees could no longer stand the strain of ice hockey, and without hockey—well, what was the point of the pond, a breeding ground of mosquitoes and muskrats. The sycamores were a nuisance and one was dying. It's not crazy at all, he said. He went on about his bum knees but I wasn't listening carefully because I had had an argument with a girl and I was trying to fathom why she began it. I was replaying the argument while my father talked about his knees and what a splendid addition the teahouse would make.

I didn't know you had arthritic knees, I said.

They flared up a few weeks ago, he said. Once or twice I've had to use a cane. It's a pain in the ass.

I didn't know, I said, looking at him in the darkness. Only a month before, I would have known. I would have known how much he was hurting, known the name of his doctor and what his knees felt like and the prognosis and the medicine prescribed. But he had said nothing to me, or if he had, I was not listening.

Much pain? I asked.

The look he gave me was the answer.

I'm sorry, I said. I didn't know. Seen the doctor?

Live with it, the doctor said.

Don't worry about it, my father went on. You have other things on your mind. You've been busy. He took out a cheroot, lit it, and blew a cloud of smoke in the direction of the pond, and then back to me, another look of appraisal.

You look good in a tuxedo, he said.

Thanks, I said.

Look like you were born in it. Most men don't look good in one, they move as if they're in a straitjacket. They look dressed up, and've got expressions like they expect a guillotine's behind the bandstand and when the music stops the tumbrils arrive in the ballroom and that's it for them.

I began to laugh.

Squire looked good in a tuxedo. Probably you got it from him, naturalness. You can't teach it and you can't learn it. You're tall and that helps, and you're fit. You're a god damned good-looking kid and you don't act as if you know it.

My father had never said anything like that to me before, and I didn't know why he was saying it now.

At least you're not a towhead, he went on, still staring into the darkness. He said something about my needing a haircut and then asked me if I would fix him a drink, a short scotch. Have one yourself, he said.

When I returned with the drinks, he said, How's work?

It isn't work, I said. It's a circus. I described the newsroom, cigarette butts on the floor, overflowing wastebaskets, pint bottles of whiskey in brown paper bags, a side-of-the-mouth atmosphere common to a racetrack or pool hall, each day a high-wire act. And your old partner Judge Greenslat is in the news again. Nasty, nasty divorce, and his scorned second wife is singing to anyone who'll listen. "Love Nest" will figure in the morning headlines, and they tell me there's a photograph. Showgirl, I said.

Poor old bastard, my father said, and was silent.

You liked him, didn't you?

Butch? Everyone liked Butch. His nephew was nothing much but Butch was good as gold. A rogue, but good as gold. Loved showgirls, the gaudier the better. Started with waitresses, graduated to showgirls, but waitresses were his first love. It was a treat watching Butch stroll into the office at three in the afternoon, a spring in his step and a glint in his eye. Butch and I would spend hours after work talking about life. He was a philosopher, Butch was. I learned a lot from him.

And what did you learn?

Later, he said with a smile. When you're older.

I'm learning a lot downtown, I said.

I'll bet you are, my father said.

I'm learning what they put in and what they keep out.

My father laughed at that.

Sometimes they give me a hard time, I said.

What do you expect? You're a Quarterday kid. They know how you got the job and they know that when September comes around you'll be saying bye-bye and going off to college and they'll still be there, worrying about showgirls and the Mob and City Hall. Trying to make ends meet.

We sat in silence a moment and then I said, I see you're still carrying the duffel.

Yeah, he said. I don't know why. The strike went away. The threat's gone. Probably there wasn't any real threat, except Clyde and his brick. Seemed real enough at the time but I don't think there was much to it. He rose slowly and peered into the darkness. I watched him steady himself on the arm of his chair, wincing.

I was trying to imagine my father with a cane but couldn't. He had always been healthy, never so much as a common cold, and now he was talking about a cane to get around. Then I was thinking about the girl, and the argument that began at the party and continued in the car and ended on her front porch in Winnetka, what she had said to me and what I had said back. We had been talking about privacy and the newspapers and how scandal threatened to undermine the confidence that people had in the established order, democracy itself called into question, successful people held up to ridicule, even their children. The reference was to a gossip column about her older sister, harmless but snide, something to do with an accident in the kitchen that caused her to attend her debutante party with her arm in a sling. The headline read, BOUND BUD BOWS. The argument somehow turned into a litany of complaint about my secretiveness, the worldly life I led downtown, my unwholesome enthusiasm for what she called "the angles," and my morbid outlook on life generally. If I had been a true friend I would have seen to it that the cruel and offensive item was killed, and when I protested that I had no such power, that my job was to fetch coffee and hustle copy from one desk to another, she said, Don't kid me. You enjoy seeing people suffer. You're like the boy in the cartoon who throws a snowball at the banker's top hat. You think it's amusing, Wils. We had parted without a kiss or even a civil good-night, and we had been good friends, not romantic friends but friends sure enough, and now suddenly I was Trotsky, expelled from the party and thrust into exile.

My father said, One of these days I'll give it back to Tom.

You'll miss it, I said with a smile.

Shit, he said with scorn. And again, more softly, Shit no.

But I would have used it if I had to, he added, speaking again into the darkness.

I'll miss watching your skating, I said.

But he did not reply to that, taking a sip of his nightcap and staring away into the darkness.

I saw my father alone only once more that summer. We played a late round of golf, managing only six holes before the sun set. I shouldered my bag and began to walk down the fairway to our house when he called to me and motioned in the direction of the clubhouse. So I made an about-face, followed him to the seventh tee and down the slope to the road, and then to the clubhouse and the men's locker room that adjoined it. The locker room bar was deserted except for two golfers playing liars' dice at a table in the corner. They looked up and called a cheerful hello, my father giving them a wave before we settled in at the long bar. The barman, Cecil, brought drinks and we three talked about our forgettable round, bad off the tee, bad on the green, had all afternoon. When Cecil went away, my father asked me about my social life, how the summer had gone and whether it had been—productive.

I smiled and said, Productive? I suppose so.

And you've made new friends?

A few. And a few enemies.

You must be doing something right, he said.

It's hard to find your place, I said suddenly.

He nodded while he fished an olive from his martini and ate it.

I opened my mouth to say something more but could not find the words. The bar's atmosphere was congenial and no one was eavesdropping but the moment was not right. I had met a girl and I wanted to tell him about her, how we met and how close we had become and how much she meant to me.

You were saying, my father said.

The trick is, I said. The trick's to find something you know that no one else knows.

In reference to what, exactly? my father said.

Employment, I said. What you do for the rest of your life. The boys I meet at the parties, they're all going to work for their fathers. Real estate, the stock market, family businesses of one sort or another. They've already made their plans, work downtown for their fathers and live happily ever after on the North Shore. Ride the train to work. Join a club. I hope you're not planning on me working for Carillo & Ravan.

No, he said. I hadn't planned on that.

It just seems so—routine, I said.

Sounds like it, he said.

My father's voice had changed timbre and I knew then that I had offended him.

I didn't mean that the way it sounded.

My father nodded and looked down the length of the bar for Cecil and twirled his fingers, two more drinks. The locker room bar had the rosy glow of an English pub, the bar stools and tables of varnished hardwood, the floor pockmarked from spiked shoes. Watercolors of famous holes at St. Andrews and Troon decorated the walls, and at the far end a plaque with the names of the club champions. As a child I thought it the finest room I had ever seen and could not wait until I was old enough to be admitted with my father; and now, here I was. Cecil arrived with the drinks and set them carefully on cork coasters.

So your summer wasn't a success, he said.

Oh, yes, it was. Quite a success.

You were a success, he said.

Yes, I was. I knew what I was doing to get it, too.

My father seemed uncomfortable, moving his shoulders up and down like a pitcher before delivery. And do you know what it is you know that no one else knows?

Not yet, I said.

You have time, he said. And then he added, Remember what you just said. It's important.

I won't forget, I said.

That was the great thing about Butch Greenslat, my father said with a sly grin. Butch never forgot anything, just so he could repeat himself over and over again without a mistake. But you're not like Butch. You'll always be moving on from one place to another. I don't know where you get that from. Not me, not your mother. Maybe your mother, now that I think about it.

You, too, I said.

Not me. I'm a one-barn horse. Barn's called Quarterday.

So you don't have any regrets about not settling in the East?

He looked at me and laughed. Are you kidding?

Then I remembered a conversation from a few nights before. I said, Do you know Mr. McManaway?

They're friends of your mother's, he said.

He admires you. He admires you for standing up to the Reds. He wanted me to tell you but I forgot until now. I saw him at one of the parties. He was tight. He asked all about you, how you were doing.

Banker, my father said. I went to him for a loan once. Turned me down. But now I suppose I can go back and write my own ticket because I stood up to the Reds, and that enhances my balance sheet. My net worth. And I have a letter from Senator McCarthy, Tailgunner Joe himself, certifying my vigilance, my willingness to go the last mile. I'm a great American.

My father's tone was sarcastic but I could tell he was pleased. That was what he had salvaged from the strike, a letter from Joe McCarthy on United States Senate stationery, and he could tell from the weight of the paper that it was inferior stuff.

I'm going to sell the business, he said.

I said, What?

So you won't have to worry about selling stationery for the rest of your life. You won't be programmed, and there's every possibility that you'll live happily ever after somewhere else.

Cecil brought the drinks and I looked into mine without saying anything.

I have an offer and I think I'll accept it.

Good offer?

Pretty good, considering.

I said, What will you do?

My father smiled and then he laughed. Fight the Communists.

Don't you think you've already done your part? I said sharply, more sharply than I intended. I didn't like McCarthy, and the word at the newspaper was that he was drunk most of the time and that Cohn was a shit.

That's a joke, Wils. It's what your mother wants. That, and other things.

Is that what she said?

It's what she wants, he said.

Well, I said, and did not finish the thought, though the "so what" lingered in the air—what right did she have to tell my father where to work?—and he heard it and turned to me and said, You don't know what you're talking about.

I only meant, your work's your life and you have a right—

I'll decide what my rights are, he said, squeezing my arm hard, finishing his drink in a gulp. Not your fault, he added, because you've been out of touch and I'm just a little bit grouchy today. But, Jesus, it was a hell of a nice business, Carillo & Ravan. I always liked making stationery for every occasion, notes, letters, invitations, printed cards of condolence, paper that when you wrote something on it the words *counted*. But it's time to let go. Time and place for everything. No one wins a strike.

But you did, I said. You won. But the expression on his face—sardonic, the look of a man counting loose change—told me he saw things differently. Everything came with a cost, and the cost was not always apparent. Win the girl, win the lottery, win the golf match, win the strike; and always there was something left over, a residue you did not count on or even imagine. Winning was never the only thing; often, it wasn't anything.

All right, I said. But I could not resist adding, with a smile, You win.

Let's go home, my father said, signing the chit and limping to the door. I waited a moment, watching him, listening to the rattle of dice at the table in the corner, and then I followed him out.

I have not been as close to anyone since. Of course my father and I grew apart, as if the magnetic force that drew him to my mother (and she to him) had its opposite corollary, a counterforce that required we keep our distance. Is it true that there's room for only one friendship in any household? I know that the spring and summer of that year were a trial for them both, the brick through the window one sort of division and Squire's death another. I was the third. My father had his worries and my mother had hers, and each had to do with the other but not in any reconcilable way; and they were stubborn people. My mother had changed in ways I could not immediately understand. I believe Squire's death was her first occasion of profound grief, and this was not grief that my father could share. He admitted as much. When she returned from the East and took charge once again, our great comradeship came to an end, not by any agreement spoken or unspoken; it simply ended, as night falls, and in the gathering darkness we no longer saw each other clearly. Perhaps he had said all he had to say about the way of the world and how a man conducts himself in it, or anyhow all that could be said over a hand of pinochle to a nineteen-year-old. And now I was away from the house every evening, all dressed up in my tuxedo with the shawl collar, retailing scandalous stories gathered in the newsroom, learning the angles, waltzing as my father had taught me, learning to drink with style, discovering what I knew that no one else knew; and at last and finally, meeting a girl I could love.

Now and again I saw my mother and father at the dances, though only a few words passed between us. They were with their crowd and I was with mine. I was surprised at how comfortable my father seemed in his tuxedo, his expression one of faraway amusement; sardonic would be the word. I would look over someone's shoulder and see him in the shadows, leaning on his cane, usually in the vicinity of the bar. He would be watching me on the dance floor or talking with someone, his mouth arranged in his half-smile—and I had the thought he wanted to join us and hear for himself what I was saying that could make a girl laugh so. He knew I was performing, and when I raised my hand, motioning him over, saying to whomever I was with, I want you to meet my old man, I saw him turn and take my mother's arm, putting aside his cane, guiding her to the dance floor, where they began to waltz slowly and then faster, my father pausing only to point east, and they would turn to the moon rising hugely over the unruffled lake.

So that year we all grew apart, secessionist provinces of an unstable nation. The house was reorganized, the den and the terrace brought up to date, the pond and the sycamores soon to go; it was as if my mother was determined to erase history itself, airbrush the photographs as the commissars regularly did. Later that year, my father sold his business as he promised he would do, and at that moment some essential vitality left him. He gave away his skates and resigned as rules chairman of the club. He no longer arrived home with wildly improbable stories, like the one about the Persian and the basket of trembling silkworms. He lost touch with Sheriff Felsen. He lost interest in the Communists and I am convinced he felt defeated by them. He had loved his business but now the business was gone, sold like a stick of furniture, and now it lived in someone else's house. He looked to the stock market to occupy his time. My father no longer manufactured a product you could hold in your hand but gathered pieces of paper instead, shares in an automobile company, a bank, a pharmaceutical concern, a clothing business, and oil, blue chips all.

In August I saw them off on the train for New Orleans, where they were to board the boat for Havana. My father was smart in a white suit and carrying a malacca cane, my mother chic in a shantung suit and a wide-brimmed straw hat drawn down over one eye, sunglasses. They looked like a pair of middle-aged movie stars, the more so since my father had recently grown a mustache, neatly trimmed, Gable-sized. It was hard not to feel envious of them, embarking on such a glamorous journey, promising to buy me a bright red Cuban shirt, promising also to share their winnings in the casinos. My mother had been studying the rules of baccarat. We drank a glass of champagne in their compartment, toasting the success of the trip, hoping for good weather, hoping for agreeable shipboard companions, hoping that I would behave myself back home. The house is in your care. Don't stay out too late. Eat properly. No parties while we're gone.

I listened to their instructions while I looked out the window, passengers streaming by, everyone in a festive mood. A traveler in a dark suit was standing on the platform looking at my father. His expression was unpleasant, and then he turned to the woman he was with and said (I could read his lips), That's that son of a bitch Tom Dewey, and continued to stare. I looked at my father, scarcely believing that anyone could mistake him for an indoor politician like Dewey, altogether too slight a figure, not broad across the shoulders as my father was, not *solid*. My father raised his glass of champagne and turned to look at the platform and he and the stranger locked eyes. The other flung his cigarette to the ground and crushed it under his heel, gave a final sneer, and stalked off.

My father said, What was that about?

I said, He thought you were Tom Dewey.

Why the hell would he think I was Tom Dewey?

The mustache, I said.

My father's forefinger went to his upper lip and he colored slightly. He said, I'll shave it off. Jesus, Tom Dewey. That bastard wrecked the Republican Party.

Don't be silly, my mother said. I love the mustache.

The mustache and the glass of champagne, I said. It all adds up.

Tom Dewey led us down to defeat, my father said.

The mustache didn't have anything to do with it, my mother said.

The hell it didn't, my father said. He looked like a head-waiter.

Well, you don't look like a headwaiter. You look like my Teddy, only more distinguished. My mother raised her head and kissed him on the cheek.

It's the champagne, I said. Wasn't that his nickname? Champagne Tom Dewey? And that was why he lost to the Kansas City haberdasher, swilling champagne in Wall Street instead of campaigning in Pekin. Haberdashers trump headwaiters.

My father smiled at that. Even my mother gave a grin of sorts.

Hell of a way to begin a trip, my father grumbled. Mistaken for Tom Dewey.

When the conductor's whistle announced the departure of the train, there was a sudden commotion on the platform, passengers beginning to hurry. I kissed my mother and shook hands with my father, wishing them both a bon voyage and reminding them about the red shirt, maybe a pair of castanets to go with it. They gave me a last warning about the house, always lock the door at night and turn off the lights, no parties, drive safely. Then I rushed from the train, pausing long enough to wave at them from the platform. My mother had taken off her hat and they were toasting each other and were still toasting when the train edged away from the platform in an acrid cloud of steam. I watched the cars recede, then went on my way to the newspaper office downtown, filled with plans for that evening and the next and all the evenings until Labor Day, when college began and I could move into one of the university dormitories on the South Side, temporary quarters until I could find a private apartment with a bed in the living room; but I would be a Chicagoan at last, on my own in a city larger than anyone's ambition. Meanwhile, I had plans for the empty house, the terrace, and the other special places where my girl and I would not be disturbed.

The glass of champagne in the crowded compartment of the City of New Orleans was the end of our life as a family, though I did not know it then. I did not notice because I had acquired this new life of my own, the one I liked to call the wider world, in some clear sense the modern world, and one I was disinclined to share, no doubt because its utter secrecy and privacy was part of its appeal. I had an idea that this new life gained in excitement because it was lived in the shadows of the North Shore, far from Quarterday.

THE DEBUTANTE'S ARCHIPELAGO

5

IN JUNE AND JULY there were debutante parties nearly every other night, two hundred of us dancing under high-topped tents with girls in armored evening dresses, pearls swinging against their throats, the orchestra playing on and on until midnight, when breakfast was served, shirred eggs, scrambled eggs, eggs benedict, eggs daffodil, in copper chafing dishes arrayed on a long buffet table while white-coated waiters opened fresh bottles of Piper-Heidsieck. That summer the Charleston made an unexpected comeback, along with a jazz band from somewhere in Mississippi, its members very old black men. The jazz band played during orchestra intermissions and was the surprise hit of the season. They were tremendously sympathetic, the oldest well over ninety years old. He was rumored to have been born a slave, and you could believe it. He stood in a crouch and his fingers were gnarled as tree roots, as black as the clarinet he played. The jazz band played all the old standards, "Basin Street Blues" and "South Rampart Street Parade," and hymns like "Just a Closer Walk with Thee." He seemed to float above the others, his eyes neither here nor there. If you spoke to him he always nodded politely but declined to speak back. My God, you thought, he was born at the time of the Civil War.

The dances had a timeless quality, as if things had not advanced for a quarter century—Coolidge in the White House, Capone in the Loop, *Gatsby* in the bookstores. Some nights you could believe that the entire North Shore was dancing to "Mountain Greenery," the musical phrases handed off from one country club to another up the debutante's archipelago from Chicago to Lake Bluff, two thousand dancers whirling in a blur of cream and black, black and pink, aqua and white, the sound of saxophones rising and settling over the vast monotonous lake like a nervous mist; and the mist vanished at midnight, when the orchestra played its finale and the sweating musicians gathered up their instruments and left the bandstand, disappearing into the night. Then there was a sudden crush around the buffet table. The eggs had arrived.

Everyone knew each other, old and young brought together through acquaintance of the debutante or her parents or school connections or if you were on the List. The origins of the List were obscure, but it was updated every year by a committee, the object being to ensure an adequate supply of presentable young men. I remember reading somewhere, probably in Sassoon, that the great objective of Britain in World War One was to ensure an adequate supply of heroes for the Somme and the Marne; this was a weak-kneed version of that. At first I knew only about a dozen people, but by the end of the first week I had met most everyone, including the houseguests, school friends or cousins from the East and one from England. We roamed in a pack, circling the dance floor, commenting on the action. Each debutante party had a narrative and we knew in the first hour whether the narrative would be successful; that is, if we were still around for the eggs. Now and then I would dance with a popular girl, and when I was cut in on, return happily to the bar and continue to prowl the perimeter, observing the social rituals of the young marrieds. The hierarchies of these gatherings bore a resemblance to life aboard ship. We had set sail aboard a hilarious *Pequod*, young Ishmaels fascinated by the obsessions of the black-tied Ahabs and their women. The young marrieds seemed to us always in search of some fantastic grail, eternal youth or the ring of the Nibelungen, the presidency of the bank, the perfect crime, or the ultimate revenge. Their lives seemed to us unimaginably exotic, as if they were a tribe of the Caucasus or South Sea Islanders or French voluptuaries. The married life was storm-tossed and momentous and until you entered into it you were still an adolescent, becalmed.

They were rowdy, drinking heavily and dancing with abandon, as if their settled state entitled them to a valedictory spree—tomorrow they would be a day older, and the day after that the children would begin to arrive along with gray hair and arthritis and nighttime fatigue owing to various responsibilities at home and at work, too, the bank or the brokerage house where someone was always looking over your shoulder, and if you made a mistake the word would spread at once and your father would be on the telephone with a friendly word of warning and your wife would indicate disapproval in the usual ways. Naturally your father-in-law would also be informed, so there would be the obligatory lunch with him, offering sober assurances that the mistake, whatever it was, would never happen again. The excuses were well honed from years of use with headmasters and university deans and highway patrolmen. The married men never failed to dance with the debutante, if she was pretty or if her father was influential, and the deb was usually delighted because married men were so at ease and amusing, experienced as they were, not left-foot clumsy and looking down the front of your dress like the boys your own age. The married men treated you with courtesy even as they flirted a little, reminiscing about their college years, driving five hours from New Haven to Vassar or Bennett, arriving at dawn for a breakfast of doughnuts and scotch, weekends in New York and meeting under the clock at the Biltmore and going on to Jimmy Ryan's and ending up at someone's apartment and talking seriously about the state of the world, the war in Korea and how the Reds were trying to take over, the toll taken by the Yale class of '51 when so many boys joined the Marines, a life-altering experience. Like whales, they knew the secrets of the deep.

The other reason the young marrieds drank heavily and danced with abandon was because next year there would be fewer party invitations and the debs would be even younger, a rebuke to husband and wife alike. My friends and I were not welcome in their company, in the way that sergeants were not welcome at the Officers Club. The married men—they were only a few years older than we were but seemed middle-aged—were sarcastic, spoiling for an argument, and their wives were condescending, as if they knew something that we didn't, that something being, of course, married life, its ardor, its pleasures and miseries, its intimacies, its compromises and boundaries and burdens, its envied seriousness. They knew the score and we didn't. During intermissions they would press close to the jazz band, nodding to the beat, listening with perfect nonchalance, managing to imply that they and the old black men shared a certain knowledge of the wider world of hard knocks and disappointment, casual slander and crimination for imaginary offenses and the simple struggle to stay on top—and although they could not aspire to the natural rhythm of Negroes, they could certainly appreciate the melancholy soul of the blues, an American birthright. The blues were part of every life, even a privileged life on the North Shore; and while it was unnecessary—pointless, really—for one of them to imagine a sharecropper's life in Mississippi (everyone was dealt a particular hand, and how you played the hand was the acid test of character), it was no less pointless for one of the Negroes to imagine their life—the expectations that went with kinship in a good family and matriculation at a fine prep school and an Ivy League degree and the right sort of marriage and all the rest of it, a lifetime of measuring up, with the temptation all the while to say the hell with it, and that decision came with a price also. Not that the price wasn't sometimes paid, and with unpredictable, often hilarious results. Point was, even the North Shore wasn't all it was cracked up to be. Whatever hand you were dealt, someone at the table always had higher cards; and the stakes were not small. You went through the mill the same as everyone else, including the Negroes, though it would be a stretch for them to understand that. In any case, the blues crossed racial lines, even the divisions among the classes; each group would have its own special affinity. Behind the finger-snapping façade of the blues was a glum house of betrayal, thwarted ambition, sexual totalitarianism, lies, and misprision.

82

The idea was to stay at the table to get what was coming to you; that was the lesson of the blues, especially the stoic example of the clarinet player, born a slave at the time of the Civil War.

There was a man I wanted to meet, a silent presence at all the parties, always standing in the shadows off the dance floor, a gin and tonic in his hand and a cigarette burning in his fingers. He was gaunt with gray hair, crewcut, and I estimated his age at somewhere in the vicinity of fifty, ten years either side. It was impossible to be more precise. He seemed to have a prematurely aged head on an athlete's sinewy body, as if his head had lived an entirely different life. He was evidently unmarried. Now and then during the evening a woman would join him for a few moments of one-sided conversation, her attitude solicitous, looking up at him with something like awe. And then she would touch his elbow and drift off, leaving him alone and watchful in the shadows. I had learned his name, Jason Brule, and I knew he was a doctor, a psychiatrist with offices off Lincoln Park on the North Side, downtown. I knew nothing of psychiatry, except for my father's view that it was a shabby discipline one step removed from voodoo. Jason Brule did not seem to enjoy himself. He was often lost in thought, staring at his shoes or off into the distance. He rarely danced and usually left before the eggs. But he was present at most every party, and I came to think of him as a sentry on night watch. I wanted to meet him because he looked and behaved so out of the ordinary, but no one I knew was acquainted with him and it was not done to walk up to a stranger and introduce yourself, not at these parties, and certainly not if the stranger was an older man. His distant manner discouraged familiarity anyhow.

One night I was dancing with a girl I had not met before. She gave her name as Aurora and her conversation instantly set her apart from Debbie, Mimi, Gigi, and Dana. Dana was the girl I had argued with weeks before and this was her party at her parents' house, one of the lakefront mansions in Lake Forest, a perfect evening in July. I was trying to stay out of her way, and when I saw Aurora standing alone I asked her to dance. She had been watching the floor as if she expected a knife fight or other bloodletting, and when I asked her about it she said there was trouble among the bachelors and the benedicts and if I was smart I'd keep my head down because they were drunk and unpredictable, the benedicts particularly. Honor was at stake, she said, and she was trying to discover whose honor it was. A girl was at the bottom of it. So to speak, she added with a smile. And that's all she knew about that, subject closed. We were dancing well and getting to know each other better when I felt a tap on my shoulder and yielded to one of the wolfish benedicts. I recut a dance later, and asked her if she wanted a drink, that way we could talk without being interrupted by men who should be dancing with their wives. We fetched drinks—she took a Dubonnet and soda, a drink I had never heard of—and wandered to the shadows of a great oak and stood with our backs to the dance floor and watched the lake ruffle the moon's reflection. When Aurora told me she lived in Chicago, I asked her if she knew the gaunt man with the aged head. I turned to point him out but he had vanished.

Jason Brule, I said.

Why do you want to know? What's he to you?

Nobody, I said. He looks interesting, is all.

I suppose he is, she said. That's what everyone says.

What do they say?

That he's interesting, she said with a smile.

Bachelor, I said.

That, too, she said.

Head doctor, I said.

Is that so? she said.

See, that's interesting.

Why is that interesting?

How many psychiatrists do you know? And everyone around here is either married or too young to be married—

Not everyone, she said, and named a bachelor of flamboyant manner and ambiguous reputation, odd in that he was seen only in the company of older women.

He's different, I said. That isn't what I mean.

What do you mean, then? That smile again, insinuating something, I didn't know what.

I mean—and then I wasn't certain what I meant, except that there were different sorts of bachelors and that Jason Brule

84

was not the odd sort, and this conversation was moving in a direction I did not want to follow. I said, At any event, someone who isn't married stands out. Also, the doctor's head doesn't go with the doctor's body. It's as if they haven't been introduced. And he doesn't say much, does he? Doesn't dance, doesn't mix, drinks little. He's a psychiatrist and that isn't usual, either, around here. All these things together make someone who isn't run-of-the-mill, and therefore he's worth knowing.

If you say so, Aurora said. She took a step outside the shadows to stand near the lip of the bluff that sloped down to the lake. She wore a pale blue gown that shimmered in the moonlight, and a plain gold necklace that shimmered as well. She wound her finger around the necklace as she sipped her drink and looked at the reflection of the moon on the lake. Behind us the band struck up what sounded like the last dance. I offered her a cigarette but she shook her head.

They call him Jack, she said.

Who?

Jason. Jason Brule. Thought you'd want to know.

I haven't seen you around, I said.

I don't get up here very often. But I'm a friend of Dana's, so here I am, dancing in the moonlight. She smiled thinly and added, But I know you. You're the boy with the stories, Wils Ravan, the boy with all the gossip from downtown. Dana was telling me all about you and how you wouldn't go to bat for her sister at the newspaper. Dana thinks you're a bad friend and a menace. Subversive was the word she used, though she was probably just repeating her father. Dana said that if we met I was supposed to give you a piece of my mind, and I promised but now I don't know. You don't look subversive to me. Are you subversive?

I do my best, I said.

Try harder, she said.

Aurora was silent a moment, rocking on her heels, and suddenly threw her glass high in the air. We watched it rise and fall to the underbrush near the water's edge. We heard a faint explosion when the glass hit a rock. She leaned over the lip, squinting in the darkness. She said, Where do you live?

Quarterday, I said.

Where's Quarterday? I never heard of it.

The other side of Half Day.

I never heard of Half Day, either.

You've been missing something, I said. You've led a sheltered life.

Not as sheltered as yours, she said, and I had an idea this was a reference to the confusion of bachelors. She said, As a matter of fact, I do remember now. Quarterday. Where they ride horses.

We need them for the spring plowing, I said.

She smiled at that and said, Why don't you tell me one of your stories?

It's Saturday, I said. I didn't go to the office.

That's where the stories come from?

Well, it's a newspaper office. A newspaper office is a story factory. You make stories the way a furniture factory makes chairs. The stories are supposed to be well made and comfortable, so that you can sit in them without fear that they'll break down or disappoint you in any way.

Consoling, she said.

Definitely, I said.

Tell me an old story, then.

I never tell old stories, I said. My stories are all fresh stories. Today's news, not yesterday's news. Nothing deader than yesterday's news.

Behind us people were clapping. The orchestra had stopped playing. I lit a cigarette and blew a smoke ring into the moonlight. Aurora was staring into the darkness and frowning, as if she had seen something there that annoyed her. But the only visible movement was the running lights of an ore boat bound for Duluth.

I said, Do you want some eggs?

She said, I want to go home.

I'll take you home, I said.

I don't live anywhere near your Quarterday, she said. I live in Chicago. As I told you.

That's all right, I said. I've been there. I know the way.

All right, she said.

If we skip the eggs we can stop at the jazz club on Bryn Mawr. Listen to the last set and I'll drive you home. It's a wonderful band in the old style, you'll love it. I smiled at her, waiting for an answer, explaining that the Eleven-Eleven Club was located under an El station in a rundown neighborhood near the Edgewater Beach Hotel, the crowd always noisy and friendly, and sometimes Georg Brunis played the trombone with his toes. The bartender had become a friend and every time I came in late in my tuxedo, he shouted, Stop the presses! Mr. Hearst is in the house!

I've been there, she said. I was put out, having the idea that this very well-known jazz club was my own private discovery, and my expression must have shown it because Aurora raised her eyebrows and added, But we can go there anyway.

Let's go now, I said.

You mean—no eggs?

I'll get us some champagne instead. For the car.

We walked back to the house and made our goodbyes. The buffet table had a crowd around it and the bar was doing a brisk business. Dana was nowhere in sight but her parents accepted our thanks with curt nods and no handshake from him. It seemed to me that Aurora was included in the general frost but it was hard to tell because they turned almost at once to say an effusive goodbye to a young married couple, both drunk and cute as buttons. They had the Englishman with them and everyone was laughing at something he had said. I fetched two glasses of champagne and waited for Aurora while she spoke to a friend, explaining that she had a ride home, not to worry. The friend looked dubiously at me and leaned forward to say something to Aurora, taking her hand in a kind of warning gesture. As we walked to the car, Aurora shivered slightly so I took off my jacket and put it around her shoulders. The breeze off the lake was cool.

I said, What was that about?

She's been talking to Dana.

Bad news, I said.

I'm a fool to trust anyone as unreliable as you.

Mr. Nobody from Nowhere, I added.

Exactly, she said.

When we were settled in the car, I said, I don't know your name.

Aurora, she said. I told you. And then she added, Aurora Brule.

I didn't say anything but I was thinking, Idiot. Ahead of us the married couple and the Englishman were struggling to fit themselves into a green MG, the Englishman driving and the woman sitting in her husband's lap, her slippered feet riding high above the windshield. I was silent a moment, watching the antics in the MG, the wife hilarious and the Englishman trying to put the key into the ignition, dropping the key, and pushing the wife's foot out of the way while he rooted about on the floor of the car. The husband was drinking from a flask, and when his wife reached for it he held it away, out of her reach.

Your bachelor father, I said.

She nodded. The head doctor, she said.

Oh, Christ, I said.

I'll take that cigarette now, she said.

I passed her the pack of cigarettes and my Zippo. Ahead of us the green MG lurched off in a cloud of exhaust, trailing laughter, the woman's crinoline skirt billowing in the breeze. The policeman at the end of the drive gave them a friendly wave but they ignored him. A cigarette sailed from the car and landed at his feet.

The Palshaws, Aurora said. Oscar and Lizzie. And the rude Englishman at the wheel. I forget his name but I heard he was a lord and he seems to be their permanent houseguest. I dated Oscar once. Once was enough. That MG, you might as well be riding in a coffin. He has trouble locating the gearshift and there's no escape.

You dated Oscar?

Last summer, she said. And the next thing I knew, he was engaged to Lizzie.

Not a success, I said.

Definitely not a success, she agreed. And you won't believe my father's enthusiasm when he said, I told you so.

Their favorite words, I said.

88

Fathers, yes, she said.

I'm sorry what I said about him.

It was funny, Aurora said. For a minute I thought you were putting me on. When it was clear you weren't, I just went along for the ride. Aurora lit her cigarette and exhaled in a long thin stream. She put her head on the backrest and looked at me, her eyes owlish behind thick-lensed glasses. They had materialized from nowhere and I decided she was more attractive with glasses than without, though I had not paid much attention to her looks beyond a general impression that she was pretty. At these formal dances it was difficult seeing beneath the party skin, the tulip-shaped dress, the corsage, the coiffure, and the forced laughter, except Aurora's dress was more lily than tulip, she wore no corsage, and her laughter was not forced. In the quiet of the car I could smell her perfume and give attention to her voice, which seemed to me to have the timbre of an oboe. Her voice, the music of her personality, carried an odd cadence and inflection—

The Pal-shawzzz, Oscar and Lizzzzzie—

that on first hearing sounded affected but the longer I listened did not seem affected at all, simply a signature. She was small-boned and small-faced, made smaller by her short haircut. Her sheath dress was cut low and not made for a debutante. In the light of the dance floor her hair looked dark blond but now seemed merely dark. She looked nothing like her father, save for a tightly wound quality softened by her smile. Her mouth curved up at the edges as if she knew a secret and the secret was amusing and hers alone. Looking at her now, I had the sensation of stopping at a portrait I had seen often at a gallery, taking the time now to observe instead of look. Aurora had opened the glove compartment and was peering into it, muttering that she needed a Kleenex. When I handed her my handkerchief she began to slowly polish the lenses of her glasses.

She said, What about the champagne?

I handed her one of the glasses I had on the floor between my feet. I took the other, we clicked, and she said, Luck.

Luck, I said.

So don't feel badly, she went on. It's not worth it.

Sometimes I talk too much, I said. Without thinking.

Forget it, she said.

I've wanted to meet him—

I can arrange that, she said. I'll make an appointment. Not that it'll do you much good. He doesn't talk much. Talking isn't his long suit. I assume it's a conversation you want, not a consultation.

God, no, I said hurriedly, throwing the car into gear and backing off the lawn and into the driveway. The policeman had moved off into the shadows, his uniform making him nearly invisible. Aurora was laughing at my "God, no."

I said after a moment, Is he good at what he does?

She said, I guess so. They say he is. He has patients all day long and often into the evening and they swear by him. They send him flowers on his birthday.

Well, I said. He must talk to them.

Not necessarily, she said.

He must, I insisted. That's what psychiatrists do, ask leading questions about your dreams and so forth and so on. Your sex life.

He's a Freudian, she said wearily. Freudians listen, the patients speak. It's a technique. The patient is led to her own discoveries, and dreams would be one of the routes. All dreams are sexual, by the way.

All dreams? I asked skeptically.

No exceptions, she said. Sometimes he'll go fifty minutes without saying a word and then he looks at his watch and says, See you next week. Now will you please give it a rest? Aurora was sitting with her feet on the seat, the glass of champagne resting on one knee and her fist with the cigarette on the other. Now and again she jerked her hand out the window to flick the ash from her cigarette.

But I didn't want to give it a rest, preoccupied as I was with the sexuality of dreams, including one I had had about falling from a great height. I said, I suppose it's the quality of the listening, then. Listening well, concentrating hard.

She said, You can usually tell when they're bored. They try

not to show it but they don't succeed. At least, they don't succeed with me. You can feel their attention wander and suddenly they aren't there, they've gone away. Their heads are there, and their crossed legs, and their notebooks and pencils and shirt cuffs and shoes. The creak of a chair when they shift their weight. Their breathing's there. But they aren't.

You've been, then, I said.

Of course, Aurora said.

What was it like? I had an idea it was an all-consuming experience like a serious illness or sex. And I was surprised by her casual "of course," as if psychiatry was as normal as homework.

She turned to give me a long wary look, and then hesitated before she replied, Not all it's cracked up to be.

Was it—I sought a neutral word—helpful?

Told me things I didn't know or even imagine. Whether the things were helpful, we'll see.

My father thinks it's voodoo.

Well. She thought a moment. In one sense, it's like sticking pins in dolls.

She was silent, winding her index finger around her gold necklace. I wondered if that had any special significance that a voodoo master could spot and, with a blinding flash of insight, explain.

We were driving slowly along Lake Road, most of the houses dark except for lawn lights, somehow out of focus, that gave the grass an unnatural amber cast. The effect was amateurishly theatrical, a midsummer night's dream on the lawn of a banker's mansion, Caliban cavorting in the moonlight. Unnatural too was the architecture, European souvenirs, here a mansard roof from a château of the Loire, there a stone arch from a manor house in East Anglia, up high an eyelid window from the brothers Grimm, down below heavy double doors fashioned by the bearded Norwegian cabinetmaker in his shop on Skokie highway. You could lose your way inside these houses, corridors without end, rooms that had never been looked into. Now I noticed a single light burning in a downstairs room of the nearest house, and I imagined an insomniac ill at ease in the library, a book in her lap, listening to the clock tick, wondering what happens next or if anything happens. The time was past midnight, the moon a sliver among the trees, the lake out of sight back of the houses.

Fortresses, Aurora said. You stay in and the world stays out. No admittance to the world without an invitation. That's the point. Did you see the cop back there? Oscar threw his cigarette at him. What a place. I'd call it a Potemkin village but it's all too real. And what it conceals, not very successfully, is a lack of imagination.

They like it in there, I said.

They surely do, she agreed.

They feel safe. And the world envies them.

The genius of capitalism, she said.

My father says that money isn't everything but it's way ahead of whatever's in second place.

Aurora smiled in the darkness. She said, My father wouldn't agree, I'm afraid. But then again, he sees the results.

I suppose he would, I said.

She said, What does your father do?

Not psychiatry, I said. He owns a printing business.

Are you going into it?

No, I said.

That's a start, she said.

What do you mean by that? I asked, annoyed at her presumption.

She looked away and didn't reply. I'm outspoken, she said at last. Always have been. It's the way I am, take it or leave it. But I don't see you in business. She had thrown away her cigarette and was moving her right hand sideways out the window, catching a balloon of air and releasing it. Now she bent her head close to the dashboard and switched on the radio, Hit Parade music. I turned off Lake Road and headed inland, picking up speed on the deserted streets, waiting for her to continue.

He takes me to school, she said suddenly. He thinks buses are dangerous so he drives me to school and then turns around and goes back to the apartment so he can prepare for his first patient. He's never said much on these drives until lately, my last three or four weeks of school. He's decided to open up.

He'll stop at a light and point at some poor pedestrian and say, Paranoid, and at another and say, Repressed, and at a third and say, Hysteric. When I asked him how he knows, he said by the way they carry themselves, their gait, and the expression on their faces. A certain aura surrounds them. Everyone has an aura, a particular style, a signature that belongs only to them. When I pointed out that the paranoid one had his hat pulled down over his eyes in such a way that you could not see his expression, my father said he knew what the expression was without seeing it because he knew the aura, and the angle of the hat confirmed it. He was quite definite. And he did this every day while he was taking me to school, analysis on the run. Isn't that strange? But we're very close.

Aurora finished her champagne and carefully put the glass under the seat. She continued to sit with her hands on her knees, except now her chin was resting on her hands. He was in the war, she said, and the way she said it I knew she meant World War Two. They were going to call him up for Korea but they didn't. My father has terrible headaches and perhaps that was the reason, but I never heard of missing a war because of a headache, did you? He was in the Pacific. And he won't say a word about it. None of them do. Another conspiracy of silence.

She said, Was yours?

In the war? No.

Why not?

I thought a moment. I don't know, I said.

Medical deferment, probably.

I suppose so, I said. My father had no medical problems that I knew of except for nearsightedness and, now, his knees. Probably it was his age. I imagined my father at Guadalcanal or Iwo Jima, a second lieutenant like Sassoon's infantry officer, recklessly brave, wounded in the chest, and at the end of it a pacifist. His war would have made him a different man, not the father I knew but another personality altogether. Sassoon's nerves were shot—

Won't say a word, Aurora said. Won't say where he was or what he did. But he was trained as a surgeon, so I imagine that was what he did, care for the wounded. I know when he got out he went back to school to become a psychiatrist. He's a lonely man but he won't admit it.

Maybe that's the essence of loneliness, I said. Not admitting anything.

Maybe it is, she said.

Lonely, you speak only to yourself because you're the only one who'll listen. And then it becomes a habit. Aurora said nothing to that, and after a moment I said, Can I meet him?

Sure, she said. Don't ask about the war, though.

I won't, I said.

He's only told me one thing, when I asked about it. And I've asked him more than once. He said he was on a hike. That's what he called it, "the Hike." She was quiet again, looking out the window and humming to the music on the radio, one of Frank Sinatra's old wartime songs. She said, You're simpatico.

I said, So are you.

I don't meet many boys who are simpatico.

I said, You scare them away.

Why did you ask me to dance?

I was avoiding Dana, I said. You were alone and you looked like you wanted to dance and I liked your looks. It wasn't a bad idea, either, because here we are drinking champagne without anyone cutting in.

You didn't like it when I made that crack about your father's business.

Sore subject, I said. He's had some trouble with his business. A strike and some minor violence, so he hasn't been himself.

She didn't say anything. She looked to be counting her toes, one by one. Then she said, I have a hard time with my father. There's one way, his way. And one story, his story. And if you don't fit into his story, well then, you don't know what you're talking about. It's hard to discuss anything with a man like that. Plus which, his grandparents were Dutch. He's hardheaded and so am I. Difference is, I'll admit it and he won't.

Even so, she said, we're very close.

I put my arm on her seatback and she made room so that her head was resting on my wrist, and then her hair was in the palm of my hand. Her hair was rough against my fingers. She moved her head slowly and I knew without looking that she was smiling. I wondered what it meant, being Dutch, or if it meant anything. I realized that we had a story that, with luck, no one else would fit into. The story was only beginning, an hour or so in duration, but it was ours.

She said, Will you tell me one of your stories?

I said, I'll make one up.

Not make-believe, she said. A real one from the newspaper, the story behind the story behind the story. What do they call it? The inside skinny.

The inside dope, I said. All the stuff that doesn't get into the paper because of the libel laws. Questions of taste, questions of propriety, maybe because the subjects are friends of the publisher. Or the daughter of an advertiser or the son of an alderman we support. All sorts of reasons why the inside dope never sees print.

Tell me one, she said.

I'm thinking, I said.

Aurora raised her head suddenly to look around, then turned and stared sourly at me. Where are we, Wils? This is not the way to Chicago.

I said, We're going to Quarterday. I thought you ought to see it.

I thought we were going to Chicago.

We were. We aren't now.

And who decided that?

I did, I said.

I don't like surprises, she said.

You'll like this one.

How do I know? What if I insist you turn this car around?

I'll argue and you'll win. We'll go to Chicago. But you'll miss your one chance to see Quarterday at night. More romantic than Venice.

She shrugged unhappily and continued to stare out the window at the fields and the farmhouses scattered here and there. We met few cars. The farmhouses were dark. West of the North Shore a curtain descended, the air saturated with smoke from the smoldering Skokie peat bogs, the road rising some and falling, moving in a line so straight that the car seemed to be steering itself. There was breathing room here, I thought, even if what you were breathing was burning peat. The North Shore was hemmed in, each breath a kind of gasp, closely observed from behind eyelid windows. All in all, this anonymous countryside had an attraction; the attraction was its undefinition. When we stopped at a railroad crossing I counted the freight cars, ninety-nine, bound for the Chicago rail yards. Aurora was silent beside me, smoking a cigarette as the monotonous fields flew by. We drove on, unobserved.

Indian country, Aurora said at last. We might as well be in the middle of Kansas. And just think, at this very moment we could be listening to jazz on Bryn Mawr Avenue. Are we at the Mississippi River yet? Aurora asked, and then I stopped at the golf club entrance.

Aurora's head touched my shoulder. I kissed her tentatively, and again, not so tentatively. I drove slowly into the club grounds, past Sixteen and Seventeen and Five, the short par three. All the houses were dark, including my own. I pointed it out and explained the layout of the holes while Aurora yawned flamboyantly. It felt strange to me, being in these familiar surroundings with a girl. The men's locker room was dark and I drove into the empty parking lot, stopping at the far end. I had an idea we could take a swim in the club pool, strictly forbidden after dark but there was no night watchman to check. Aurora took off her glasses. She said something I didn't hear, and when I looked at her questioningly, she murmured, I like you. We like each other, I said. At that instant I did not want to be in the swimming pool or anywhere else except where I was. She took off my tuxedo jacket and threw it on the back seat and then she loosened my tie. When I moved to turn off the car's headlights, Aurora's hands flew from my shoulders and she screamed, a high-pitched wail such as a child might make. Staring at us through the window was a deer, its eyes blood red in the brilliance of the headlights. The animal did not move, mesmerized in the light; and then it turned and loped away, graceful leapings to the hedge that surrounded the parking lot, and over the hedge to the fairway on One, where it seemed to ascend into the darkness and in a moment was lost to view.

Aurora's face was buried in my neck, her arms tight around me. She was trembling. I spoke softly to her, explaining about the deer everywhere around the club. Still, this one was alarming with its blood-red eyes and wolfish snout, tawny coat like a lion, so silent and static, as if it were staring into a mirror. But it was only a harmless deer after all.

Finally her arms relaxed.

Are you all right?

I'll be all right in a minute, she said. Is it gone?

It flew away, I said.

My God, Aurora said. I didn't know what it was. One minute I was kissing you and the next, there it was. Those *eyes*.

Here, I said, and handed her my champagne. Only about a quarter inch was left in the glass but she took it and drained it, her hands still trembling. She said, I didn't know what I was looking at. I didn't know what it was, some creep standing and watching us or what. She shook her head.

Sorry, she said, with an attempt at a smile. Gosh.

It's gone now, I said.

That's what happens when I take off my glasses. I can't see a thing without them. Plus which, I was with you. I wasn't thinking about wild animals, at least not that one. Where are we, anyhow?

I said, Come on. I'll show you the pool, and pointed to the portico and the semicircle of cabanas back of it. We could smell the chlorinated water. She didn't say anything but the expression on her face was not encouraging. I lit a cigarette for her and one for myself and we sat listening to the night insects and, far away, an owl. After a while, Aurora opened the car door and began to stroll in the direction of the pool. She turned and asked me to bring her eyeglasses; and then she removed her high heels and walked off on tiptoe, swinging the shoes from their straps.

When I caught up with her she was sitting on the low board, her toes just touching the water, squinting into the darkness. A silent audience of canvas chairs and sunmats was arrayed around the pool. The moon was gone and the stars were fading. I handed Aurora her eyeglasses but she did not put them on right away, preferring to squint into the darkness. I began to describe for her this swimming pool on a Saturday afternoon in midsummer, indolent teenagers and young mothers and their small children, pool boys present with fresh towels and a drink if you wanted one. We were drowsy from the sun and the syrupy odor of suntan oil. At five the children were ordered out and the adults took over, men just in from a round of golf, their wives from the tennis court. The men would show off their diving skills from the high board; and those who had no skill would cannonball. The bar did a brisk business until six o'clock, when everyone dressed for dinner, usually some affair in the clubhouse; there was a dance every Saturday night. I pointed to a cabana at the far end and told her that was where I had my first taste of tobacco and, the next year, scotch. I was eleven the first year, twelve the second. That was a naughty cabana, owned by a family called Cordes. They had two teenage daughters, older than me and eager to corrupt. I was a kind of mascot and fell in love with both of them. Later on, the older daughter started sleeping with the lifeguard. The lifeguard was infatuated but good, and had bought a ring and was planning elopement when the summer ended and Suzan—everyone called her Suzan-with-a-z, and eventually just Z—went back to Northwestern, and that was that with the lifeguard. He returned the next summer but it wasn't the same. Suzan had found another boyfriend, a senior at Purdue, a football player as big as an oak and just about as dumb. Each summer had its own story, usually centering on a romance that didn't work out.

Aurora smiled but didn't say anything. She still held her shoes from their straps.

The summer after that, the lifeguard was gone. He moved up to one of the better clubs in Winnetka. Better pay. But the manager was quite specific, no fraternizing with members. The lifeguard had had it with members and the members' wives and daughters, so he didn't mind. That was what Suzan told me.

Aurora said, I don't understand about *perdu*.

It's that university in Indiana.

98

Oh, she said, laughing. I thought it was the French, *perdu.* Lost.

Perdu in West Lafayette, Indiana.

I never heard of it, she said.

You don't know what you're missing, I said.

What happened to the football player?

He graduated, I said. Married a Delta Gamma.

What's a Delta Gamma?

Sorority, I said.

So you were here every summer, she said.

Watching the comedy, I said. I took a long look down the line of cabanas at the Cordeses', all the furniture tucked away for the evening. I remembered that the cushions were royal blue and the tables white. The daughters wore identical yellow Jantzen swimsuits, and by the end of the summer their skin was brown as mahogany, their hair bleached white. Every hour or so they would walk together to the bar for a Coke or an iced tea, enjoying the attention from the pool boys and the lifeguard and every other man in the vicinity. Sometimes they'd ask me to fetch the drinks and I would return to find them painting each other's toenails, concentrating fiercely as if they were looking through microscopes. Suzan and—I had unaccountably forgotten her sister's name. Those summers when I was eleven, twelve, thirteen, we were inseparable at the swimming pool. The summer after the year I had been sick, they had been very kind, wanting to know all the medical details and shuddering when I invented a few. They said they had always wanted a kid brother and now they had one. I spent hours listening to them gossip in a sisterly language, difficult to decipher; but I thought if I listened hard enough I would learn about girls. What I learned was the inevitability, the curse, of menstrual cramps and that the sisters had them at identical times of the month. Then they would both retire to the cabana's interior, avoiding the sun. Men had it so easy, Suzan said. Men didn't know how easy they had it. Men could do what they wanted whenever they wanted to do it, so darned *unfair.* Don't you agree, Wils? Yes, of course, I said. It was a tragedy, a neverending wrong. Then the girls would continue their indecipherable conversation. The next summer their family took a house in Wisconsin and I didn't see them at all. And the summer after that, the girls spent less time at the pool because they had summer jobs and busy lives on the weekends, and who needed the pool? Our great friendship was ended.

Donna, I said.

Aurora said, What?

I'd forgotten Suzan's sister's name. It was Donna.

I stepped off the low board and lit a cigarette, leaning against the lifeguard's elevated chair. I had not been to the pool at all this summer and I wondered if the routine was the same, and who were this year's Cordes girls.

Come on, I said. Let's go to Chicago.

I like it here, Aurora said. I like the silence.

Shall we take a swim?

No swim, Aurora said.

We drove to Chicago in near silence, through the acrid smoke of the peat bogs, through the farmland and villages to the edge of the North Shore. The roads were empty, the night as dark as it had ever been, until we approached the city. We drew close, the spell between us unbroken. I wanted to confide in her, believing in her completely, but I had not the words to reprise the rush of memory when I looked at the empty chairs and sunmats and the Cordes cabana bare of furniture. Those girls had brought me up, whether they knew it or not. I went on to describe our conversations and I could see Aurora nod in the darkness, and I knew she was back in her memory, too. I thought to ask her where she was going to college in September, and when she said Barnard I laughed and said I would write her from the University of Chicago, one urban bohemia to another; I said I knew she'd fit right in and so would I. All this time we held hands and I was so glad she was there in the darkness beside me.

We passed through Half Day and Winnetka and Evanston. I drove to Lake Shore Drive via Bryn Mawr, the jazz club closed now, the El station empty, the streets deserted. I told her about the bartender and his greeting and about the time Georg Bru-

nis let me sit in for Hey-Hey Humphrey, one number only, "Big
Noise from Winnetka," where all you needed from the drum-
mer was supercilious percussion. It was my eighteenth birthday,
legal drinking age at last; and I had been a customer for three
years already, Chicago as wide open as it had ever been. Aurora
said she had been to the Eleven-Eleven Club just once, with a
man her father did not approve of, an intern at Passavant Hospital. He wanted to sit in for Hey-Hey Humphrey, too, but
Brunis wouldn't let him. Brunis and Humphrey looked at him
as if he were a bug in a tweezers. She said this with a wide grin,
and I leaned over to her and kissed her on the mouth, flying
through the red light on Sheridan Road.

He didn't take it well, she said.

An embarrassment for him, I said.

Terrible, she said. He thought being a doctor entitled him
to play Hey-Hey Humphrey's drums. He had beautiful hands,
long fingers as supple as rubber. I mean Hey-Hey Humphrey.
The intern was a brute.

So your father was right.

That one time, Aurora said.

And Oscar Palshaw, I said.

Two times, she admitted.

I'll bet you liked the green MG.

A coffin with an engine like a sewing machine, she said.

We swept down Lake Shore Drive, the city spread out before
us glittering with nervous energy, its relentless industrial hum.
Chicago never closed down completely and now it seemed swollen with potential, crouched beside the black void of the lake,
void all the way to Canada. The wind came off the lake and
rushed through the open windows of my car and I was as happy
as it was possible to be. I began to speculate on the marital arrangements of the Palshaws and where the green MG and the
rude Englishman fit, if they fit at all. Aurora added a thought
about Oscar's habit of drinking three martinis before dinner
and proposing marriage before the dessert.

Did he ask you to marry him? I asked.

All but, she said.

What did he say exactly?

He said he'd have to sleep with me first.

As the precondition to become Mrs. Palshaw, she added.

Lucky you, I said. Didn't you find him—old?

Not as old as you, she said.

What do you mean by that? I said.

It's a compliment, Wils. She leaned over and bit my ear. And you, she said. What do you think about Oscar? What was I supposed to say to him? Gosh, let me just get my pants off and we'll see where this leads.

I think that's what he thought, she said. Aren't they amazing?

Boys, I said.

Boys, she agreed. Now's your turn in the confessional.

I waited a long time before answering. I had an easier time with other people's stories than I did with my own. I had yet to find a narrative to my life, certainly no narrative that advanced in any coherent order or in which I played anything but a winning cameo role, kid brother or newsroom raconteur. It did not seem to me that you could fashion a life until you could make the decisions that governed it. Until that time you lived quietly in your father's house.

No stories that can match that one, I said.

No girlfriends? she said.

A few. Not very serious.

Why not? Aurora said.

Bad chemistry, I said with a smile.

Too young, you mean.

They're inexperienced. Like me.

But you tell them stories. You flirt with them all the time, I've watched you. It's quite a performance.

I like it when their fathers are around. They get so pissed off.

She grinned and turned up the volume on the radio and we began to sing along with Ella Fitzgerald, Aurora's head on my shoulder. I was still thinking about the debs and their irritated fathers, and then about Oscar Palshaw. I could not believe he had said what Aurora said he said; no one behaved that way. Then I wondered if there were different rules on the North Shore. Aurora told her story with conviction and a nonchalance that suggested—extravagance. Gosh, let me just get my pants off and we'll see where this leads.

I remember now, she said. He winked at me.

Who? I asked.

Brunis, she said. Georg Brunis with his bad skin and dinky mustache and bartender's belly. He put his trombone to his mouth and winked at me. He made sure the intern saw it, too.

And did he?

He did. His face got red. Then he said it was past my bedtime and we would have to go home right now. And I said I didn't want to go home, that I liked it at the Eleven-Eleven Club and wanted to stay through the set. He could go if he wanted but I was staying, because Georg Brunis was so great.

Aurora and I held hands in the darkness, the wind rushing into the car. We passed the marina and the Lincoln Park Gun Club and I accelerated, anticipating the turn into Lincoln Park. The skyscrapers of the Loop loomed over us to the south, behind the Drake Hotel. Summer was not ended and before too long my parents would leave for New Orleans and the slow boat to Havana. I thought the promised red shirt would look marvelous on Aurora and more than marvelous if she wore it without a bra. I shot up the long curve of Lake Shore Drive and into the turn with her head touching my shoulder, and when we arrived at her apartment building on Lincoln Park we were both as wide awake as if it were noon. When I parked and turned toward her she put her finger to her lips and winked.

6

A THREE-WEEK STRETCH that summer was unusually warm and I imagine it was for that reason that people told stories of their winter ordeals, the commuter trains that did not run and the basement pipes that burst. Too cold for the paperboys to deliver the *Tribune*. Too cold to walk the dog. People stood limply in their evening clothes, sweating under the high-topped tents, too enervated to dance. Men removed their dinner jackets as a matter of course, and Meyer Davis and Lester Lanin often played to empty dance floors. The heat gave rise to confusion, people losing their bearings and drinking more than was good for them, a gin and tonic a kind of oasis in the tropical heat. Everyone had a story but it was the same story, details altered; and all the stories were remembered with an amusing twist, the nuthatch belly-up in the birdbath, the absence of gray squirrels. Where had all the squirrels gone? Palm Beach, old Mr. Bartlow said. They've gone to Palm Beach.

He was dancing with one of the debs. He had not danced all evening and decided to select the prettiest girl he could find so he could tell her about the squirrels in Palm Beach. They were dancing a tango, one of the two dances he executed really well, a dip and a reverse, elbows flying. The girl loved it because boys could not tango, they didn't understand the Latin spirit of it, a kind of concentrated abandon. Only experienced older men knew how it worked. People made way for them, watching enviously because the girl was completely in synch and that was so rare. They made a handsome couple, the girl laughing, her head next to his as they broke into a little foxtrot. He was telling her about the squirrels scrambling aboard the—and he forgot the name of the train, either the Florida Limited or the City of Miami. Bar car, he said, and ordering drinks all around before bedding down for the night and then, two days later, disembarking in Palm Beach and being taken at once to the Breakers, where a floor had been reserved. Squirrel floor, each room with its vase of roses and dish of acorns. Once they were settled they made a run for the beach, where they would sit under umbrellas. He spun the story out, what the squirrels had for cocktails and dinner and the sports they enjoyed, shuffleboard and miniature golf. The deb laughed and laughed but people noticed that an odd expression had come over her face. When the dance ended she kissed old Mr. Bartlow on the cheek, a warm kiss, thanks for the dance. He was winded but pleased about the kiss. She stood waiting, and when he thanked her— You're a fine dancer, young lady, let's do this again sometime soon—she looked at him with an expression somewhere in the vicinity of dismay leaning toward amusement and said in a strangled voice,

Bill? It's me, Marcie.

Marcie?

And he saw at once that she was Marcie Lamb, his stepdaughter, and all this time he had thought she was just another pretty deb in an alice-blue gown with pearls and a white orchid, so they collapsed together in laughter and he led her to the bar for a congratulatory drink because they had danced so well together, everyone commenting on how cute they were in the strut. The story went around the floor, everyone amused, old Bill so caught up in the tango that he didn't recognize his own stepdaughter, and that was what the hot weather did to you. Even Marcie's mother rolled her eyes. Bill could be so damn dim sometimes.

Brutal heat following so closely on the brutal cold caused people to wonder if the weather was not undergoing some fundamental change, perhaps a return to the Ice Age or worse, the seasons themselves no longer reliable. Florida had been cold and damp, ice in the sand traps. Migratory birds were not following their usual patterns, canvasback ducks disappearing from the Mississippi flyway, other anomalies. It made you wonder about the monkey business above the Arctic Circle, Russian nuclear testing, one explosion after another and no one called them to account.

Don't tell me the Russians don't have something to do with it.

Rads in the atmosphere interfering with nature's rhythms.

There's a lot we don't know.

And here someone would turn to the older man who hadn't said much but had been listening with mounting alarm.

Don't you think so, Charlie?

Anything's possible—

That's exactly what I mean.

But not actually, no, Charlie said in a voice that commanded respect.

Aren't you hearing the same thing?

No, I'm not. It's just—weather. Weather's changeable. Don't you remember the winters we had years back? And everyone's testing nuclear weapons, even us.

Charlie Smithers was a lawyer who had clients in Washington. There was a rumor that Ike had wanted him for a very sensitive position in the Justice Department but he had turned the White House down. He didn't want to leave the North Shore for Washington but he was reported to have said that he could be helpful to them in other ways. So he was often in the capital on unspecified business with the Justice Department and other government agencies; and in the spring Charlie and his wife had been invited to a state dinner at the White House, and the next morning he and Ike had played golf together at Burning Tree. Charlie knew whereof he spoke; not that he spoke often or at length, he was much too discreet for that. But if you asked him a straight question you got a straight answer. Now half a dozen people had collected around Charlie Smithers, including Aurora and me, Aurora listening intently.

Sometimes you don't know what to believe, Aurora said with an ingratiating smile that hinted at an ulterior motive, I didn't know what.

That's the way they like it, Charlie said firmly. I did not know if he meant the Russians or the White House, but when he added, It's a fudge factory down there, I assumed he meant the White House or perhaps Washington in general. He was a large man and spoke in a lawyer's careful baritone, leaning forward in the way he would lean into the rail of a jury box.

The one thing you can't believe is the papers, he went on, to a murmur of agreement.

That's so true, Aurora said. Don't you agree, Wils? This, with the smile I had come to know so well. She loved to put me on the spot, and always signaled her intent with the smile.

But before I had a chance to answer, the lawyer was rocking on his heels and lowering his voice to confide that "the president"—the formal title implied an intimacy that the familiar "Ike" could only pretend to—was struggling with unimaginable burdens, responsible for the domestic economy and the Cold War and that was why the office was called a splendid misery, too much really for one man, and thank God for the team he had assembled, George Humphrey at Treasury and Charlie Wilson at Defense and the Dulles brothers elsewhere. He deserved every American's support and confidence, and also it was wise to remember that in Washington those who speak don't know, and those who know don't speak, and that was why the papers were worse than useless.

Aurora had hooked her arm through mine and gave me a pinch as she said, Gosh, really? Did you hear that, Wils?

Only a few people knew the score, Charlie continued, and then, with a wide smile, he added, How the fudge is made, and the ingredients of the fudge and who it's sold to and for how much—and here the company began to laugh, the metaphor so apt, a suggestion that fudge was only a convenient synonym for the various aspects of governance and statecraft, everything from the interstate highway program and rolling back the captive nations of Eastern Europe to keeping taxes low and the State Department under control and, most important, giving the president a Republican Senate at the midterm elections. Dick Nixon will be carrying the ball on that, Charlie concluded, and fell silent. There seemed nothing more to say and everyone nodded thoughtfully, having been given a privileged look behind the gray façade of the national government. Of course it was no more than a look, a glimpse into the shadows; and a good thing, too, because the more discreetly the administration went about its work, the better. Thank God for men like Charlie Smithers, whose soundness was not in question. Charlie would keep them up to the mark, and it was good of him to share his insights. Wasn't it worthwhile to talk politics occasionally?

And then people turned to the dance floor, red-faced Bill Bartlow dancing a tango again, this time with his wife, stepdaughter Marcie watching from the sidelines. They flew into a double reverse, the bandleader clapping and trying to encourage more dancers onto the floor. But Bill and his wife remained alone, it was so damned hot.

At some point during these evenings a woman would think to ask what had happened to the colored girl found frozen in the alley and taken to the city morgue where her heartbeat was miraculously discovered and she was revived, thawed as you would thaw a piece of meat. Where was she now? There was general agreement that she had no doubt returned to her self-destructive ways and was even now lying dead drunk in some alley on the South Side, probably the same alley, except now the weather was warm and she could sleep it off like anyone else. The point was, you couldn't change people. People would do what they wanted to do regardless, the natural consequence of a lack of self-discipline, a moral compass, and a failure to imagine the future and prepare for it, and a likelihood also of unfortunate breeding and, in that one sense, inevitable. There was nothing to be done about it. People simply had to pull up their socks and when they didn't, well, the results were tragic all around. It was like watching a train wreck; you were helpless in the face of it. Yet Chicago had a big heart. A few days after the story appeared a Help-Her-to-Hope Fund was established and everyone gave what they could, a matter of civic pride. No one was left behind in Chicago. New York wouldn't do as much.

Still, fact was, people had to look after their own.

Where was the girl's family?

Absent. AWOL.

Thing is, there's too much reliance on government.

Among the colored, someone put in.

Everyone's looking for a handout. And when they get one, they buy a Cadillac.

The evening was ending. The bandleader looked at his watch and announced last dance, but only a few people drifted to the floor. This weather, bad luck for the deb and her parents, and they'd made such an effort, the flowers, the orchestra. The men had taken off their jackets but even so, their shirts were soaked with sweat. The group I was with, Paul and Louise Binning, their houseguest and her date and his brother, loped over to the bar for a last drink and it was there, everyone laughing, that I spoke up at last.

I said, She was in her thirties, so she wasn't a girl.

Who's that, Wils?

The woman who almost froze to death. The one who wouldn't pull up her socks.

Well, Paul said, seemingly at a loss.

And she's disappeared, I said.

What do you mean, disappeared? People can't just disappear.

She did, I said. She put on her clothes and walked out the front door of the hospital. Disappeared. The doctor wanted to follow up but couldn't because no one can find her. She had no address. No one knew her name because she had no ID. No one has come forward. They have her fingerprints but the fingerprints do not match any fingerprints they had on file. It was in the newspapers.

That's what I mean, Paul said. Someone saves your life and you can't be bothered to stick around. Can't be bothered to say thank you very much for your trouble. You just say, The hell with medical science. Where would we be if everyone behaved like that, no sense of responsibility?

She had no money, I said. No family, either, at least none that showed up.

She had the fund, he said. The Help-Her-to-Hope Fund.

The fund's still there, I said. It's her that's missing.

How do you know all this?

The paper, I said. We've had two reporters on it for months. No one can find her. The police can't. She's vanished.

It's obvious, Paul said. She's on the South Side somewhere. And that's a place your writ does not run, bud. He laughed loudly, the cords of his neck bulging from the strain. His eyes narrowed, too, his head cocked to one side as if he were hearing something unearthly. If he were another kind of man he might have tried to put an image to the sound, violins under the horns in *Tannhäuser* or one of Picasso's morbid one-eyed horses, but as it was he heard only the blank rustle of disorder, Genghis Khan and his ten thousand horsemen, foreigners, foreign ideologies, bad breeding, people not from here, people who wanted things that didn't belong to them, a most unpleasant sound at odds with this unusually warm night attended by a full blue moon rising over the bland skin of our lake, pretty young girls in crinoline dresses and orchid corsages and pearls gleaming in the soft glow of lanterns, the tinkle of their laughter reminiscent of so many superb summer nights on the North Shore, a spectacle consoling in every way, like church bells on Sunday morning. Yet in his mind he heard marching feet, the low growl of a mob creeping like beasts from a disheveled wilderness to the boom of jungle drums, prepared to seize by force what had been gathered by fathers and grandfathers over decades of hard work, self-denial, individual responsibility, and civic pride. None of this went unnoticed. You had to be watchful every minute of every hour simply to keep things as they were. So it was a matter of maintenance.

And then Paul returned to the present moment, managing a thin smile though his fists remained clenched at his sides and a light sweat had broken on his forehead. He moved his shoulders back and forth like a prizefighter. He said at last, You go down there, try to find that girl, you'll get your white throat cut ear to ear. No one will give a damn. They're savages.

No one has a picture, either, I said. No one knows what she

looks like, except she's slender. In that way she's a species of phantom. You could meet her on the street tomorrow and not know who she is. There are rumors that the coroner has one photograph, taken when they thought she was dead. But that photograph is unpublishable.

Not even in your paper? He laughed, a kind of bray.

Your paper prints anything, his wife said. Sometimes I wonder how you get away with it, Wils. The stuff you print. Really, you should be ashamed. I don't mean you personally, but the paper. It's scandalous.

I'm just—at a loss, she concluded.

I'll tell the managing editor, I said.

I wish you would, Louise said.

But I'm afraid we don't have much circulation on the North Shore.

And I don't wonder, she said.

We certainly hope you find that girl, husband Paul said. And I know you'll spare no expense. It'll sell papers and of course that's what you want. I sell stocks and bonds, you sell grief. And what I want to know is, what's the P-E ratio on that? You find that girl, you'll be doing well on the bourse. But I wouldn't take any bets. She's gone, she's flown the coop. You'll never see her again. Your genie's out of the bottle, good riddance. He threw a massive arm around his wife's shoulders and guided her away, but then she turned to face me.

What I don't get is, Why are you working there? What's possessed you? You don't have to. Your father has a perfectly respectable business. Why would anyone want to be a newspaper reporter? It's so sordid, what you have to see and do. It's so— vulgar. That colored girl, for example. The stories about her throw such a bad light on things, accentuating the negative, makes us all feel rotten, as if we're being accused of something. I'll tell you this. I won't allow your paper into the house. I don't want the maid to see it.

She shook her head angrily and for a moment I thought she would break down in tears of frustration or anguish. But she gathered herself, took her husband's arm once again, and marched off to say good night to the deb and the deb's parents.

That kid's trouble, the husband said.

It makes me sick, said his wife.

That left the houseguest, her date, his brother, and me standing together in an awkward zone of silence. The houseguest announced that she didn't know what *that* was about because she didn't read newspapers. Who was the colored girl? She hadn't heard anything about any colored girl where she lived, Pittsburgh. The date and the brother said it was a local story, a Chicago story. But they were so angry, the houseguest said. She looked at me and said, What was it about?

I was searching the dance floor for Aurora and finally saw her near the bandstand talking to Charlie Smithers. She seemed most intent on whatever it was he was saying, and when she caught my eye made no sign of recognition except a minute raising of her eyebrows before turning again to the lawyer, listening hard.

What was it about, Wils?

I was still watching Aurora, her focused expression, and said the first thing that came to mind, Fear.

Why, they don't have anything to be afraid of!

More than you think, I said.

Well, the houseguest said. That's silly-billy. Look at this beautiful house, the grounds, and everything about it. And then she, too, turned away in frustration.

When we left the party, I asked Aurora about Charlie Smithers.

He's not what you think, she said.

He's a bully, I said.

Of course he's a bully. *Dick Nixon will be carrying the ball on that*. Touchdown assured. But he's something else, too. I like listening to him. What's between the lines.

He's an idiot, I said.

No, he isn't, Aurora replied. She walked on, and when we were settled in the car she said that, as a matter of fact, Charlie Smithers wanted very badly to go to Washington. He was bored with his law practice. He had always thought that if you could contribute to a cause you believed in you should do it as a matter of conscience, civic responsibility. Wasn't there more to life than making money? And Washington was exciting, not the gray city of government you read about. He told me to visit the Lincoln Memorial at night and look at Lincoln's ruined face and read the writing on the walls, the Gettysburg Address and the Second Inaugural. Also, the Metropolitan Club was agreeable for lunch and in the evenings there were dinners where the business of government was conducted over brandy and cigars, women excused to powder their noses. Aurora raised an eyebrow at that and continued, But Charlie's wife refused to leave Wilmette because of their son, who was troubled. Charlie went on and on about the boy, Aurora said, an intelligent boy but self-destructive. Not a lovable boy, Charlie said, except to his mother and me.

So I said that sometimes adolescents grew out of their problems.

He said his son was twenty-five.

I said I knew a doctor who might be able to help.

He said he knew the same doctor. But the boy was very difficult.

So there we are, Charlie said.

Sometimes, he went on, whatever you do, it isn't enough.

Nice talking with you, Aurora. Say hello to your dad for me.

Aurora managed to put herself on the same footing as older people, I don't know how. She had a manner older than her years, but it wasn't only that. She had a talent for listening and understanding what was between the lines, like a musician with perfect pitch. And what she heard, she remembered. Whenever I thought about our future, which was often, I thought of us in this serious grown-up world, people telling Aurora their secrets. Meanwhile, I went to the newspaper office downtown as if I were attending classes at a progressive trade school. I had no intention of becoming a newspaper reporter, then or later. The work was repetitive and easily grasped and didn't lead anywhere I wanted to go. I was in it for something else, I wasn't sure what. I suppose I wanted to observe the down-and-out—the vulgar and the sordid, as Mrs. Stockbroker would have it—to see how their lives were lived actually, the terms of the deal; and who was shuffling the cards. Yet I discovered soon enough that you necessarily observed from the outside and the glass was opaque, unless you were someone like Aurora Brule in whom people confided as a matter of course. What I had was second-hand stuff, vital statistics on a police blotter or the phoned-in report from the firehouse. Actual life as it was lived actually was missing in action.

I worked as a copy boy for an afternoon paper, the one that would die a few years later, victim of its own excess. Readers were loyal but advertisers were not, the State Street merchants worried that the paper's enthusiastic coverage of the interminable Red Scare and the city's nightly mayhem—the crushed skull in the garbage pail, the Norway rat in the infant's crib—compromised the hoped-for sobriety and civic equilibrium promised by the new Republican regimes in Washington and Springfield. Who saw progress and prosperity in a Norway rat? Did the page one photograph of the rat baring its teeth from a bloodstained layette encourage the Winnetka housewife to visit Marshall Field's for a new bedroom suite? The paper seemed mired in Chicago's criminal past, refusing to recognize that the Republican landslide signaled a new optimism, progressive, forward-looking, constructive, and good for business. So the paper was on the skids and the response in the newsroom was to uncover ever more revolting examples of municipal disorder and enemies within. The Norway rat in the spring and Judge Greenslat in the summer were but grace notes to the continuing search for the colored woman who had vanished so mysteriously from Cook County General.

When I remarked to one of the reporters that the case was fascinating, romantic almost, a woman with no identity, who had left no trace upon the face of the earth, who had managed to elude the posses of police and newspapermen sent to run her to ground, he looked at me sourly and said, She has an identity, son. She knows who she is. She knows where she is. It's only us who don't. And there's not the least thing romantic about her.

She's a down-and-out, Henry Laschbrook said. We'll never find her. He hesitated a moment, looking at me, I thought, with something approaching interest. He said, Do they like this story up where you live?

They do, I said. And they don't.

Well, he said. Which is it?

They read it. But they don't want to be seen reading it.

Like a girlie book, he said.

Like that, I said.

They don't read our paper up there, do they?

Not much, I said.

We're a little too raw for them, I suppose.

The Norway rat, I began.

You ever see a bigger god damned rat?

Never, I said.

They lead sheltered lives up there on the North Shore, he said.

They don't have rats in the bed, if that's what you mean.

And they don't want to read about people who do, he replied.

It upsets them, I said.

But not enough for them to do anything about it.

That's why they live on the North Shore. So they don't have to.

Henry laughed unpleasantly and said that was certainly one way to look at it, though not necessarily the best way.

It was suddenly important to me that Henry Laschbrook get one thing straight. I said, I don't live on the North Shore.

You don't?

I live in Quarterday, I said. Farther west.

Quarterday, Henry said. That's not the North Shore?

No, I said. Quarterday's another place altogether.

Well, Henry said. I'll be damned. You could have fooled me.

I led an appealing double life, bon vivant by night, workingman by day. I owned two uniforms, the tuxedo and a seersucker jacket and khakis, and most mornings only a few hours separated the one from the other, when I hurried to my car for the long drive to Chicago, anticipating the day's unruly events. I strolled into the newsroom to report to Ozias Tilleman, the city editor. Tilleman: fiftyish, saturnine, surly, always badly shaven, nursing a wildfire of a hangover. He had a wife somewhere and children, too, but no one had ever seen them. I handed him the paper bag with a Boston coffee and a jelly doughnut, took his money, and waited for whatever assignment he had for me, usually research on an obituary or some oblique angle on the night's bloodletting. Tilleman had been in the navy during the war, so his language was sprinkled with maritime expressions, loudly delivered. A story was either running at flank speed or in dry dock, and if you missed something important you were aground, at anchor, lying to windward, up shit's creek without a paddle. I was happy enough working away in the morgue, scouring the clips for tempting facts, all the while eavesdropping on the ribald conversations at the water cooler, office romances and after-hours escapades, and rumor upon rumor of the paper's probable demise. In the afternoon, when the reporters wandered back from their assignments, I hustled copy from their desks to the pencil editors on the rim, fanatical grammarians who, when they discovered a split infinitive or a misplaced comma, chirped like canaries in a mineshaft, whispering the offender's name or nickname, Moron, Idiot. No one at the paper knew of my nighttime life on the North Shore, though Tilleman guessed, and, when the time came, cashed the chit.

What the devil are those? he asked one morning, pointing at my feet. God damned bedroom slippers in my newsroom. Take 'em off. Wear 'em again, you're in the brig.

You look like a fairy, Tilleman said.

Tinker Bel Air, he added.

In my haste and confusion that morning I had mistakenly slipped into my dancing pumps, the ones with the little bows, and when I discovered what I had done I was already halfway to Chicago. I was always on thin ice at the paper, and careful to do nothing that would cause Tilleman to fire me. I seemed to know instinctively where the line was, and while I often walked up to it, I never crossed it. I loved my job—grace and favor from the publisher, who was a golfing friend of my father's—and the atmosphere of the newsroom, never quite real, as if the people we wrote about were characters in a play or a novel who did not exist outside the narrow columns of type. Its atmosphere was as special and specific as the locker room or infantry bivouac with its own language and code of conduct, as disheveled as life itself, a man's cruel world where the odds were eternally six-to-five against. The paper was a carnival of love nests, revenge killings, slumlords, machine graft, and Communists deep in the apparatus of state and national government. The city itself was thankfully Red-free except for the degenerate intellectuals at the University of Chicago, rootless cosmopolitans whose primary allegiance was to Europe. It was easy enough for me to believe that the world of the newsroom was the real world, wised-up and unforgiving, brutal as a matter of course, life's mediator, but always with a reassuring insinuation of the indomitable American spirit asserting itself in countless miniature acts of selflessness, the fireman who climbed all fifty-one rungs of the ladder to rescue the cat in the tree or the nun who spent her weekends praying with unwed mothers or the hero doc who discovered the faintest of heartbeats in a body frozen solid. Surely it was a public service to present this wholesome world to the readers, poor saps, in order to—the word would be "console."

The stories translated wonderfully at the parties I went to in the evening. North Shore girls knew nothing of the ambiance of a big-city newspaper devoted to sexual mischief, crime, life's terrors, a chronic melancholy among the city's down-and-out. It was a netherworld to them, a sinister murk invisible from Lake Forest or Winnetka, and many light-years away from their boarding schools in Connecticut or Massachusetts except for the insights gained from the assigned reading, *Tess of the D'Urbervilles*, for example. Of course they were fascinated, being invited backstage at the burlesque. The reporter's telephone call ("Deputy coroner calling") to the distraught mother whose children had "perished" in a tenement "blaze." The businessman who—the word was not "fell" or "jumped" but the immaculate "plunged" from his tenth-floor office on Division Street following a visit from the friends of Sam Giancana.

Gosh, really?

Who's Sam Giancana?

Perhaps their fathers were a little less impressed, and now and again one of them would interrupt my aria with a gruff comment, correcting a newsroom rumor related to municipal corruption, favors given and favors received in the matter of a tax break, a zoning variation, a property assessment, a favorable ruling on an ambiguous section of the city building code—all the grease for the great wheels of commerce. I assumed they did not like the idea of a nineteen-year-old instructing their daughters on the way of the world as observed by newspaper reporters, and once I heard myself referred to as "that wiseacre Ravan kid, Teddy's boy, what he doesn't know about Chicago would fill Soldier Field . . ."

This hinted at another level of reality in Chicago, a parallel world more sinister even than the one I had discovered, but I didn't take the hint. If I was wised up, the bankers were necessarily naïve; the naïveté of the American ruling class was an appealing idea, a cohort of dimwitted La Salle Street financiers jumping through hoops held by aldermen and Mob muscle. I believed I represented a threat to their vision of civic order, my arias hitting a little too close to the mark, the corrupters believing they were victims of a process whereby an honest businessman couldn't stay honest and also stay in business, owing to the genius of the Democratic machine and the Mob, whereas perhaps the reverse was true. I specialized in stories that were better left untold, or at least not told to their young and impressionable daughters just now embarking on life's great journey and whose very expensive educations were designed to shield them from life in the city, and specifically how things worked. That part was true enough. But that part wasn't the half of it.

Aurora listened to my stories, too, but tended to drift away when my audience of debs was at its most attentive. Gosh, really? she would say later, batting her eyelashes after listening to yet another description of one reporter who kept a pint of whiskey in his desk and another who was having a love affair with an alderman's daughter, this one a male Mata Hari who came back to the newsroom with stories of how the alderman conducted his business from the corner saloon and was never known to pay for a drink, though there was always money on the table. She did not find my newsroom yarns enthralling but conceded that was no doubt because she did not attend a boarding school in Connecticut or Massachusetts but a private day school in Lincoln Park, a city school where aldermen's daughters were her classmates. There were bankers' daughters as well, she said, and lawyers' daughters, and she often had difficulty telling them apart. There were loud ones and shy ones in each group.

Bankers' daughters often wore pearls, Aurora added thoughtfully, and the others gold. The pearls tended to come off more quickly than the gold but that was surely because the aldermen's daughters tended to be strict Polish or Irish Catholics and the bankers' daughters amorphously Protestant. The lawyers' daughters were often Jewish and somewhat mysterious, unclassifiable. There were exceptions in all categories, as any conversation in the locker room after gym would demonstrate. All that sweat, she said, loosened inhibitions. When I said, Gosh, really?, Aurora smiled and said, Really. But I was imagining the after-gym conversations, girls sprawled on benches and in chairs in their underwear, disclosing the secrets of the deep.

Sometimes I think the Midwest is a nation apart, Aurora said, and the North Shore is a hidden valley inside that nation, protected on all sides. It's undisturbed. They have all the stuff that everyone else has, radios and movies and newspapers, and the books are the same coast to coast. But we do not listen or read in the same way.

We listen and read defensively, she said.

I don't know why I say "we," she added. I don't live in the hidden valley.

They hold on to what they have, believing that it can't be improved upon.

I have affection for the South, she said. What they aren't up to down there! Probably it's the heat and humidity, like the locker room sweats. She had a cousin who lived in Texas, went to the local high school, changed boyfriends every week, loved being a cheerleader. What a time she has. Full of life, that southern cousin. The only thing she wants is that thing just out of reach and absolutely forbidden, except down there the forbidden sign comes with a wink attached. Her father owns the bank, as a matter of fact, Aurora said, and laughed and laughed.

She did listen carefully when I told her about Henry Laschbrook, star reporter, who began his day at the pool hall on Wabash, down a flight of stairs to a large basement room, quiet and cool as a library, taking the high chair in front of table number six, requesting a cup of black coffee, lighting a cigar and sitting quietly for a little while in order to contemplate the green baize field and mahogany rails of the table, as full of mystery and potential as a waiting chessboard and as violent as Antietam.

I go there because when I am there no one knows where I am.

An hour of serenity, Henry said, before the racket of the newsroom.

The thing about a game of pool, the playing field is small, the variations infinite.

Unlike the newsroom.

What does he look like, your Henry Laschbrook?

Tall, I said. Very thin. Wears double-breasted blue suits and a fedora.

Aurora looked at me and asked, Jewelry?

A pinkie ring, I said. One small diamond.

What else? she asked.

Well-groomed. Barbered, I'd say.

Shoes?

Wingtips, I said. Black and white. Why are you asking?

Thank you, Wils. It's for my archives.

The party season ended and my work at the newspaper was soon to end. Most days I met Aurora after work for long walks along the lakeshore, Lincoln Park to Michigan Avenue, and down the avenue to the Water Tower and, farther on, the Art Institute, where we would wander through the rooms until closing time. Aurora was taking courses there in the morning, the Impressionists at ten, Persian miniaturists at eleven. There was a sultan in a turban and red robe that reminded us, in his girth and stillness and imperturbability, of Richard J. Daley. Aurora and I would dine somewhere nearby and go to a movie on the Near North Side and then I would take her to Lincoln Park and drive home alone. My parents were soon to leave for New Orleans and Havana and I was busy devising a scheme whereby she could spend a few days with me in the empty house in Quarterday with its terrace and screened-in porch, the one with the white shag rug, the soft lighting, and the matching chaises.

Were we absorbed in each other? Here's how much:

On our third or fourth date — it seemed to me that we had been talking for half our lifetimes and I could not remember what I had talked about before I met her except it was surely inconsequential and she believed the same, and wasn't it remarkable how many variations there were on the philosophy of the Midwest when you had a sympathetic listener, one who picked up where you left off, building on the idea the way a composer builds on a simple melody, the notes coming so fast and with such intensity that you had to concentrate like a virtuoso because the worst thing would be to say something foolish or inattentive — I asked Aurora when I could meet her father. Parents, I corrected myself. Your mother, too.

My mother? Aurora asked. My mother does not live with us. My mother lives with her new husband in Detroit. Grosse Pointe, rather. They're particular about it being Grosse Pointe and not Detroit. He does something with cars. And they have a child of their own, a boy, five. His name is Dwight. Named for our general, much admired by her husband. His name is Robert. Probably he was named for a general, too, but I can't be sure. He's from the South so you can probably guess which general, if it is a general. Aurora spoke as if she were reciting from a prepared text, and it took me a moment to understand what I had heard. She had never spoken of her mother but I thought nothing about it because I never spoke of mine. Our parents were absent during the long conversations concerning the philosophy of the Midwest. Aurora had paused, waiting for me to catch up. She said, When they separated I was given a choice, him or her, and I chose him. My mother is a very modern woman. At least, that's how she sees herself.

She didn't always, Aurora added.

The place she wanted to live more than anywhere in the world was the North Shore. She liked its apartness. She liked the North Shore for the opposite reason your Henry Laschbrook likes his pool hall. When she was there, everyone knew where she was.

But then Robert came along and she had to settle for Grosse Pointe because they don't make cars in Chicago.

We were walking up Astor Street in the late afternoon, the air most mild. The street was quiet but all around us were animated voices heard clearly through open windows, people at predinner cocktails. Now and then a phrase of music drifted by, and the ballgame, second half of a double-header at Wrigley, bottom of the seventh, one out, one on, count two-two, outfield deep for Cavarretta, fouls once, fouls twice, steps back from a breaking ball inside, count three-two, and the noise from the stands rises a decibel and falls when Cavarretta steps out of the box, looks to third for the sign, steps back in, the tedium of waves on the surface of a windless sea and the sea is bottomless. We walked on. That part of the Near North Side was like a village, none of the row houses more than three or four stories high, looking like filing cabinets back of the great stone wall of Lake Shore Drive apartment buildings. You expected to see village shops, a shoemaker's or an ironmonger's, but commerce was not allowed. Baby carriages and bicycles crowded the front stoops, gate-bounded gardens facing the sidewalk.

I said, Do you see her often?

Christmas and Thanksgiving, Aurora said, except I missed last Christmas because they wanted to take Dwight to Key West. He's a swimmer. And I didn't want a Christmas without snow. My father is not exactly Mr. Ho-ho-ho Christmas Spirit but he makes an effort and the big thing is that in Chicago there's always snow for the holidays, mountains of it. You can count on it, set your watch by it. We always went to the Drake for Christmas lunch when my mother lived with us, so each year my father and I go, just us two, and have a fine time. Last year he ordered a bottle of champagne to go with the goose and analyzed everyone in the room, even the maitre d'hôtel. The dining room was full, all the waiters tricked out in tuxedos, season's greetings at the Drake. There were plenty of people for him to analyze. We had a baked alaska for two but he gave his portion to a little girl at the next table. Her parents tried to protest but he insisted.

Aurora was quiet a moment and then she said, So there are those two holidays and whenever else I feel like it.

There's no formal custody agreement, she said.

They share custodial responsibilities.

I always thought a custodian was a kind of janitor, she went on.

My parents promised the judge they could work it out between themselves, and after listening to them, the judge agreed. He was a friend of my mother's and knew my father, too, though they were not friends. My father does not have many friends. Later on, I had my say and Judge Maxwell called me a very poised young lady and consented to the Christmas-and-Thanksgiving-and-whenever-else-I-feel-like-it, which I don't, often. They have their own life and I don't like suburbs, the lawns and the empty sidewalks and you need a car whenever you want to go anywhere, even to the movies. That's all they talk about, by the way, cars and the advertising slogans for cars. Did you know they call a Buick "the doctors' car"? Bet you didn't.

So that's the story of my modern mom and her modern marriage, where she lives, and who she lives with for now.

I was trying to form a picture of Aurora and her father at the Drake Hotel drinking champagne on Christmas, the room full, a tinseled tree in the corner. That was as far as I got.

I know what attracted her to him, Aurora said. He's big, as tall as my father but thick. Beefy. He has that molasses accent, always sounds like he's making a speech on the floor of the Senate. He has a big mane of yellow hair that he's proud of. He believes good grooming is an essential part of success. He plays the piano. Probably the most important thing about him is that he isn't my father. He chain-smokes, for one thing. And he talks all the time.

Like us, I said with a smile.

Not like us, Aurora said firmly. Not anything like us. He talks to fill the air. No silence so golden that a word from him wouldn't improve. And since my father rarely talks at all, I suppose she was attracted to someone who does. Talk all the time. Even when he plays the piano, which, incidentally, he's good at. They chatter together like a couple of railbirds and they're always trying to get me to join in but I don't. I listen to my own thoughts. I'm sitting at their table and I'm wishing I was home where it's an event when my father says, Please pass the salt. I began to laugh but Aurora put up her hand, palm out. She said, Yes, there is one other thing. I think he's afraid of my father.

I nodded. I knew at once she was correct.

Unpredictable, she said. He thinks my father is unpredictable, "not right," and he's not alone. People worry about my father, men and women, too. I'd say he enjoys it but I'm not sure he's aware of it.

I wouldn't call him unpredictable, I said.

It's not my word, it's Robert's word. But it's more than that.

I said, Unreliable?

No, she said. Not at all. That's the last thing he is.

Are you? I asked. Afraid?

She looked at me crossly. No, she said. Of course not.

We strolled on. The air and sky had an end-of-summer look and feel. I was conscious that our time together was short. After Labor Day she was headed east to Barnard and I was remaining in Chicago and that was that. We rarely discussed the matter but it was always with us, uncomfortable baggage.

She said, I worry about him but I'm not afraid of him. Why would you think I was afraid of him? I'm not afraid of him or anybody.

I was only asking, I said.

You should have known the answer without asking. He would never do anything to harm me. Never. Not ever.

I know, I said.

Then why did you ask?

We walked on, quickly now, not in tune. I remembered our conversation of the night before, when she told me she could read my mind. I said I believed it but the reverse was not true. She had said, Try harder.

I said, Do you think a lot about New York?

She said, Now is not the time to talk about that.

It was not the time last night, either, or the night before. I knew she wanted out of Lincoln Park as badly as I wanted out of Quarterday, and I wondered if she had chosen Barnard to spite her father, as I had chosen the University of Chicago to spite mine, and how passionate was her desire to leave all else behind, making her way in New York. But this was not a subject she cared to discuss, beyond saying that we would write letters to each other and plan to meet at Thanksgiving. Of course I was afraid she wanted to cut all ties to Chicago, including me, in order to arrive in New York unencumbered. Listening to Aurora, I knew she was in distress, preoccupied with the life her mother led and the life she herself had made with her father, a difficult personality who frightened people though he did not frighten her. She had waited all this time to tell me of her split-up family life. It occurred to me that we were suddenly a crowd, my family and her two families including a stepfather and the swimmer, Dwight. When I looked into the rearview mirror now I saw a multitude, all of them with competing claims. Last night we had been at the jazz club to hear the closing set but the band was off so we sat at the bar. I wanted to talk about the future, her life in New York and mine in Chicago and how these would fit together. I wanted the future to begin at once and she said that wasn't possible. We had to take things on faith. We had to assume that our life together would work out, and meanwhile she was going to New York alone and that was the end of it. Discussion closed. Earl, the bartender, had been listening to us and put in that the future began with the first night you spent in jail. Same as losing your virginity, you never forgot it. I smiled, thinking of Earl, and explained to Aurora that I was thinking about this crowded past we had suddenly acquired, but I did a bad job of it because she did not reply. I was not certain she was listening carefully.

I said, What's his name, anyhow? Your stepfather?

Robert Elliott, she said. Two *l*'s, two *t*'s.

I thought I ought to know in case I become a doctor and need to drive a Buick.

She smiled marginally and said, Give it a rest, Wils. I should have kept my mouth shut.

No, I said. I put my hands on her elbows and turned her so that we were face to face. I said, We must have no secrets between us.

She said, Everybody has secrets.

I'd like it if we didn't, I said.

She shrugged and turned from me.

Honestly, I said.

Secrets are what get you from one year to the next, she said, pulling away. Secrets are what make the difference, one person to another. That's what a personality is, secrets. One mask after another. Secrets known and secrets kept. Secrets treasured. Secrets honored. Otherwise, what's the point?

There shouldn't be secrets between us, I said stubbornly.

That's impractical, she said.

What's impractical about it?

It sounds too much like work, she said.

And now we're having our first fight, she added brightly. She was smiling and looking over my shoulder at someone across the street.

Look there, she said. It's Adlai Stevenson.

He was alone, lost in thought, carrying a heavy briefcase, hatless. We watched as an older woman approached him and nodded, the governor grinning cordially, moving on. I thought he would be hard to pick out in a crowd, a nondescript middle-aged man in a gray summer suit that looked a size too small, his face pale and fleshy, his hair thinning. He looked like any tired businessman on his way home after a hard day at the office. Not so long ago he had been a presidential nominee, Americans attending to his every thought and deciding at last that they were the wrong thoughts, perhaps too precise for the perilous times and that, all things considered, muddled syntax from a five-star general was preferable. On the night of his defeat he quoted Lincoln to the effect that he was too old to cry and it hurt too much to laugh, and with that quip returned to private life and now, on a warm August afternoon, was strolling up Astor Street alone, a common citizen once again. I wondered where he was bound at this hour, imagining that he had an appointment with his advisers, perhaps to contemplate another campaign, perhaps only to complain about the last one, out of time, out of money, harassed on all sides by the miserable Republican press. The ghosts of a hundred secrets would be present at such a meeting, secrets among the advisers, secrets of the candidate, secrets concealed from the public and the press, secrets shadowing every word uttered. They were the war plans in the commander's tent, and would never be disclosed. The reason given would be "confidentiality."

There he goes, I said. A tomb of secrets.

But Aurora did not reply. She was watching him.

Then I decided that Mr. Stevenson was done with all that and was en route to his farm in Libertyville, a pretty rural community on the margins of the North Shore, there to meet an attractive young woman, a refreshing gin and tonic in his backyard garden, dusk falling, something on the phonograph, cornfields all around, hummingbirds in the air. There had been rumors in the campaign of his liaisons with women, society women from Chicago and New York. They were fond of Adlai, having known him for years, and discovered soon enough that there was raw romance in a political campaign, a festive highstress atmosphere not unlike an opening at the Art Institute or a premiere at Orchestra Hall, a rush of adrenaline observing America from the rear platform of a Pullman car and of course all America watching back and deciding it did not like what it saw, a nondescript middle-aged man in a summer suit that looked one size too small, a Princeton man, an egghead, a quipster. Not a man of the common experience, a stranger to ordinary American life. I remembered hearing that the governor's advisers were divided on the value of news photographs of the candidate with women. Voters might get the wrong idea, not that he was a libertine, exactly, but that the bedroom or even the suggestion of the bedroom had no place in a political campaign. Impossible to know where such suggestions would lead. The other side argued that was exactly the idea the voters should have, the image of a country gentleman irresistible to women, owing to the other rumor, baseless but persistent. He was a bachelor and that raised troubling questions. A president was president of all the people, not only the bachelor portion. The divorce was worrisome also. Something turbulent about it. A divorced bachelor could not relate to the troubles of the average American family and so it was helpful to have photographs of the candidate with attractive women, normal middle-aged women with children of their own, along with the usual gallery of Nebraska farmers and Pittsburgh steel workers and, now and then, a Negro. The other rumor, the baseless but persistent rumor, rarely spoken out loud, was especially worrisome. Rumors in a political campaign were like airdropped propaganda leaflets in a war—exhausted troops read them and said, Well, it's possible, isn't it?

I said, Do you think he's attractive to women?

Aurora said, He's attractive to me. I don't know about women generally. But he likes us, so naturally we'd like him back.

Aurora waved at the governor but he did not see her. He had paused to admire a black prewar Cadillac convertible at the curb, its top down, the same model FDR used in his travels around Washington. Adlai Stevenson's expression was unreadable, only a trace of a wistful smile as he turned abruptly and continued on in the dappled sunlight of late afternoon, until he turned the corner and was lost to view.

There's a man with secrets, I said.

Secrets *kept,* Aurora said. And she waited a moment before adding, He's a friend of my father's. Jack was a sort of adviser. Adlai appointed him to one of his task forces on mental health or something.

Have you met him?

Of course, she said.

Did he tell you any secrets?

She laughed and said he hadn't, except for jokes.

Wonderful raconteur, she added.

I told Aurora my carnal speculation concerning the destination of the former governor of Illinois, an attractive woman in his back yard at the Libertyville farm, dusk falling, hummingbirds in the air.

A woman definitely, she said.

Do you think so really? He's old. He's way over fifty.

Do you think they stop at fifty?

I don't know, I said.

I don't think they do, Aurora said.

Probably not, I agreed.

Most definitely not, she said.

Aurora paused and looked sideways at me, nodding suddenly as if she had come to a momentous decision.

I think it's time you met my father, she said.

THE KING OF CHICAGO

7

YOUR FAMILY had some trouble, didn't they?

We were sitting in the living room of the Brules' third-floor apartment, the failing sun casting long shadows in Lincoln Park. The crowns of the trees in the park seemed close enough to touch through the open windows. Dr. Brule was fussing at the cocktail table, breaking ice into a bucket, cutting lemons, and inspecting the bottles. He had poured a scotch for me and a Dubonnet for Aurora and now he was uncertain what to prepare for himself. He had greeted us in the foyer and after kissing his daughter had said, Hello, Wils, without any introduction from her, motioning for us to follow him into the living room. He was dressed casually in khakis and a faded green polo shirt. His feet were bare. I did not recognize him at first without his tuxedo. Aurora had excused herself and now we were alone, Dr. Brule at his drinks table and me on the long couch, the walls crowded with abstract paintings and a sculpture I recognized as one of Brancusi's birds in flight. The room had the look of a professor's parlor, academic journals on the coffee table, the couch well-worn, the far wall thick with books floor to ceiling with a sliding ladder to reach the high shelves.

The room was in deep shadow and Dr. Brule's voice seemed to come from it, a doctor's voice, I thought, a bored baritone. I did not answer right away when he asked about my family's troubles because I did not know what he meant, other than Squire's death, and he would not have known about Squire. The silence lengthened and finally I asked him if he meant the strike.

Yes, he said. The strike.

Thank God it's over now, I said, and when he did not reply I added, It was hard on my father.

Dr. Brule was silent again, concentrating on feeding ice cubes into a shaker and pouring the gin over the ice and waiting while it settled.

Hard on all of you, I imagine.

My father mostly, I said.

He poured the contents of the shaker carefully into a goblet and brought it brimming to the cocktail table, where he placed it on a coaster. Then he stepped to the window and stood staring over Lincoln Park, the trees moving in a light breeze, a sliver of Lake Michigan beyond. The silence lengthened. I wished Aurora would return. The ice in her Dubonnet was melting and I believed I was not far behind. The examination had begun and I did not think my newsroom anecdotes would carry me very far. I remembered Aurora telling me of her father's terse descriptions of people he saw in the street and imagined him sorting through the ones that might fit me, "anxiety neurosis," for example, or "chronic maladjustment." Whatever test he was devising, I was failing badly. His posture at the window reminded me of a military man's. I noticed him slip his feet into loafers, the loafers highly polished, a professional soldier's spit-shine before taking review of the troops.

When I took out a cigarette and flipped the top of my Zippo, he said sharply, Not in here. No smoking in here.

House rule, he added, all this without turning around.

I put my cigarettes away while Dr. Brule continued to stare out the window, raising and lowering himself on the balls of his feet, an athlete's exercise, his hands clasped securely behind his back. I listened to the clocks tick and traffic sounds coming through the open window, and, far away, the bleat of an ambulance. Apparently he was waiting for Aurora because he had not touched his drink; and mine was already half gone. I had never heard of a house that forbade smoking, except my father's aunt's house and that was for religious reasons. She was a Methodist.

I said, My mother was upset. It's understandable.

That earned a grunt from the window.

She was disappointed they couldn't go to Havana.

He cleared his throat and said quietly, I would have thought Havana would be the perfect place to forget. The casinos, dance bands and nightclubs, swimming pools and other distractions. A sandy beach.

That's what my mother thought, I said.

But your father didn't agree.

He agreed but there was nothing he could do. It was a strike. My father couldn't leave his business. Would not leave his business while it was under attack. He had production quotas to meet, things like that. He had to fight. His back turned to me, Dr. Brule did not move and appeared not to have heard.

I hesitated, sipping my drink, and then with as much nonchalance as I could muster, I said, For a while, he carried a gun.

Dr. Brule turned slowly, a sort of theatrical turn, a double take. But he said nothing and presently resumed staring out the window. Somewhere in the apartment I heard a rush of water.

He needed it for his own protection, I said.

They threatened him? Dr. Brule said.

Yes, in a note. Then in a phone call to the house. They threatened my mother over the phone.

Dr. Brule nodded gravely and said in a voice scarcely louder than a whisper, And how did your father react?

I thought a moment, remembering him with his hands on my mother's shoulders, attempting to comfort her. I said, He was upset, naturally. A telephone call not to his office but to the house, and whoever it was had mentioned me, too. So he had us to worry about along with everything else. I hesitated, trying to remember what he had said to my mother that night at the dinner table but I could not remember his words. I said, But he had the gun. A long-barreled Colt .32, I added unnecessarily. He carried it with him wherever he went.

And did he have occasion to fire it?

No, I said. He never did.

That's fortunate, Dr. Brule said.

But he would have used it if he had to.

Is that what he told you?

I know he would have, I said.

No doubt, Dr. Brule said. I know that weapon, he went on in his soft voice. I know it very well. It's reliable and well balanced. It does not have the stopping power of a Colt .45, but the .45 is heavy, almost forty ounces, and awkward to use. It's a brute of a gun, not accurate beyond twenty yards. He was silent a moment and then he said, Did your father carry it in a holster?

A duffel, I said.

Yes, of course. Dr. Brule continued his vigil at the window, his glass of gin on the table growing warmer by the minute as the light failed outside. He cleared his throat and said, It was difficult for your father, wasn't it? The letters and the telephone calls, his family threatened. And his business, too, of course. So it's normal for him to be frightened.

My father? No.

But it's rational to be frightened when someone's threatening to kill you. Bring harm to your family. Don't you see?

He wasn't, I said loyally.

An unusual man. Hats off to him.

He's tough, I said. He was a hockey player in college.

Did he see them face to face? The ones who wrote the letters and telephoned?

Not exactly, I said. They followed him in a car and then, once, they threw a brick through our terrace windows. We were at dinner. My father was cut, not seriously. Most of the time, during the day, he had a sheriff's escort. The sheriff and my father are old friends.

The sheriff, he said.

It was the sheriff who gave him the gun. From his inventory.

I see, he said.

Tom Felsen, I said.

And did Sheriff Felsen give your mother a gun, too?

My mother wouldn't know how to shoot a gun, I said.

Yes, Dr. Brule said. Of course.

It wouldn't be safe, I said.

Dr. Brule nodded agreement. So, he said. They threw a brick.

While we were at dinner, I said.

And he never saw them.

No, he never did.

Their faces.

I shook my head.

Invisible men—

Yes.

Lucky him, Dr. Brule said. Lucky, lucky him.

Excuse me, I said. Why is that lucky?

Dr. Brule raised his athlete's shoulders and let them fall, bending forward until his forehead almost touched the window. Beyond him, through the trees, were the rushing lights of Lake Shore Drive and here and there points of light on the water, pleasure craft. He said, The world is anonymous to us. We walk our own paths for the most part. Family, friends, colleagues, the woman at the post office window, the cop on the beat. That's our orbit. God help us when we slip from it and enter someone else's and it's unfamiliar. They do not wish us well. They have decided we are a blood enemy. Of course we know there is evil and malevolence in the world but most of us do not see it up close. We read about it in a newspaper article or hear about it from an eyewitness. We watch a newsreel and are moved or not depending on the quality of the film. It's a different thing entirely when you see the devil face to face, snake-eyed, malignant, merciless. He wants to erase you, destroy your soul. He'd do it in a second, without a moment's thought or a backward glance. If your father was not frightened, it was because he never looked into their eyes and saw the absence of reason. They are dead eyes. It's a terrible thing, hatred. Terrible. But in the witness of malevolence, it is inevitable. It is the product of fear.

It is, yes, I said.

Not their hatred, he said loudly. Your hatred. *Yours.* You cannot possibly understand fully at your age, the way you live and where, your country at peace. It's your hatred *of them,* and this hatred becomes an obsession to you, a passion that you can only know when you see them, see their faces, listen to their speech, watch their hands, these degenerates, so-called members of the human species. In your passion you become like them. No difference between them and you, and you find yourself thinking thoughts that are unimaginable and committing acts that are more unimaginable still. The line dividing them and you vanishes, except they are powerful and you are not. The abnormal becomes normal and you are—reduced. And you enjoy it, this reduction. The more extreme, the more pleasure you take. This does not occur at once. You do not recognize the change day to day, and then one morning there's an encounter and you know your heart's grown cold. In such circumstances pleasure and pain are the same thing. You need only a context. So do not believe for one minute that there is very much difference between one human being and another. We all have a will to survive, but it is stronger in some than it is in others; and the urge for revenge, that too is stronger in some than in others. As a father I have tried to keep this knowledge from Aurora. Dr. Brule raised his timeworn head and sighed deeply. He was silent at last, his thought concluded. He remained standing with his back to me and then, at a noise somewhere in that many-chambered apartment, he wheeled and left the room, motioning for me to remain where I was.

I watched him hurry off, and when I was alone the room seemed to exhale, and settle, exhausted. I was trying to make sense of what he had said to me, his monotone growing louder with each sentence. Of course my heart went out to him. I felt an intruder into some terrible private grief but I had no idea what had given rise to it, other than my father's trouble and how lucky he had been. Aurora's father had told me too much and not enough. He unnerved me and I wondered why I had told him about Havana and the brick, the note and the phone call, and the Colt .32 from the sheriff's arsenal. I had never told Aurora. I had never told anyone. Certainly, psychiatrists had a way of eliciting information, that was what they were trained to do, although Aurora had said her father rarely commented himself. Rules of the game. What had begun this sermon—I could think of no other word to describe it—was my stubborn insistence that my father had not been frightened. But he had been; anyone would be, blood on his hands, blood on his shirt, an attack without warning. I knew that at some time in his life Jason Brule had been frightened profoundly and had never forgotten. I could understand why people were bothered by him, his emotions so deeply buried but seething all the same. I wondered if he was in the paper's morgue. If he had ever been in the news. Henry Laschbrook had assured me that everyone was news once in their life, a birth or a marriage or a lawsuit or some scrape with the police, unless they had the clout to keep their names out of the paper. Otherwise they're in there somewhere, Henry said, pointing at the room filled with filing cabinets. You only have to know the alphabet, you want to find them.

I looked at my wristwatch, almost eight o'clock, dusk falling rapidly in Lincoln Park. My drink was finished and I wondered if I was allowed to fix another but decided that would be presumptuous. I had already begun to think of Dr. Brule as a prospective father-in-law and wanted to make a good impression—but his passionate and coiled manner suggested to me that that was not how he saw himself, and I already had the suspicion that he knew much more about me than I knew about him, so I went ahead and poured the drink. I had a question or two for Aurora as well, Aurora whose disappearance was ill-timed and had lasted far too long. I couldn't imagine what she was doing, unless it was a séance with her father, discussing matters that I couldn't possibly understand fully at my age because of the way I lived and where, a nation at peace. A subtle change in the room's atmosphere, and a whiff of familiar perfume, told me I was rescued at last. I rose at once from the couch, turning to the door, and said, Where have you been?

Why are you sitting in the dark? the stranger said.

Good question, I said.

Who are you anyway? Where's Jack?

The woman in the doorway looked to be in her early thirties, indisputably a city woman, tall and slender, fashionably turned out and made up, nothing sporty about her. She had a trace of an accent, Italian I thought, or Spanish. She looked Italian, smooth olive skin and a long thin nose and the blackest hair in Chicago, worn loose so that it fell carelessly over her shoulders. She wore heavy rings on her fingers, gold at her throat and wrists, and a knee-length black dress. The dress was as snug as the hair was loose. She stood in the doorway as if she owned it, an expression of anticipation on her face. She carried a little gold purse slung over her shoulder on a chain. The house key she held in her hand disappeared into the purse, and now she stood looking at me, a frank appraisal. Her posture reminded me somehow of a circus performer, feet wide apart, hands on her hips, prepared to execute the daredevil stunt as soon as the applause died down.

Wils Ravan, I said.

Ohhhh, she said, and gave a provocative giggle. You're the nice boy Aurora goes out with, the one she talks about all the time. The one that's different from the others. The one who works for that dreadful newspaper and visits pool halls and racetracks in order to learn the ways of the masses. The one who does not believe in the present. You're the boy who came to work in dancing shoes and was almost fired for it. What a riot. Happy to meet you. Her hand flew to her mouth and she giggled again.

I said, And your name?

Consuela, she said. Connie.

What else did Aurora tell you?

Much, much more, Connie said. But I'll never tell, she added, and made a gesture as if to say, That's all for now but not forever. She looked around the room and said again, Where's Jack?

I don't know, I said. He was here and then he went away.

Where did he go? He didn't go out?

Somewhere in the apartment, I said.

We have a dinner date—

I expect he'll be back. There's his drink. I pointed to the untouched glass of gin on the table.

She sighed and shook her head. He's impossible. He makes them and doesn't drink them. Can you beat it? I have been with Jack one year and I must have thrown out a gallon of gin. But he is not always predictable, and he does not like to explain. Also, he does not like to be searched for. So I will await him here.

She strode around the living room turning on lights, the two lamps on either side of the couch and the standing lamp near the drinks tray. She straightened the journals on the coffee table, lit a cigarette, and flung herself into the chair by the window and said, Make me a drink, darling Wils. Cinzano and soda, light on the soda, lemon peel, one ice cube. I've had a ghastly day, just ghastly.

She went on to describe the ghastly day, something about a fitting gone wrong and a canceled lunch date with an editor who was in town for only about three seconds and couldn't spare one of the seconds for a bite at the Buttery to discuss the contents of her book, taking shape at last after so many interruptions and false starts. Rush, rush, rush all day long. Cabs were impossible, and this midwestern heat, a furnace from hell, how do you stand it? It's worse even than Famagusta.

When I looked at her blankly, she said, Cyprus.

Where I spent my summers in a white villa by the sea, my little brothers and sisters always underfoot, a grove of lemon trees, owls in the trees, butterflies, too. A boiling sun. Homer's sun. The nights were almost as warm as the days, yet the air was always beautifully fragrant. In the afternoons we drank clove tea and played backgammon while we listened to the news on the radio. That's the book I'm writing, summers in the villa at Famagusta, a walled city, the destination of refugees for thousands of years. For refugees, Famagusta was a paradise. Of course there was unrest. There has always been unrest in Cyprus owing to Turkish provocations. They are not gemütlich, the Turks. They are lethargic and cruel, a morbid combination. My father's family is Greek in origin. My mother is Hungarian, mostly. And I can still see the butterflies in the lemon trees and taste the clove tea in Famagusta. So now you know all about me, including my irritation that Jack is absent and unaccounted for.

So you must come sometime to Famagusta, she said.

I would be delighted, I said.

When I handed her the Cinzano, she smiled and said, I was only teasing, what I said about you and the proletariat. The dancing shoes.

Aurora talked too much, I said, but I smiled as I said it.

She makes up for her father, Connie said.

He talks to me, I said.

Does he? Well, it's natural, isn't it? You are his daughter's friend. It's natural that he should want to know you, what kind of boy you are. He and Aurora are very close. He's protective of her, as fathers are. He has not had an easy time. He struggled terribly with that cow of a wife. She is in no way agreeable. She misbehaved when Jack was away in the war, and misbehaved again when he returned. She is a low personality, concerned with herself alone. So Jack worries about Aurora, surely you can understand that. He feels responsible for her, and that's why he attends those wretched parties in the countryside. He does not make a fetish of it, however. Do you like her?

Yes, I said. Very much.

Of course, I can see that. I am not an idiot. I don't know why I asked. Forgive me for asking.

She's very special, I said.

Jack, she began, but did not finish her thought. She said instead, You, too, are reserved with your opinions. You're quite grown up, that's obvious. Everyone in America grows up faster now, it's one of the good things about this country. At last.

So he goes to the parties to watch after Aurora?

To be present, Connie said. Aurora looks after herself.

But I've never seen you, I said.

I do not care for children's parties.

You'd like them, I said. There's music—

I am not invited, Connie said stiffly.

But that's absurd, I said. You have as much right as anyone else.

And if I were invited, she said, I would not go. Jack tells me about them, as much as I want to hear, the orchestras that are playing . . . She hesitated, listening, then rose from the couch and stepped to the open window, where she pitched her cigarette into the street, leaning over the sill to watch it fall. When she turned back to me, she was smiling broadly.

He doesn't like tobacco, she said.

I know, I said.

But he has a terrible sense of smell, so it is possible for me to enjoy tobacco without his knowing. This is fortunate.

I can see that, I said.

So he tells me who is dancing, she went on. The tensions among families, who is straying from the marriage bed. The banality of the conversations. The grief, I should say. Who Aurora danced with and whether she had a good time and if she had a ride home. That is what Jack tells me. It's enough for me to hear about the parties from him without having to go myself. We have another sort of life, Jack and me. Parties do not figure in it.

I was nonplused by these revelations—no one in my straitlaced family would ever tell such stories to a stranger—but before I had a chance to reply, Dr. Brule was in the doorway, freshly showered, smart in a tuxedo. He moved nervously to Connie's side, murmuring an apology, kissing her lightly on the mouth. She straightened his bow tie and adjusted the handkerchief in his breast pocket. He took her hand, smiled pleasantly at me, and escorted her from the room, both of them moving with the weightless self-absorption of ballet dancers, all this without a spoken word. Connie winked at me as they swept by. I heard them pause in the foyer, and then a rustle of clothing and a low laugh from Connie. The front door opened and closed, and I was alone again in the living room.

8

I STOOD at the window and watched them on the sidewalk, Dr. Brule standing on the curb with his hand raised, Connie beside him saying something. I heard their laughter and when he said something back, she gave him a playful shove. A cab arrived and the doctor opened the door, Connie still talking; she bent, taking her time, and I watched him slip his hand under her skirt while she paused a few more moments. The cab disappeared and I turned back to the room thinking about their other sort of life in which parties did not figure. Now there were three untouched drinks on the coffee table. I made another scotch for myself and a Dubonnet for Aurora and stepped into the empty hallway. Connie's scent hung in the air and I paused, wondering if she had returned; she was not quite real to me, an imaginary woman along with her owls and butterflies in restless Cyprus. A long corridor led to the interior of the apartment. I called softly but there was no response from Aurora, so I set off down the corridor, peering into rooms as I went. I did not feel as if I were intruding. Thanks to Connie's shared confidences, I felt like an honorary member of the family, a country cousin or other poor relation. There were bedrooms and a large bath and a library, more bookshelves and framed photographs on the walls, with a leather chair and a sofa and a Webcor phonograph, a man's room, as private as a locked desk. I wondered if this was his consulting room, but it didn't look like a consulting room and no woman would be caught dead there. I paused and looked in but did not enter.

I'm here, Aurora called, her voice coming from no obvious location, so I continued down the corridor, the two drinks cold in my hands.

She was lying on her bed reading *Lie Down in Darkness*. The bed was populated with dozens of stuffed animals, bears mostly, but also lions and other African beasts, and a yellow bird with a blue beak. Aurora seemed small and childlike in the big bed surrounded by her menagerie. She put the book aside and raised her eyebrows.

So you met Con-su-e-la, she said, drawing out the last syllable, *laaaa*.

We are great friends, I said.

I'll bet you are, Aurora said. Line forms on the left.

She's Greek, I said.

No kidding, Aurora said. She moved her legs and two of the bears fell off the bed.

And where have you been? I asked. Not fair, you know, leaving me alone with your father.

He wanted a private word and asked if it was all right with me and I said it was, and before I knew it he was back in his bedroom and I heard her voice. Hard to miss it, that screech. She was a nightclub singer. But I bet you guessed that. I'll bet when you heard Consuela's voice you said, Nightclub singer. Not out loud of course. I didn't hear you saying much out loud.

You were listening, I said.

From the corridor, she said. But I couldn't hear everything.

She told me about Famagusta and the lemon trees. Her book. A missed luncheon date. Much else.

She had a word or two about my father, didn't she?

And the parties, which she thinks of as children's parties. She isn't invited to them. Not that she'd go.

Well, Aurora said, and smiled. Consuela's not dumb. And what did she say about my father?

She talked about how much he cares for you.

It's not up to her to say that, Aurora said. Who does she

145

think she is, saying that? Then, after a smoldering silence: What are you looking at?

She meant well, I said.

Consuela does not *mean well*, Wils. She means a lot of things but well is not one of them. But you should know that yourself, being so grown-up. A perfect specimen of American grown-upness. She drives me crazy. She drives me up the wall. You better get used to it. Aurora was silent a moment, her eyes narrowed and her mouth working, talking to herself. So how did it go with my father? she said at last.

He asked me about trouble in my family, I said evenly.

Did he? I didn't tell him.

How did he know?

My father knows things, she said. Maybe one of his neurotic patients said something. People talk. He listens. That's his occupational specialty, listening. But it wasn't me. I've spoken to him about you but not about that. Because you've only given me the bare bones. It's tough enough as it is, Wils. Don't make it harder. She cleared a space on the bed, animals tumbling to the floor with soft plops. I sat down and handed her the Dubonnet. In the harsh glare of her bed lamp her face looked flushed and when I said I was sorry, she gave a weak smile, almost a grimace, an expression I did not recognize. When I took her hand, she seemed not to notice.

All these animals, she said. Did you have toy animals as a boy?

One bear, I said.

I have eighteen, she said.

So I notice.

My father always gives me a bear on my birthday, no two alike. She picked up a tiny black bear by the ears and let it fall. One of these days he'll be forced to buy a duplicate, and I'll notice and call him on it. And we'll laugh and he'll blame his memory. You probably had fire engines, chemistry sets, and a football. Boy stuff.

War stuff, I said. Battleships, lead soldiers, artillery pieces, and an enemy-plane spotter kit so that when the Luftwaffe bombed Quarterday I could tell my father that they were Messerschmitts, not Stukas. Dive for cover! They're after the sand traps! That won a tired smile from Aurora, and a squeeze of my hand, but she was still far away. She had not touched her Dubonnet and I wondered if it was a tradition of the Brule family that drinks were made but never consumed, prepared for decorative purposes only, like a bowl of terra-cotta apples.

I said, Probably you had a dollhouse, too.

No, only the animals. I was never interested in dolls because I was never interested in playing house. Or mom. That worried my mother and was the occasion for a conversation with my father. He said she wasn't to worry, I was all right. That was the expression he used, "all right."

Do you want a cigarette?

I don't mind, she said. He hates smoking but he never comes in here, so I smoke whenever I feel like it. I handed her a cigarette and lit it for her, then lit my own. She opened the drawer of her bedside table and put an ashtray between us and we sat smoking in silence.

I said, Where are they going?

A recital. Someone hired a soprano and a pianist for the evening. Supper after the recital but they won't stay. They'll go someplace else for dinner alone. Probably the Pump Room, where they can sit in the darkness and hold hands, eat steak flambé, and not have to talk to anyone.

I said, Where does she live?

Aurora looked closely at me and gave a long exasperated sigh, rolling her eyes. She lives here, dummy.

I could feel my cheeks redden and there seemed no suitable reply, so I smoked and sipped my drink and inspected Aurora's room, schoolbooks stacked in the corner next to a tennis racket and a field-hockey stick, a Princeton pennant on the wall between a *Viva Zapata!* poster and an African mask, photographs in frames on her dresser and desk, and a Toulouse-Lautrec drawing of a dancer in full fling. A bulletin board held ticket stubs, matchbooks, and a drying corsage. The room was heavy with her scent, even with the window thrown open to the air. I had never been in a girl's bedroom and did not know what to expect. But I was surprised to see a studio photograph of Marlon Brando with an inscription I could not read, his bold signature beneath.

Another friend of my father's, Aurora said, following my eyes.

What's he like?

Very nice, she said. Sexy. Very amusing, wonderful storyteller. Beautiful manners, beautiful eyes. He grew up around here, you know.

I didn't know that.

Yes, she said. But he doesn't live here anymore.

We listened to the night sounds of Chicago for a while and then she turned off the light. More animals tumbled from the bed and suddenly we were kissing in a tangle of sheets. The sheets smelled of her and of stuffed animals. Her bedroom door was open and soft light filtered in from the corridor, more shadow than light. We were hurried, as if breath were rationed and if we didn't rush we'd run out, and then unhurried, as if we had been making love for centuries, our own discovery along with Peyton Loftis and the characters in all the books on her shelves, even Marlon Brando. At that moment I felt like someone else's creation, guided by some imagination more powerful than my own. Aurora was whispering something in my ear but I could not hear owing to the rushing in my head. She was saying Wils, Wils, and I was nodding as if I understood but what I saw and felt overcame what I heard. She was telling me to take off my shirt and whatever else was between us, so I impatiently rid myself of the shirt and all else, one by one until I was stripped. In the half-light from the corridor I saw her smile, an inward smile for herself and for me, too. She was very strong. She arched her back and gave a cry that seemed to come from the center of her heart. Her eyes popped open and closed again at once but I did not follow because I did not want darkness, the darkness of aloneness. I was so close to her I could count her eyelashes. I unbuttoned her blouse, button by button, and when I was done I thought I had never seen anything in the world as lovely as her skin. She had a shiny black barrette in her hair and I removed that, and a wristwatch and bracelet and I removed those also, looking at her closed eyes and inward smile that now seemed unruly, fierce in its desire. We paused then, hesitating; and from somewhere in the street we heard swing, Benny Goodman I was certain. The horns went on and on behind Goodman's soaring clarinet but when I whispered his name she shook her head so vigorously her hair flew on the sheets. But it was Goodman all right, and the world was suddenly with us again. The music became part of the room's darkness and then it faded and the car drove away into Lincoln Park. We heard a siren but that faded, too, perhaps actually, perhaps because we weren't paying attention. We were only with each other. The world went away, leaving only the rustle of bedclothes and her sounds and mine as we continued until we could continue no longer. The animals fell from the bed, one animal after another, and the apartment's stunned silence closed around us, the seconds advancing, drawing us into our no longer mysterious future. The roaring was still inside my head. I was not thinking clearly except I knew, and I knew she knew, that this night was a great discovery, as momentous as any we would experience together, a dividing line. Precisely what it divided did not call for explanation, except I never wanted to be on the other side again. That was settled. I thought it was hard in this world to know what it was you didn't know, and now there was one less unknown unknown. I was in a state of restless contentment, overloaded, not trusting myself to speak. I stretched out on the bed, holding her as we rocked slowly from side to side. She was humming the Goodman melody we had heard from the car in the street. While she hummed, she beat a soft tattoo on my chest. She was smiling, her fierceness disappeared; or perhaps it was only in hiding. We were surrounded by her scent and mine, so dense you could not separate them. She looked at me and back at herself, murmuring something about negative space, things that were inside and things that were outside. Then she began to laugh. Now I watched her draw a cigarette from the pack, light it, and blow a smoke ring in the darkness, watching the ring slowly dissolve and collapse, her inward smile intact and her eyes glittering.

When I moved to disentangle myself, she laid her hand flat on my chest.

No. Don't.

Be still, she said.

So we remained together in her bed, smoking and interviewing each other. Not all the questions had answers and some of the questions were make-believe. After a while she excused herself and disappeared into her bathroom. I heard nothing, then her humming something jazzy, bah-da-dada da. I lay on my stomach and looked down at the books stacked on the floor. The one on top was leatherbound, ARCHIVES printed on the spine. I opened it at random, the page filled with a minute script, difficult to read but certainly Aurora's handwriting, long paragraphs prefaced by a date. I closed the book at once and replaced it, realizing I had stumbled on a diary, passages of description and dialogue. I knew that Henry Laschbrook was there somewhere and Charlie Smithers and, I hoped, me.

In a moment she was back, leaning against the doorjamb, finishing the cigarette. I did not move, watching her in the half-light of the corridor. But when I opened my arms wide she did a little shimmy and launched herself as if from a diving board, landing across my body, giggling wildly. She had an idea we could pretend we were at summer camp, so we had a pillow fight and following the pillow fight whispered confidences, inventions of one sort or another.

Later we decided to prowl the apartment, the bedroom that Aurora's father shared with Con-su-e-laaaa, the anonymous guest room, and the doctor's consulting room with its private entrance. The consulting room was austere, a chaise with a small table to one side, a box of tissues on the table. No ashtray, I noticed, but there was a shallow bowl with sticks of Wrigley's gum. The doctor's ladder-back chair was back of the chaise, out of the patient's line of sight. There was a formal Sheraton desk bare of paper and a glassed-in bookcase filled with medical reference books and journals. The atmosphere of the room was dour, discouraged and somehow lifeless. I could not imagine how Jack Brule sat in his chair for an hour at a time; and I imagined his disembodied voice behind the patient when the hour was up, So long, see you next week. The voice of God or of

Oz. The walls were bare except for two framed certificates, the doctor's medical diploma and a license from the state of Illinois. The carpet on the floor was a faded green with an indeterminate pattern. Heavy curtains covered the windows. The chaise had a Turkish bolster at one end, the bolster with a head-sized indentation. We stood in the doorway in our bare feet and suddenly Aurora nudged me, beginning to chuckle. She explained that inside the glassed-in bookcase, pushed back on the rear shelf where you couldn't see it, was a human skull. Supposedly taken from an Indian mound out near Galena. Her father's joke, but the point of the joke was unknown. Her father wouldn't say.

An honest-to-God skull? I asked.

With teeth, she said.

Does he have a name for it?

Not that I recall, Aurora said.

We stepped down the corridor to his study. I looked carefully at the photographs, a wedding picture with a smiling woman who did not fit Consuela's description of Cow, pictures of Dr. Brule and Aurora, and watercolors of empty rooms—a bedroom, a foyer, a dining room with a long table and a single chair, modest rooms that looked as if they belonged in seaside cottages in Ireland or in Spain. The pictures were delicately done and water was visible from the windows, the water a flat washed-out turquoise. There was a photograph of the doctor reading a newspaper in a Paris café, and one of Consuela on horseback, a Stetson on her head and a polo mallet in her hand. I looked back at the photographs of Aurora and saw for the first time how much she resembled her father, the set of her shoulders and her way of standing and her look, filled with curiosity, eyes wide open, always maintaining a certain distance in public. Their features were similarly compact, especially the smile that curled up at the edges, the one the doctor used so sparingly. Her mother had an outdoor look, a guileless athletic expression somehow at odds with the wedding dress, low cut, yards and yards of tulle, the train gathered at her feet. Her expression said, All in all, I think I prefer the golf course. Aurora and her mother were identically built, and that gave me something to think about; her mother looked to be a few years older than Aurora was now.

Dr. Brule's discharge paper was framed in plain wood painted black, the sort of frame you bought at the dime store. It was hung behind the desk. Next to it were photographs of three young soldiers, unshaven and in filthy uniforms, pistols hanging from web belts next to field canteens. The men looked exhausted and I saw that the one in the middle was Dr. Brule, taller than his comrades, his face drawn, his eyes hidden in shadows. The men were loose, slouched as if they had completed an arduous day; and there was still a way to go. There were palm trees in the background and a battered army jeep partly concealed in the trees. The shadows were sharp from a merciless sun. I looked closely and saw that all three men had the caduceus insignia on their shirt collars, along with the bronze leaf that signified the rank of major. But the sad-faced men, in their weariness and boredom, did not look like doctors. They looked like ordinary foot soldiers; and then I noticed the cigarette in Dr. Brule's fingers, as much a part of him as his wedding band and web belt and unsoldierly slouch. There were four photographs of the doctors. All of them appeared to have been taken on the same miserable summer's day.

Aurora had put on my shirt and given me one of her father's robes. When she moved to peer closely at the photographs, I slipped my arm around her waist, feeling the material of my own shirt and the warmth of her body beneath it. We continued to stare at the photographs of exhausted men in filthy fatigues, the grainy texture reminding me of Mathew Brady's compositions of the Union infantry. Aurora said she had no idea where they were taken or the year or the circumstances. She did not know the names of the other doctors. Her father would not identify or explain, saying only that he would tell her about them someday but that day had not arrived. When she complained that he was secretive, that she deserved to know what he was doing all those years he was away, he replied sharply that he was under no obligation to confess the facts of his own life. The war was on a strictly need-to-know basis, that was how things were set up. That was the agreement. So, still wondering who or what was involved in the "agreement," she stopped asking and filed the question under Unmentionable in her archives. There were Unmentionables in all families, she said, probably even yours, events and situations that were forbidden. I smiled at that.

Secrets, I said.

Secrets, she agreed.

The definition of personality, I went on, reminding her that Odysseus wept when he heard the poet sing of his great deeds abroad because, once sung, they were no longer his alone. They belonged to anyone who heard the song.

I suppose, she said doubtfully.

Probably your father did something great in the war, I said. Some act of bravery or sacrifice—

She made a dismissive gesture. You should have seen him when he came back. He was a mess.

There's a cost, I insisted, remembering what he had said to me earlier about hatred and observing the enemy up close. "In your passion you become like them." It's a private experience, I said, and he doesn't want to share it and shouldn't have to. I was surprised at my own vehemence and knew that I had intruded. I said to her, Sorry. I really don't know anything about it.

Aurora did not reply. We stood silently, looking at the photographs, making of them what we could. I felt a subtle change in her and in me, too, standing half stripped in her father's private study, wondering when he and Consuela would return from dinner. Of course I liked it where I was, with Aurora in the bright light of the desk lamp, my arm around her waist and her head on my shoulder, a delicious immodesty. It seemed to me that anything was possible now that we were on the right side of the divide. I remembered reading somewhere of one of the Italian hill communities, inhabitants of a region overrun again and again by alien peoples, Austrians, Hungarians, Serbs, Turks, Germans. The true test of character in that region was the ability to step outside one's own identity, go beyond one's roots to another realm altogether, a kind of transcendence. Such an ability required the severest sort of self-knowledge coupled with the will to survive. Your soul would be multilingual, not to mention your conscience. I felt one identity slip away and another take its place, and I was certain that Aurora felt it also, and with the same excitement. I knew we would make our own way in this fabulous undiscovered country, fortified by these new identities as yet undefined. We discarded the robe and the shirt. I kissed her, all the time wondering if her father had heard the poet and was afraid or was afraid of hearing the poet.

She bumped me with her hip while she thought things over. She said, It's your first time, isn't it?

Oh, no, I said. Not at all. I stand around naked all the time with beautiful girls in their fathers' private studies, looking at war photographs. It's the normal thing in Quarterday. We've been doing it for years and years. When she smiled wickedly and raised her eyebrows I knew at once that I had misunderstood the question, not for the first time that evening.

What if it is, I said.

Nothing, she said.

What about you?

What if it isn't? she said.

With my newfound identity, my multilingual transcendence-into-another-world-altogether, I summoned what I hoped and believed was a manly smile, the prelude to a most intimate exchange—and then I knew I did not want to hear this poet's song, not then, not ever. Somewhere behind me I heard the tick of a clock. I was aware of the heavy silence between us, Aurora turning slowly away from me, waiting for the answer to her question; I could not see her face, but I knew she was grinning. The men in the photographs stared out in vacant indifference. I pulled Aurora close and bent toward the photographs, believing that if I looked hard enough I would find—I suppose the word was inspiration. But nothing came and after an interval I said, It's the Pacific theater.

Yes, she said quickly. That's where he was. I know that much.

I was looking closely at the second photograph, the doctors standing in front of a military building, a flag hanging limply in the heat.

I said, That's the Philippine flag.

Aurora said, He's never mentioned the Philippines.

The last of the photographs did not include the doctors. It was taken by a professional, a posed picture of an American general and his aides. The general seemed to be composed of skin and bones but he stood alone and unsupported, a little apart from the others with his ghostly dignity, his eyes averted from the camera. His posture, his great height, and the boniness of his skull reminded me of Aurora's father as he was now. The general's face was familiar. And then I knew for a certainty where Dr. Brule had been and what he had endured.

I said, Your father called it "the Hike."

That's what he calls it, Aurora said. Another joke.

I took a step forward to look at the photographs more critically. The war was close in time, but it seemed part of another era. Today's war was Korea. Books came one after another and there were articles every day in the newspapers, an anniversary of a battle or the death of one of the great commanders or a fresh analysis of this tactic or that, the Ardennes or Guadalcanal. The agreed-upon silence not to contradict the Hollywood version of events was giving way at last, yet even the firsthand accounts were written with circumspection and most veterans declined to speak at all of their wartime life, the experience too personal, too frightful even now to relate for the education of civilians, spectators really, bystanders who listened out of a sense of duty or simple curiosity or pity. What self-respecting veteran could look into those faces, so filled with sympathy and noncomprehension, and tell the exact truth? The exact truth was profoundly private, as closely held as the most shameful secret; and to speak of it would be to lose it, a truth so hard won. The hard facts of the matter were etched on their faces. I looked at those long-ago photographs in their dime-store frames and knew that "the Hike" was the Bataan Death March and that Jack Brule was one of the survivors and that his stoic silence was the means of that survival.

I said, Did he ever mention Bataan?

No, Aurora said. What's Bataan?

I volunteered nothing further, preferring instead to join the conspiracy of silence. There were so many conspirators, would one more make a difference? Somehow Jack Brule's secret had become my secret, and if he did not care to share it with his daughter, neither would I.

What's Bataan? she said again.

A battle early in the war, I said. The Philippines.

Was my father in it?

I don't know, I said. Might have been.

The name's familiar—

Let's go back to your room, I said. They'll be here soon, your father and Consuela. We can go around the corner, have a bite to eat.

Will you tell me about Bataan at dinner?

I don't know much about it, I said, and turned from the photographs. How I enjoyed telling stories about municipal corruption and the Chicago Mob, describing the way of the world to North Shore debutantes. But this was different. This was serious, a war in which many thousands died and Jack Brule was one of the walking wounded. I had an idea that it was some form of patriotism that caused him to withhold the facts of his own life; and it was not my business to interfere, though as I thought about it I knew I had made a choice. The choice was between Jack Brule and Aurora, and I had chosen him over her, preserving his privacy and her—I suppose the word was innocence.

You know more than you're telling, Aurora said. You have that *look*, the Wils look. It's a wiseguy look, and it's unbecoming. She was grinning and went on about my look, furtive, sly, a smile that was becoming a smirk, signals of a guilty conscience. I wasn't listening to her. My hands were around her neck, then slid to her waist, and for now all else was forgotten in a full avalanche of desire. I knew so little of women, and that little I knew now seemed illusory. It had never occurred to me that seduction could be cooperative.

We remained in her father's study for a while, until Aurora went away on some unspecified errand, gliding from the room on her toes with a knowing glance over her shoulder. I watched her go, then rose lightheaded from the couch and turned off the table lamp. I stood in the darkness a moment longer, wishing I had a cigarette and remembering then that I had tucked a pack and lighter in her father's robe, and as I fished for them I noticed his scent, an old man's sour smell mingled with bay rum. The robe looked to be many years old, as worn and frayed as any favorite item of clothing was bound to be. I stepped to the window and looked out, Lincoln Park mostly dark but through the trees I could see headlights on the Outer Drive and, close in on the surface of the lake, the running lights of sailboats and yachts out for an evening cruise. I lit a cigarette and blew smoke rings into the darkness, still thinking about Jack Brule's secret that had become my secret, and the guilty conscience that went with it. I wondered if I would always associate a guilty conscience with bay rum and an old man's sweat. Well, it was his business. The choice was his, not mine. I had only gone along, as I had every right to do. But my God, Chicago was beautiful at night. The breeze from the lake was soft, a sickle moon rising in the east. The city seemed as tranquil as a country village. All that was missing were church bells and a town crier. I heard the purr of an airplane far away but I could not hold it and the sound disappeared into the silence.

I was thinking of the life we would make together. I wanted to live in an apartment like hers, elevated from the street, a private place in the city where you could live as you pleased. Standing now at the window, watching smoke from my cigarette drift away on the breeze, I felt like the king of Chicago, looking down on my private park with the silver sliver of lake beyond, a line of sight all the way to Canada. I saw Aurora and me in an apartment like this one, smaller naturally, but well situated and comfortably furnished to our own taste. The bedroom would have the lake view. We would have exciting jobs, Aurora too, but we would have a life away from the jobs. Her father and I would become friends and I would keep his every confidence. He and Consuela would come to us for Sunday lunch or drinks on a Friday evening, the apartment alive with laughter; and one day he would bring Brando or even Adlai Stevenson and we would all tell riotous secrets, cocktail glasses filled and refilled, even Jack's. Our apartment, Aurora's and mine, would be the place to come for Sunday lunch, and when we tired of the routine we would drive to Wisconsin, somewhere around Fish Creek, for a long weekend. We would own a cabin in the woods and a runabout and the cabin would be for us alone, no guests. The cabin would not have a telephone, only a phonograph. Aurora's Toulouse-Lautrec drawing would go in the bedroom. I thought this was a grand idea, living and working in Chicago and avoiding the North Shore and Quarterday. Away on Lake Shore Drive, whirling red lights sped north, the sirens faint and rhythmic in the distance.

I heard Aurora in the corridor and turned from the window, pitching my cigarette into the street. The telephone rang and she answered it, her voice curt; and then I heard her say, Oh, no, everything's just fine and we're leaving in a few minutes to get a bite to eat. We didn't realize the time was so late because we were playing backgammon and listening to music, your Goldberg variations. No, don't hurry. Take your time, you and Con-su-e-laaaa. We're having a fine time, don't worry about us. We've been delayed but we're leaving now. Poor Wils is tired and hungry. He's had a long day at the office.

When she rang off, I said, What are the Goldberg variations?

She said, Private joke. He didn't believe a word of it. He heard something in my voice. And what he heard was insincerity. He's good at that, you know. He's an expert. It's what he does for a living, listen to lies. Probably I shouldn't've mentioned the Goldberg variations but I couldn't resist.

She looked into the study and asked what I was doing in the dark.

I turned on the desk lamp and said I had been thinking about an apartment in Chicago and a cabin in Fish Creek as the venues for our future life together. The bedroom gets the water view.

Fish Creek, she said, making a face. Black flies and mosquitoes.

And Indians, I said. Don't forget the Indians.

There are no Indians in Fish Creek, she said.

I was misinformed, I replied.

She laughed at that and said, What makes you think I'd live in Chicago?

I looked at her blankly. Where, then?

I intend to live in Greenwich Village, she said.

I suppose Greenwich Village would be all right, I said.

Glad you approve, she said. She smiled wickedly and pulled on my arm. Come here, she said. I want to show you the skull.

In the consulting room once again, we peered into the bookcase. The skull rested on the bottom shelf. It was well formed and well cared for, as slick and polished as ivory, a small ragged hole just above the right eye. Of course I wondered whose skull it was, and the identity of the killer, and the circumstances of the death, time and place and cause. I wondered if Jack Brule knew, or whether his skull was an anonymous casualty, an unknown soldier of an undetermined war. Or a commonplace neighbors' dispute, an argument over a fence post or water rights or an insult to someone's wife or daughter. Or the wife or daughter.

Aurora closed the bookcase and said it was time to go.

Get something to eat, get our clothes on.

They'll be home soon, she went on. They were just finishing up at the Pump Room and unless I miss my guess, they're in a cab at this very moment. He's complaining about the Goldberg variations and she's in a snit because he wouldn't give her time to finish her peach flambé. It wouldn't be a good idea if they found us here undressed.

Stripped, I said.

Yes, stripped. And he doesn't like strangers in his consulting room.

I think I know why, I said.

What does that mean?

But I did not answer directly. I said instead, Were you serious about Greenwich Village?

Yes, I was.

You never mentioned it before.

You never asked me. What did you mean about knowing why?

Everybody has a place they don't want people going into. Your father's study is private. I put my arm around her, her skin damp to the touch. Her hair was damp and I felt a sudden chill in the room. Aurora tugged gently and I stepped back from her father's glassed-in bookcase with its grinning memento mori that had nothing to do with an Indian mound near Galena or, I was convinced, anywhere else on the American continent. In the lower jaw was a molar with a gold filling, twentieth-century dentistry. I wondered if the skull belonged to a comrade or an enemy and if it was there to remind him of the war or to help him forget. Familiarity, the object present every day, bred absent-mindedness.

You said you liked Chicago, I persisted.

I do. Chicago's where I'm from. It's not where I'm going. Chicago's large, Wils. It's just not large enough.

I was at a loss. Greenwich Village had come from nowhere. Probably Aurora had a friend who lived there or she had read something, a novel or a biography, that had mentioned Greenwich Village in an attractive way, an unbuttoned neighborhood where a young woman could go about her life unsupervised. Greenwich Village was often in the news, usually something to do with outrageous bohemian conduct. Maybe Brando had said something amusing about Greenwich Village, making it seem as exotic as a foreign capital—though it did not appear that Aurora had found Chicago especially confining. How large, exactly, did a city need to be? But I could see the appeal of Greenwich Village, a cosmopolitan appeal reaching across class divisions; no doubt Brando would have had something to say about that as well. When you came down to it, Chicago was still the Midwest, the landlocked heartland—and suddenly the University of Chicago looked drab, a provincial backwater no more than an hour's drive from Quarterday. Henry Laschbrook had told me that even the Reds came from small towns like Hibbing and Ely, wintry Norwegian and German boys heavy with grievance owing to the industrial struggles of the Iron Range. There would also be a contingent from Chicago itself, earnest high school valedictorians who did not wish to study physics too far from home. Meanwhile, my Aurora would be in Morningside Heights, the edge of the continent.

I said, Who told you about Greenwich Village?

Nobody, she said. I've always liked the idea of it.

What, particularly—

It's not-here, she said briskly. That's the first thing. And the second thing and the third thing. When I did not reply, she tugged at my arm. Time to go.

I said, That skull's a bad omen.

It can't be a bad omen for you. It doesn't belong to you.

It doesn't belong to your father, either. It belongs to whoever lived inside it.

Whatever you say, she said.

It could be anybody, I said.

I don't believe in omens, she said.

We dressed in her bedroom. I finished first, happy to be rid of Jack Brule's robe, and wandered again into the corridor and stood looking into the consulting room once more. What could you know of a human being from the room where he did his work, listening hard to the deepest fears and the most private secrets and struggling to find coherence and, from coherence, a remedy; and out of sight on the bottom shelf of a glassed-in bookcase, a memento mori. An outsider could only guess at the contours of his life, the hills and the valleys and the caverns beneath them. I had known him only as an aloof presence at North Shore dances, a slender figure in a well-cut tuxedo who refused to dance. Now I knew that he had found himself in the occasion of danger and survived. He had not sought it but had not excused himself, either; and the event stayed with him. He carried it around like a wallet. How much of him was passed down to his daughter, other than the wide-set eyes, the pride, and the refusal to let things go? I knew that the training of psychiatrists included their own psychoanalysis and I wondered if that had been, for him, a success. And what, in his terms, would constitute "success"?

I'll only be a minute, Aurora called from the bedroom.

At any moment I expected the front door to fly open and a French farce to ensue, a hasty retreat, shouts, threats, mistaken identities, and finally a rowdy exit from her bedroom window.

Take your time, I said.

I felt as if I had been in this apartment half my lifetime, and knew it as well as I knew my family's house in Quarterday. I realized I was making too much of too little, but that was my habit. Loving Aurora, patrolling her father's rooms without his knowledge or permission, searching for his past—what of it I would gather through the photographs and framed documents and souvenirs, and what he had said to me and how he had said it, and what Consuela had disclosed—I knew I was trespassing, but suspected also that Jack Brule had invited me in. I had been staring at Aurora's photograph, a candid made when she was little, perhaps six years old, her fists at her side, hair wet from a bathing pool, an expression of utmost truculence, cheeks ballooning in disappointment. Something had been withheld, or a promise broken; and if I had asked her about it, I had no doubt she would remember what it was. I felt like an astronomer at a telescope watching the birth of a star changing shape before my eyes. She in no way resembled what she became, except for the truculence.

I heard a door slam in the street and Consuela's complaint delivered in a throaty contralto: *Jackie, I think we should get up there right now.* I turned unwillingly from the consulting room and went in search of Aurora. She appeared from her room wearing a skirt and a shortsleeve sweater, running a comb through her hair. Her glasses were perched on the end of her nose. When we heard the whine of the elevator, she turned and pointed down the corridor, the private entrance for the doctor's patients. We hurried through it and waited, then rushed down the stairs to the lobby. We fled the apartment like thieves in the night except we were laughing, pausing in the street long enough to look up at the third-floor windows. Jack Brule and Consuela stood in the half-light of the living room in their formal clothes looking like any well-to-do couple home from an evening out, the theater and dinner later, and only moments before bedtime. Consuela said something and Aurora's father seemed to shake his head in disgust; and then his hands went to his temples and his shoulders sagged as if from a great burden. Aurora had told me of his headaches and I supposed this was one. Then the lights abruptly went out and Jack and Consuela were visible no more. Aurora and I hurried off down the street in the direction of the all-night restaurant on Clark Street. I could not erase the sight of Jack Brule's fingers on his temples and the sway of his body. I was in awe of him, yes; but I was afraid of him also.

9

A WEEK LATER, my last day at the paper, Tilleman in-
structed me to be at the state's attorney's office at ten
o'clock sharp to pick up two copies of a grand jury indictment and return at once to the newsroom, flank speed.
Word was that the grand jury had charged one of Chicago's
leading Mafiosi with racketeering, loansharking, extortion, and
intimidation of witnesses. This is news, Tilleman said. It's been
a long while since anyone thought to enforce the law on our local hoods. Our readers will want to know the particulars. It'll be
chaos at the state's attorney's office, so arrive early, and here's
fare for the taxi back.

And then you can have the rest of the day off, in recognition
of your valuable assistance this summer.

Tilleman gave me a worn dollar bill from his own wallet, a
kind of ceremony signaling the importance of the assignment.
The paper rarely gave cab fare for anything except a four-alarm
schoolhouse fire or a love-nest slaying.

Thank you, I said.

We've never had anyone in the office quite like you, Tilleman said. You're a North Shore kid, one of a kind, hard to figure out. Tell me this. Did you enjoy yourself in my newsroom,
Ravan?

I did, I said.

Like the atmosphere, do you?

I do, I said. I've learned a lot.

What? he said. What have you learned?

I hesitated, uncertain exactly what it was that I had learned except how to place a bet with a bookie and how to hold a telephone tucked between my shoulder and my ear and speak so that I could not be heard five feet away. Then I remembered the colored woman found frozen in an alley on the South Side, the woman without a name or an address, now a missing person. I said, I learned there are some stories you'll never get to the bottom of. You'll try and try and come up empty. And those are the most interesting stories of all, and the ones that people remember because the question remains unanswered. Years later, they'll say, What do you suppose ever happened to that woman, found frozen solid?

Tilleman said, Horseshit. Those are the stories that people forget. You'll never be a reporter. He pronounced the word ruh-*porter.* Tilleman smiled thinly, and thought a long moment while he tapped his pencil against the paste pot. He said, You're the oldest god damned nineteen-year-old I've ever met. I think you were born middle-aged, and that's your trouble. Curiosity is child-like. My best reporters never grew up. I don't think you enjoy *finding things out.* Finding things out is for the proles. Find something out, you do away with guess work. You do away with romance. You like guess work because you think everything's a mystery. You like mystery. You don't care much for the truth. But that's not what reporters do. When reporters find things out, they demystify. They don't have to like what they find. In most cases, they don't care what they find. Liking and caring don't come into it, the reporter's trade. When you're on the job, you dig; and what you dig up goes into the newspaper. If it's gold, it goes on page one. If it's brass, it goes inside. That's the incentive, you see. Page one. But you're not interested in digging, one crisp fact after another until you have a story that people will buy the newspaper to read, because the story's satisfying. It's nourishing. It's scrambled eggs and bacon. It's well told. But you don't care what satisfies people, what makes them buy the paper day after day. You don't want to be below decks, doing the digging, shoveling coal into the hotbox, making the engines run. I think you're interested in topside. You're interested in navigation. You want to be on deck with the sextant, charting the course. You want clean hands. And you want the wheel.

The skipper, I said.

Tilleman waved his arms in great arcs, his face red with anger. Skipper! he shouted. You couldn't skipper a rowboat. Hell no, the hurricane's blowing force nine but you don't notice it because you're trying to find the stars with a fucking sextant. There aren't any stars, Ravan. It's a hurricane and you can't see the stars. They might as well not exist.

Maybe they exist on the North Shore, he added.

So you better go back to Lake Forest, or wherever you come from.

Help that daddy of yours break the union.

Goodbye, Ravan. Good luck.

Good luck to you, I said, a reply that in the circumstances was just this side of insolent. I decided to fire two last shots.

You're wrong, you know, about the colored woman. And wrong about my father.

But the city editor had already turned away to say something to one of the reporters standing patiently at his elbow, feigning indifference to the tirade just concluded—and I noticed now for the first time that Tilleman's desk gave no hint of his private life. Instead, it was an inventory of the tools of his trade, a Royal typewriter with copy paper next to it, a paste pot, a box of paper clips, a Swingline stapler, number one pencils points-up in a plain white coffee mug, Scotch tape, a gum eraser, a Webster's dictionary, Fowler's *Modern English Usage*, Lennart's street guide to Chicago, a railroad schedule, and a telephone directory. There was nothing personal on the surface of his desk, no mementos, no pictures of the family or of himself with local celebrities, a saloonkeeper, alderman, or sports hero, unless you counted the ashtray with a faded logo of the Chicago White Sox. The same was true of the reporters' desks, strictly anonymous, some desks messier than others but otherwise interchangeable. It was as if the occupants of the newsroom had no life beyond it, certainly no life worth being reminded of, and nothing therefore to compromise their professional objectivity. A photograph of a wife or sweetheart or parents or children would be considered unforgivably sentimental—and then I wondered if the reverse was also true, that their homes would contain no hint of their daytime life, and somehow I doubted that. The pull of the newsroom was a twenty-four-hour affair.

I left at once for the state's attorney's office, thinking all the while of Tilleman's animus and wondering how much of it was personal and how much related to my father's business and deciding to have a final word with him; but when I returned to the newsroom, Tilleman was nowhere in sight. I put copies of the indictment on his desk and headed to the cashier's office to collect my last week's wages, thirty-five dollars and seventy cents. Along the way I stopped to say goodbye to the reporters I'd come to know, Henry Laschbrook and Ed Hoskins. I knew in my bones that we would never meet again, and so did they. For me, it was the last day of summer camp. I was leaving but the counselors were staying on, and as we talked I got the idea that this newsroom world would soon expire like a dying star. The rattle of the wire service machines in the corner, the pop of the pneumatic tubes that rushed copy to the composing room, the eyeshades and Tilleman's paste pot and gum eraser, had the antique look of a silent movie. Windows were thrown open to the heavy August air, and you could hear horns and sirens and the clank of the El and all the notes of Chicago's industrial hum.

Henry and Ed had heard the exchange between Tilleman and me—in the newsroom, no conversation was ever private, except telephone conversations—and said I shouldn't worry about it. Not everyone was cut out to be a newspaper reporter, a specific craft requiring a specific outlook on life, low pay, long hours, deadlines, anxiety, with nothing to show for it at the end of the day but a piece in the paper, edited by cranks, read by straphangers, here today, gone tomorrow. Most reporters were burned out at fifty, no good for anything but the obit desk, and the only thing to be said for the job was that it was—just a hell of a lot of fun, being in the know. In any case, the city editor's bite was worse than his bark, ha-ha, but he wasn't such a bad guy really, underneath. He was worried about his job, same as they all were. Ozias Tilleman had a reputation to maintain, "that of prick."

But we were all a little surprised, Henry said.

He was rougher than he needed to be, Ed put in. What the hell, you were here as a copy boy, special circumstances.

Aren't you the publisher's nephew? Henry said.

No, I said. The publisher is a friend of my father's.

Not the nephew?

No, not the nephew.

We heard you were the nephew, Ed said, eyes narrowing, suspicious of my story. Naturally he suspected a cover-up. The rumor was widespread and too plausible to dismiss because of a dubious denial by an interested party. Surely there was something more to it, something left unsaid. In every story there was something concealed, the inconvenient or incriminating fact.

So your father and the publisher aren't related in any way, Henry said, nailing it down. That's a shame because we were hoping you'd know something about where we stand. If the paper's going to fold, or what.

No, I said. They're just friends. They talk about golf.

And I assume your mother's not related—

No, I said.

Golfing, is it? Ed said.

And Republican politics, I said.

It figures, Ed said. This publisher is a union buster, too. But he can't get away with that here. Chicago's a union town. We wouldn't stand for it. We wouldn't stand for scabs in the plant. We'd close him down, Ed said evenly, looking at me as if he expected an argument.

My father didn't try to bust the union, I said. The union tried to bust him.

Ed Hoskins laughed sourly, turning to Henry Laschbrook. That's a new one, he said. That's not the way we heard it. But things probably look different out there on the nineteenth hole of the country club.

Take it easy, Ed, Henry said.

Plenty of kids I know, love to be making thirty-five a week

hustling copy. Fetching Tilleman his coffee and Danish. But these are kids who don't play golf, and their fathers don't play golf either.

Ed, Henry said.

Shit, Ed said, and walked back to his desk.

Henry Laschbrook and I avoided each other's eyes in the awkward silence. He said finally, This is a hard time for Ed, the uncertainty. There's more bullshit thrown around this city room than in the stockyards. He has a family, one of his kids is sick. One of Ed's kids is always sick.

My father doesn't have anything to do with it, I said.

They're going to fold this paper and then Ed's out of work. No food on the table. Baby needs shoes.

All the papers in this town, he'll find another job.

He's fifty, kid. Fifty years old, a journeyman. The other papers don't want him. And now he thinks he'll have to go into public relations, flacking for one of the department stores or the railroad, maybe even the city. Shit, Ed doesn't even own a decent suit. This paper's been his whole life, started like you, a copy boy. Wrote sports for a while, then police. There wasn't any college in Ed's future. He was the breadwinner in his family. He still is. Maybe that's hard for you to understand from where you sit, a college boy without a care in the world except deciding which dance to go to on Saturday night.

I have no idea what's going to happen to the paper, I said.

If you hear anything, let us know.

I didn't understand about Ed, I said.

No reason why you should, Henry said, turning to his desk.

And then the phones began to ring and one by one the reporters picked up, said Yeah, and began to listen hard, receiver tucked between jaw and collarbone, already inserting a sheet of copy paper into the typewriter and beginning to strike the keys, tap tap-tap tap-tap-tap tappatappatappatappa—can you spell that name again, sugar? How many injured? What's the address? Typing with one finger while lighting a cigarette and dropping the match to the floor. Smoking and typing, typing and talking, talking and smoking, weighing and measuring the information on Tilleman's Richter scale of reader satisfaction.

Hard to miss the bitten fingernails, the frayed shirt cuffs, the canny insinuating tone of their questions, and the tremendous affection the reporters had for their typewriters, personal as pocket watches. While they talked they moved their fingers from the keys to the space bar and back again, whether they were typing or not; and when they finished, the telephone in its cradle, they reviewed their notes, all the while caressing the carapace of the machine as if it were a small animal or the skin of a woman. I watched them a moment, absorbed in their utter concentration, birds building nests one twig at a time.

Then I was standing on the sidewalk in a light rain, my pay packet heavy in my jacket pocket, no assignment, no place I had to be, no specific quitting time, a free Friday afternoon at the paper's expense. I turned to look at the newspaper office one last time—gray-faced, I thought, exhausted, rain darkening the stone façade, the newspaper's logo in heavy gothic script over the entrance, upper windows thrown open to the Loop's sooty air. I stood still and listened for the rattle of the newsroom typewriters but the noise of the street swallowed it up. My summer at the paper had been a summer at the circus, acrobats, clowns, lion tamers, aerialists, magicians, and Jo-Jo the dog-faced boy, Ringmaster Tilleman supervising all of it. Who wouldn't envy such a summer, at the center of events in Chicago? And I was delighted to be finished with it. Not everyone was cut out to be a newspaper reporter. I turned my back and felt a sudden shudder, the sidewalk trembling from the huge Goss presses beginning to turn with the early afternoon edition. MOBSTER INDICTED! would be the page one headline over an unflattering photograph and a few paragraphs of essential details, hard facts to whet the reader's appetite for the second edition and the edition after that, and tomorrow's lurid follow-up already in the works. My contribution to the flow of the day's news, Tilleman's gold. But as I walked away, I was thinking of my father and his red duffel, my father the union buster, the publisher's golfing partner and confidant. I was astonished his shadow had followed me all this way. I was marked as surely as if I had a clubfoot or was carrying a white stick or wearing white tie and tails or Lieutenant Sassoon's bloody infantry uniform, and yet I had been absolutely certain that I was as anonymous as one of the newsroom's gunmetal desks, the kid who brought Tilleman his morning coffee and hustled copy from here to there, handy in the morgue, what was his name again?

You know the one. The publisher's nephew.

The college boy from the North Shore.

Bill? Will?

Of course Tilleman knew the score, thanks to my dancing shoes; and probably the dancing shoes were only confirmation of what he already suspected, having received a note from the publisher. *Hire this kid, minimum wage.* I pulled the problem this way and that, gathering twigs in my own way. But the nest would not build. I wondered if you went through life as a reflection in the mirrors of other people, and these mirrors were distorted, shaded by rumor and supposition, the way you spoke and the clothes you wore, your haircut and how you carried yourself, and you had to live with it. And I knew I was guilty of the same thing, observing frayed shirt cuffs and bitten fingernails and assembling from them a personality. What did I know of Ozias Tilleman's life really, or the lives of Ed Hoskins or Henry Laschbrook away from the newsroom—Hoskins and his chronically sick children, Laschbrook and his moments of tranquillity at the pool hall on Wabash—other than their lives were different from mine. Observing the rollers gave only a superficial understanding of the ocean beneath. Probably Aurora had all this in mind when she talked of moving to Greenwich Village, where no one knew who you were or cared, where badges of caste and class would fall away in the balmy atmosphere of—no doubt it would be artistic freedom, and a closetful of hats for every occasion, depending on the personality you chose that day.

Something missing there, I thought.

What if Bleecker Street was only Astor Street in sandals and a black beret?

All this time I had thought I was one of them, a kind of junior partner, product of anonymous Quarterday, familiar with life's hard knocks because my father had carried a gun for his own protection. But I was mistaken. I had acquired an identity that was not false, but one I had not sought, either, at least not consciously. North Shore kid, college boy, slumming for the summer. I was the enemy. But they knew no more of me than I knew of Jack Brule's skull in the glassed-in bookcase.

I walked in drizzle through the Loop to the Art Institute, intending to surprise Aurora when her class ended at noon. The Loop was as well-known to me now as Quarterday and I knew in some specific way that I would always be drawn to it, the wide-windowed department stores with plump women in gloves and high heels scrutinizing the goods on offer, the movie marquees ablaze with garish lights, the restaurants, bars, pool halls and to-bacco shops, the sidewalks crowded with shoppers and drifters, the streets damp and filthy with bits of paper that looked like the litter scattered around betting cages at the racetrack. There were fast-eyed characters waiting for buses, checking their wrist-watches, expecting a score. The buildings surrounding them were low and crabbed, many dating from the previous cen-tury, sullen in the summer rain. Chicago itself had a nine-teenth-century identity, a noisy, unlovely city of iron and con-crete, a city on the grab, fundamentally lawless, its days spent chasing money and its nights spending it; loveliness was always just beside the point. The city had elbow room but God help you if you fell behind because there was always a more muscular elbow. The city was ruled by a half-dozen old white men to suit themselves. You were permitted to go about your business so long as your business didn't interfere with their business. If it did, they invited themselves in. In its cosmic indifference, the city of Chicago resembled a mighty turbine, three and a half million souls oiling the gears and tending the works while the supervisors stood around reading the racing form. I was nine-teen years old and that was my view of things after my circus summer at the newspaper—an unlovely city, not unloved. I knew that wherever I would go in the world, Chicago was the place I would return to and recognize at once, its fedora pulled down over one eye, a wisecrack already forming in its mouth full of nickels.

A clang announced the El overhead. I thought of walking down State Street to look at the crowded racks of jazz records at Seymour's and, if I was lucky, strike up a conversation with one of the musicians who were always present. Hey-Hey Humphrey was a regular, and Jack Teagarden when he was in town, nighttime men whose days were free. The place always had a suspicious atmosphere, under-the-table business, men in porkpie hats cracking jokes you didn't understand, jiving at the punch line. I thought I would buy a record for Aurora, something advanced, Dave Brubeck or Stan Getz playing in the cool style. It was not a style I understood but I knew it was the coming thing. I thought better of the idea when a gust of wind blew rain in my face. The time was just before noon. I entered Michigan Avenue from Randolph, the great expanse of Grant Park before me, the grass bare in patches, the trees stunted and lifeless. The park was empty of people, as if it were a quarantined zone. Rain collected in puddles; and under one of the trees I saw three men in raincoats and fedoras gesturing expansively, their heavy arms moving every which way. They all seemed to be talking at once. I thought I knew what it was about, thanks to a tip from Henry Laschbrook. A State Street merchant had the idea of appropriating four or five acres of Grant Park into a parking lot for the convenience of all Chicagoans as they went about their important business in the Loop, a parking lot of the finest asphalt and ringed by stately white oaks, the Illinois State Tree. Opposition could be expected. These three were discussing how to go about things with the least fuss, meaning the most privacy. Whom to talk to. Where to talk to them. What to say. And how much the conversation would cost.

The Art Institute, spacious and softly lit, quiet as a church, was a relief; but Aurora was not there. The instructor said she had missed class. Are you the newspaperman? I said I was and gave him my name. I called the apartment but there was no answer so I decided to spend an hour looking at pictures, an exhibition of canvases on loan from European museums along with those of the permanent collection. The rooms were not crowded at midday and I was able to stroll as if I were visiting my own private gallery. I was still bemused by my unwanted identity, and I saw soon enough that there were identities aplenty in the rooms of the Art Institute, ballet dancers, cancan dancers, farmers scything fields in Provence, a dark-eyed barmaid behind a forest of bottles, her thousand-yard stare as blank as a playing card laid face-down. I thought the room represented a civilization of its own, the barmaid next to a boulevardier in a top hat, boaters beside athletes, two old women struggling up a steep sidewalk in Montmartre, the angle of their heads suggesting an exchange of scandalous intimacies. They were in no hurry to complete their climb, and then I saw that it was not the angle of their heads that suggested scandal but their locked arms and the ample curves of their backsides. A sad-faced clown, a postman, and a group of friends on promenade completed the ensemble.

I sat on one of the low benches and watched the dark-eyed barmaid look through the clown without recognition, one more guest at the costume party. Then I discovered a canvas I had somehow missed, two drinkers side by side at a plain wooden table, a bottle and a guttering candle before them. Was it the middle of the afternoon? They had been at the table a while and would remain a while longer. The woman's hat was awry but her companion didn't notice. Noticing was not what he was good at just then, and I wondered if he had a father like mine and had heard the same lecture—drinking well and not showing it because that was how you gained respect in the world and women would be drawn to you, feeling at once safe and in danger—but had decided to ignore the advice. I imagined the time as 1914, the world lit off-color, the landscape so muted that the colors could not be identified precisely, gray-green, off-red, sand-yellow, yellow-white. I had the newspaper office in mind and regretted that Manet or Degas was not familiar with the métier, tobacco smoke in the air, phones ringing, the floor trembling when the presses began to turn, the reporter with his long fingers resting on the keys, the letters of the alphabet motionless as corpses on slabs until the reporter's fingers began their tango. From the look in the writer's eyes, an artist might suggest the life behind the métier and from the frayed shirt cuffs something else and from the shapeliness of his wrists something more still, and at once a world was illuminated. I thought of Degas at the cotton exchange in New Orleans, brokers in their best clothes standing at high-topped desks. These artists were interested in labor, the workaday life and the tools of the trade. The dancers, the barmaid, and the farmer were all working people, although the dancers seemed to enjoy it less than the others. The postman looked comfortable in his official hat. I looked at the faces and tried to find a newspaper reporter, but the only face that fit was the barmaid's. She had seen much of life and that included her own life, and what she had seen was not encouraging. I had noticed the thousand-yard stare on the faces of reporters trying to compose the first sentence of their "piece," the "lede" that would bring a look of sour satisfaction to Ozias Tilleman's face; and then the editor would correct a word and add a comma, brushstrokes from a master of the number one pencil.

Painters led adventurous lives, bohemian lives on grounds no less dangerous than a battlefield, and when it got dangerous enough you cut off your ear. There was no one around to tell you that you were the oldest god damned nineteen-year-old in Provence and that you didn't belong in the atelier. You could live outside the norm in Paris or Arles and if you were successful could live very well if not grandly, and whatever the market's opinion you would always have your work or a father to advance you money. If need be, you could work as a bartender by night and paint by day or the reverse, depending on your own temperament. I sat on the bench looking at the postman, thinking the life of an artist would be wonderful to have. Despite the ear business, van Gogh certainly led a serious and productive life, though turbulent, and well traveled—wasn't it van Gogh who had gone to Tahiti? I knew nothing about him except for the ear. The postman was drawn with affection and I imagined him delivering the morning mail, handwritten letters filled with encouragement from his dealer and various important patrons, and remaining for coffee prepared by Madame van Gogh. But of course they would not be married, only living together in bohemian fashion. I wondered if van Gogh's woman looked anything like Manet's barmaid, and if the artist's turmoil caused the thousand-yard stare. But she would not have a thousand-yard stare. She would be kindly, humorous, and sexy, on the plump side, excellent with the accounts. Surely it would be thrilling for any woman to live with an artist as great as Vincent van Gogh, knowing that it would only be a matter of time before he was recognized a genius, whereupon they could move to a larger house with a garden, and a servant to prepare the coffee when the postman rang. They would have a pied-à-terre in Paris. And when the conversation of the city closed in, interfering with the artist's work, they would return to Arles and the house with its garden, and the servant, and the studio with its masterpiece-in-progress on the easel. In such a felicitous environment, Vincent's work flourished and became more dangerous still, and he was as happy as he had ever been.

There were half a dozen women in the room now, moving from picture to picture in a group. One woman was talking and the others were listening to her as she explained the artist's technique and what he intended and where the portrait of the postman fit into his oeuvre and the principles of the Impressionist movement generally, though this artist was outside the norm. The women were taking notes as the guide talked, rapt at the explanation of nervous disorders, confinement, and the ear. This was news to me and not especially welcome; so much for the bourgeois milieu of Monsieur van Gogh's domestic arrangements. Rising from the bench to take a last look around, I imagined each canvas as a miniature civilization, living cities resting on dead ones, and somewhere in the brushstrokes were graveyards and sunshine as far as the eye could see. I was drawn to this Impressionist world, its appetite and sensuality, moments profoundly incomplete, beyond reach, filled with grief. The world was only now catching up to Vincent van Gogh.

I walked from one room to another and discovered *Nighthawks*, noticing after a moment that the diner had no exit. The patrons were trapped, the coffee growing cold. Soon they would run out of cigarettes and the money to pay for them. Morning would arrive and no one would notice and night would follow and still no one moved. The counterman looked suspiciously like Richard Nixon. Eisenhower owned the place and showed up each Friday to collect the week's receipts, counting the take down to the last penny, Nixon watching him and scowling. Each time Nixon demanded a raise but Ike refused. He said, Back off, Dick. Have patience. *Wait your turn.*

Edward Hopper's other canvases, with their wintry whites and blues, suited my own bleak mood. Lonely lighthouses, women staring at their shoes in a desolate hotel room, a man and a woman together in an austere parlor unable to explain themselves, a solitary house on a bluff high above the sea, and always the same wintry white even though the season was high summer. Hopper's people were grown-up people, though. If they had had a youth, it was nowhere evident. And Hopper was not interested in work as the French artists were. The men had the demeanor of salesmen and the women of counter girls but work was only incidental to their lives, a means of making ends meet. Hopper's people were drawn after hours or on weekends, a lonely afternoon or evening, one long motionless moment, time itself as pitiless as a jailer. A minute had the weight of an hour, and all the subject knew for certain was that night would soon fall, and its coming would bring no consolation. I moved slowly around the room trying to understand from the composition of the pictures what had brought these people to their hour of fathomless melancholy. Forces beyond their control of course, the barren landscape, the glare of the light, and the emptiness of the interior spaces. Edward Hopper drew from the middle distance, giving his figures anonymity. The faces were generic, forgettable faces in a milieu of irresolution. The clown, the barmaid, and the postman were specific, recognizable anywhere. Hopper's pictures asked for your sympathy even as they conceded the futility of sympathy, and so you pulled away, a trespasser.

Pardon me, do you have the time?

I looked at my watch and said, One o'clock, surprised that I had been in the gallery an hour. But there were no windows to the outside world, and time had slipped by. Chicago itself had vanished.

Thank you, the woman said, and smiled mischievously. She was one of the group of women who had been looking at van Gogh's postman. She said, That woman's waiting for a telephone call, wouldn't you say?

I don't see a phone, I said.

It's there, she said. It's outside the frame.

If the phone rings, she won't answer.

Why not?

She knows who it is.

And who is it? The woman was looking at me strangely, tapping her notebook into the palm of her hand.

Her husband, perhaps her father.

Or her son, the woman said with a smile.

Not her son, I said. Her son doesn't have anything she wants.

And what does she want?

She wants to feel better. She wants to feel like herself.

Oh, the woman said, that's harsh. She moved up close to the picture, pulling her eyeglasses to the end of her nose and tapping the notebook against her chin. She peered at the picture a long minute, tilting her head this way and that. Her friends were gathered at the other end of the room, looking at the nighthawks locked up in the diner. She said, I think she's waiting for a call from her husband. He'll call to apologize for working late. He wants to take her to dinner when he's finished. He'll name a restaurant, a favorite where he's already made a reservation, the table for two in the corner. She's had a premonition that he'd call and that's why she's waiting patiently by the telephone. See her smile?

That's not a smile, I said.

Well, what is it?

It's not a smile. She's given up.

She has not, the woman said. Definitely not. Why, she has her whole life in front of her. Her husband is working late, trying to get ahead for *them*. He's always been considerate. Don't you see?

The phone won't ring, I said.

You make too much of things, the woman said.

But she was the one who had conjured a happy couple out of

what seemed to me a kind of purgatory. She was staring again at the picture, as if there were an encouraging detail she had missed and could pass on to me as evidence, but apparently nothing presented itself because she pulled back and shook her head, annoyed. The silence lengthened and the woman said, I've seen you before.

I looked at her closely for the first time, her hair so straight it might have been ironed, her eyes magnified behind thick-lensed glasses, dimples in her cheeks. She was attractive, not much older than I was, a familiar face from one of the summer dances, one of the young wives whose life seemed so mysterious.

We met at the Oldfields', she said.

Yes, I said. I remember.

Marnie Russel, she said. I was eavesdropping when you had the argument with Paul Binning. You remember, the argument about the colored girl, the one who almost froze to death last winter. Paul didn't have much sympathy for her, but Paul doesn't have much sympathy for anyone. Pull up your socks, says Paul. He's quite crude, you know, especially when drinking. What do you suppose it was about that girl that frightened him so? He took her as a personal affront somehow. And then Louise said that newspapers were vulgar.

She meant subversive, I said.

Vulgar was the word she used. And she wouldn't allow yours into the house. What a riot.

She didn't want the maid to see it, I said.

The maid?

The maid might get ideas.

I didn't hear the bit about the maids.

Mrs. Paul Binning was concerned for them, I said.

What ideas would they get, do you suppose?

Search me, I said. Maybe that all people were not created equal.

Cle-*ver*, Marnie said brightly. Her friends were gathered in the doorway, ready to move on to Italy. They were waiting for her with a show of impatience, glancing at their wristwatches. The docent frowned in disapproval.

Marnie said, I must go.

Marnie, one of them said loudly.

I said, Goodbye, Marnie.

Your name? she said.

Wils, I said.

Maybe you were right, back there, about the woman in the painting. Maybe it wasn't a smile. She's waiting for something important, though. But—it probably isn't the telephone.

If there is a telephone, I said.

If there is a telephone, she repeated slowly, smiling sadly, and with a wave she was gone. They moved in a group to the quattrocento, the docent already talking about religious art and where it figured in the Italian scheme of things.

I hurried off, back to the reception hall to call Aurora. Her telephone was busy, and when I called a minute or two later was still busy, and five minutes after that was busy still. I stepped outside into the drizzle and lit a cigarette. The sky was leaden but off to the west I saw a break in the clouds. In an hour the streets would be washed with light, though not Edward Hopper's light. Chicago's light was earthly, as flat and dusty as the prairie. The drizzle ended and on the sidewalks people looked at the sky and folded their umbrellas. I stood and watched the traffic, moving smartly now. I watched a young woman alight from a cab and walk slowly up the long steps of the Art Institute, her eyes down. When she reached the stone lion she paused and leaned against the plinth. She clutched a man's wallet and was evidently at a loss because she began to sway as if she were about to lose her balance. I took a step toward her and she raised her eyes, her skin drawn tight across her cheeks and forehead, looking up now and attempting some semblance of a greeting. Until she spoke, I did not recognize her—her look, her walk, the way she carried herself, all of it utterly unfamiliar.

Oh, Wils, Aurora said. Jack's dead.

10

HAILED A CAB and we slipped into Michigan Avenue traffic, stalled now. The driver was unhappy because he wanted to travel west, home for lunch with his mother. She was ill. Lincoln Park was out of his way. He slapped the steering wheel, shaking his head and muttering. I observed all this from the corner of my eye because I had my arm around Aurora. She was incoherent, trying one thought after another but unable to complete a sentence. Her face was as drawn as the skin of a drum and when I took her hands I could feel the tremor. She slumped against me, her eyes brimming. The cab moved forward by inches, some tie-up at the Michigan Avenue Bridge. Jesus, the driver said, why does this always happen to me?

Tell me what happened, I said to Aurora, but she could only murmur fragments. Her father had died sometime in the early morning. Worse beyond imagining. Ghastly. He was so young, not yet fifty. She shuddered and fell silent and I saw the cab driver—his thinning hair was the color of straw and curled over his shirt collar, his eyes were washed-out blue, and the name on the license was Homer Wyse—glance spitefully into the rear-view mirror and slap the wheel again, apparently pleased that the young woman in his cab was in distress. I glared back and he averted his eyes and threw the car in gear, the traffic moving at last. Aurora was able to say that she had called her instructor at the Art Institute to apologize for missing class and how strange it was that the most inconsequential matters assumed an outsized importance when you were half out of your mind. The instructor had told her that I had come by. "Your newspaperman is in the building." So she took a cab and the next thing she knew she was walking up the steps of the Art Institute.

I had to get out of the apartment, she said. I couldn't stand it another minute. And thank God you were there because I couldn't've climbed another step. I hardly knew where I was.

We were over the bridge now and driving past the Wrigley Building and Tribune Tower, the Allerton in the distance, and the deep blue of the lake beyond that.

When I said I had spent an hour with the Impressionists and Edward Hopper, Aurora said that Hopper was apt. To get her mind off things, I made a little story of my morning. When I explained about Marnie Russel, Aurora closed her eyes; she had no interest in Marnie Russel, the docent, or the quattrocento.

God, Aurora. I'm so sorry.

What will I do now? she said.

What was that address again? the driver said.

I gave him the Lincoln Park number and the cross street.

Jesus, he said, and slapped the steering wheel.

I said, Shut up.

What did you say?

I said, Shut up now.

What's going on back there?

I said, None of your business. Just drive.

Aurora said, Wils, please.

Move it, I said, but the driver slowed to a crawl and we continued in that way until we arrived at the apartment building on Lincoln Park.

The apartment was crowded with friends and a few relatives. Aurora took me around for introductions, Mr. Uh, Aunt This, Aunt That, people smiling automatically and shaking hands, offering their names to me, murmuring a condolence to Aurora. So sorry, so sorry, we'll miss him so, embracing her, holding her gaze until turning away with weary smiles. The room was humid from the afternoon rain and fragrant from the flowers placed in vases here and there. We were in the dining room, the round table laden with a coffee urn and cups and plates of dainty sandwiches at one end and an ice bucket and glasses and bottles of whiskey and gin at the other. Most of the men were drinking whiskey, solemn in their dark business suits. They appeared to have come directly from their offices downtown or from the hospital; a number of them were doctors, colleagues of Jack Brule, gruff dark-eyed men who seemed tightly wound. Some of them spoke with foreign accents and wore suits of heavy worsted, cut in a boxy European style. One of the doctors offered another a cigarette with the comment that it was all right to smoke, Jack wasn't there to give them grief, though if you observed carefully you could find the aura of his disapproval. The doctors used coffee saucers for ashtrays and held their cigarettes ash-end up between thumb and forefinger. When we left them after the introductions, they resumed their conversation where they had left off, something about Dora and a case of hysteria and Fred making too much of Dora's dyspnea. Fred made too much of things generally because he was afraid to face the *truth*. Viennese inhibitions; and I understood then that they were talking about Freud.

The doctors Bloom, Aurora said. They're brothers.

They don't look like brothers, I said.

Nevertheless, Aurora said.

What's dyspnea? I asked.

Inability to breathe, Aurora said. I've got a case of it right now.

Let me get you something, I said.

Aurora shook her head.

Do you want to lie down?

No, she said sharply, and looked off down the corridor. Will you be all right here for a while? I have to talk to—

Of course, I said.

—some men from the city.

What can I do to help?

Stay here, she said.

I will, I promised.

Maybe you could watch the buffet. Make sure there's ice. You know where the liquor is. And if anyone wants anything, give it to them.

Don't worry, I said.

They'll go in a while, I don't know when.

I'll be here, I said. I think you ought to rest.

Stop telling me to rest, I don't need to rest. You don't know anything about it, Aurora said angrily, the same tone of voice she had used when she told me her father would never, ever do anything to hurt her. Then a hand appeared on her shoulder and we turned to see Charlie Smithers with a strikingly handsome young man, blue-eyed, golden-haired, tall, bronzed as a lifeguard. Charlie nodded at me and took Aurora's hand in both of his and murmured something, then moved to introduce the young man, his son, Albert. Albert smiled broadly, a smile that you might see in an advertisement for toothpaste. His smile seemed enormous, larger than life, and he held it until both Aurora and I looked away in embarrassment.

I prefer Al, he said. Al. Al Smithers. Remember that, please.

Of course, Aurora said.

We'll only be a minute, his father said. We just wanted to pay our respects. Such a terrible shock—

Let Wils get you something, Aurora said.

No, thank you, Charlie Smithers said. We must be on our way.

Do you have bourbon? Al said.

Yes, I said.

Find me a bourbon, then. No ice. No water. Al's smile had remained in place, as unnerving as if he had had a knife in his teeth. He looked directly at Aurora and said, I didn't like him, you know. I didn't like him one bit.

We'll be leaving now, Charlie said.

He was mean to me, Al said.

Goodbye, Aurora, Charlie said. God bless.

How was he mean to you? Aurora said dully.

He said things.

What things? Aurora asked.

That's for me to know and for you to find out, Al said.

This is not the time, I said coldly, but at a look from Aurora said nothing further.

I'm sorry, Aurora, Charlie said.

Thank you for coming, Aurora said softly.

We watched Charlie Smithers move off with his son, who seemed unaware of the surroundings. His gestures were mannered, as if he were onstage, his chin high and his smile frozen, waiting for the house lights to dim and the curtain to fall. Now they were at the door, Charlie suddenly looking very old and unsteady on his feet, though he had a firm grip on his son's arm. You shouldn't've said anything, Aurora muttered to me. You should have let him speak. I didn't mind. What do I care what he says? Poor Charlie. Then she gathered herself and walked slowly down the corridor to her father's study, closing the door behind her.

I was at sea, a room full of unfamiliar faces, Aurora in shock. I wanted to help her but I seemed unable to find the right words, beginning in the cab at the Art Institute. She was inconsolable, and I was helpless. So I emptied the coffee saucers and fetched more ice and generally made myself useful, mixing drinks for those who wanted one, passing the sandwiches. The company became more animated, clustering around the drinks end of the round table. Many of them were discussing Jack Brule, how long they had known him, his skill as a psychiatrist, his reserve, his love for his daughter. Others were replaying everyday events in their own lives, the second grandchild, *Aïda* at the Lyric, the long summer, the Labor Day weekend, the Red Scare and the awful Rosenberg business—and in the middle of everything, the Korean War at an end at last thanks to Ike, at least he was good for something. The deceased was also present in conversations tête-à-tête on the perimeter, the conversations conducted in confidential tones, ceasing when anyone drew too close. The women looked stricken, and I was surprised that so many were drinking cocktails, the glasses held in both hands, the hands gloved. When they talked, they talked in hushed whispers. Twice I heard Consuela's name mentioned but when I looked for her in the room, she was not to be found. The noise level rose a pitch when a thick-bodied younger man entered, walking with a seaman's rolling gait. It was Marlon

Brando, instantly recognized but not otherwise noticed. On such an occasion anyone was entitled to anonymity. The great actor had the wary look of a wrestler circling the ring but was taken in hand at once by the doctors Bloom, who shook hands with him in turn and ambled off toward the window. When one of them indicated the bar, Brando shook his head, and when he turned his heavy eyes to the corridor and asked the obvious question—Where's Aurora?—the doctors began to speak in quick bursts, finishing one another's sentences, Brando turning from one to the other like a spectator at a tennis match. Finally, he asked another question and both doctors were silent, evidently searching for the correct answer, and when it came the actor shook his head and slumped as if he had been struck physically, everyone watching but making a show of not watching, and so the noise level rose to a higher pitch.

A few guests left and others arrived. I rummaged in the kitchen for more flower vases and another bottle of scotch. Now there were thirty-odd people in the room and this surprised me because I did not think of Jack Brule as a man who had a wide circle of friends. Of course some of them would be patients, and still others medical colleagues. I noticed there were more women than men, and some of the women were weeping openly, trying and failing to maintain a brave face. The conversations around me seemed ever more bizarre—

Two overweight older men, both wearing white short-sleeved shirts with a forest of pens in the breast pockets, were arguing about tattoos and which regimes required them and which did not, but when I approached with a cheese board, the men turned their backs and began to speak in German. When I went away they continued in German, their voices rising. One word was repeated and I tried to remember it so I could look it up later. Their abrupt manner discouraged familiarity and the others in the room did not join the argument.

I moved off, worried about Aurora, wondering what had become of her. I was in a room full of strangers. Near the window, the doctors Bloom were talking and Marlon Brando was listening, nodding fractionally, his heavy-lidded eyes unreadable, straying now and then to the door, the way out.

Then Aunt That was at my elbow, smiling encouragement.

I said, What are they talking about? The German men.

The war, she said.

It was something about tattoos, I said.

They're always arguing, those two. Friends of Jack's. Jack knew all kinds. Have you met Mr. Brando?

No, I said.

A good friend of Jack's, she said.

I started to say that I had seen a picture of him in Aurora's bedroom, but caught myself. I said, Aurora told me.

It's nice of him to come. I heard he was in town, something to do with one of his films.

Yes, I said. How did they all—hear about this?

My sister Emily, she said. She thought it would be better if we were not alone. I suppose she called Mr. Brando, or one of the Blooms did. I've never been introduced to him but with a face like that, in the films, you feel that you know him. You know him but he doesn't know you. It's strange, don't you think?

I muttered something noncommittal. I did not think I knew Marlon Brando. I knew Zapata and Stanley Kowalski but I didn't know him any more than he knew me.

The Blooms are taking care of him, she said. I don't need to interfere.

Do you think you can make me a drink, Wils? Scotch, soda, lots of ice?

I made Aunt That the drink and she said she was happy to meet me at last, her brother had spoken warmly of me. He said you were a good-looking boy. Considerate. That was the word he used. He was happy that Aurora had a beau. She's had others but Jack never liked them. Drugstore cowboys and pseudo-intellectuals, he said. Either too old or too young, too rich or too poor, or too full of themselves. Jack was protective of Aurora, and why not?

I liked him, I said. We only met one time.

Only once?

He was—fierce.

Jackie? *Fierce?* Oh no, he was gentle as a lamb. He was never fierce.

He was fierce when he talked about the war.

You talked to him about that? He rarely mentioned the war, the war was verboten, ancient history. Jack always said it was a mistake to live in the past. I believe the war was too painful for him. Jack was sickly as a child. You should have seen him when he came back, all skin and bones, a fright.

I think he was at Bataan, I said.

It was somewhere in the Pacific, she said.

The march, I said.

I don't know what it was. Jackie was never a great talker. Not a great talker at all. He kept things to himself. She sipped her drink thoughtfully, hesitating, and then she said, You'll have to take care of Aurora now.

I will, I said.

It'll be worse for her tomorrow and the day after.

I know, I said.

It's a terrible thing, she said, just hideous for her. I worry about how she'll get on after this, who will look after her, where she will go. She certainly cannot stay here, with all the memories of her father, and Consuela. Aurora and Consuela do not always see eye to eye, and now . . . She turned her head when she heard the ring of the telephone, but it stopped almost at once; someone had picked up. Jack was not good with women, she continued.

She said this in a bitter whisper, peering at me as if she were sharing her darkest secret.

Aurora knew it, too, she said. Consuela is so—spectacular. No one knows who she is or where she comes from. Jack met her at some concert, and before you could say Jiminy Cricket she'd moved in. She was not a good influence on poor Jack, as events have shown. Her voice trailed away as she angrily dabbed at her eyes with a balled-up piece of tissue.

I'm sorry we had to meet under these circumstances, she went on.

I am, too, I said.

I have a boy about your age, Oliver. He's at Princeton. Jack's school. You'll meet him at the funeral if he gets back in time. Aunt That paused to nod at someone across the room. She said, His father died when Oliver was very young. Jack was a kind of surrogate father until he went away to the Pacific. I married again, a rat. Welch was his name and never in this world was a name a better fit. A wartime romance, except romance would be the wrong word in this instance. Oliver never liked him, told me he was a four-flusher. One day Welch walked out the front door and never came back, good riddance . . .

Aunt That went on about second husband Welch but I didn't listen carefully. Bright shafts of light fell through the dining room window, touching the edge of the round table, and when I looked at my watch I saw that it was almost five o'clock. The room was very warm but, preserving the formality of the occasion, none of the men had removed their jackets except for the Germans, now talking in whispers. Conversation was low-key now, with a tangible sense of unease. This was Jack Brule's room, the chair where he sat, the table where he ate his breakfast. But he was not present. At a certain moment, the company felt they were intruders, invited but not necessarily welcome. The pictures on the wall, the china, the ice bucket, the coffee urn, the bottle of Gordon's—all Jack's, except they were now orphaned objects. The dead man's disapproving spirit was all too present, an unnerving feeling for those who had come out of sympathy. Where was Aurora anyhow? The dead man's sisters were the only family in the room. Emily remained at the door, greeting new arrivals.

. . . and I don't know if he's alive, or what.

I said, Is Consuela here?

I believe she is in the apartment somewhere, Aunt That said brusquely. How long she'll stay is something else again.

And Aurora?

She's with Consuela and the gentlemen from the city. I expect they'll be a while longer. But there's nothing to be done about it.

I nodded as if I understood.

What you must understand is that it would be impossible for Aurora to live here alone, quite apart from her memory of what happened here this morning. This apartment is not suitable. It's too large and expensive to maintain. It should be sold, that's obvious. I want Aurora to come live with me, I have a comfortable place in Hyde Park, plenty of room. It's near the university, where you'll be, so it's convenient. But I don't think she will. And I can't force her to. I don't know what will happen to her now. And I do think it would be good if you would speak to her.

I can't tell Aurora what to do, I said.

Nevertheless, she said.

But I will look after her.

Aunt That looked at me with a whisper of a smile and nodded doubtfully.

She said, Jackie and I were not as close as we should have been. We were very close when we were growing up and then our parents died and we grew apart. He is closer now to my sister Emily. It was awful when our parents died but Jack kept us together as a family until he went away to war. He didn't have to go. He volunteered. Can you believe it? I did not approve. He had a young daughter and other responsibilities. But Jack always made up his own mind about things, no matter what anyone else said. He did not like to listen to people. I am bound to say that as a boy, Jack did not play well with others. And when he grew up, he no longer tried. Still, he was an attentive father to Aurora, and Aurora was not an easy child, her mother's bad influence. Olivia was an impetuous woman, an egoist and a materialist. I never liked her because she talked behind my back and turned Jack against me. Poor Jack, she led him a merry chase, and finally he kicked her out. For some reason, Olivia and my sister Emily got on. Emily made excuses for her, so they were simpatico, cheaters together. Jack's strategy with Aurora was simple: he let her do whatever she wanted, no restrictions at all on her behavior and very little guidance, though he insisted on knowing where she was at all times. He has been very lucky with Aurora so far. We were a wonderful family, Wils. But we are no longer the family we had been and I don't know how that happened, and now this.

I was having trouble keeping track of the betrayals but I nodded thoughtfully each time I heard a new one. I glanced over at the window, where the doctors Bloom were arguing energetically with each other. Brando had vanished. The noise level had dropped and the animation with it, air from a balloon; people were at a loss, remembering their grief, oppressed by the atmosphere of the dead man's room. I felt myself a trespasser once again, and Aurora still out of sight in the consulting room with the gentlemen from the city. I wondered if the actor was with her, giving what comfort he could. Zapata and Stanley Kowalski were both sympathetic characters and probably he was also, speaking to Aurora in that damaged mumble, the voice of a wounded animal. Marlon Brando would be just the thing for her, an experienced older man, and if his performances were any guide, no stranger to grief himself. He would know what to say and how to say it, and I could imagine her drum face softening and becoming beautiful again as she listened to him speak of grief. An actor would have an instinct for grief, how it was felt and how it was expressed, its appalling vacancy and privacy. You wanted to let go of it and hold on to it at the same time, words bringing a measure of consolation. But that actor's instinct would come from surrendering a certain essence of yourself. You would need the courage to ignore your own personality, having confidence that something more worthwhile— really, more sincere—would come with the surrender, finding your way into another soul, even if it was only a soul on paper or on the screen or stage. I knew I could never do it. I feared disintegration. Even now I could not feel grief at Jack Brule's death. Pity for Aurora, yes, and tenderness toward her. But I had no understanding of grief because I had never felt it in my heart.

I remembered Edward Hopper's lonely woman, trying to feel better and failing; all she had was her empty room and the knowledge that night would soon fall. The telephone would not ring. No one would knock on her door. I felt myself in a bewildering netherworld, neither here nor there. Too many names and family stories had come at me too quickly. I felt short of breath and wondered if I was having an attack of Dora's dyspnea, the room so warm and airless, the atmosphere as heavy as an anvil. Aunt That and I stood uncomfortably in a closed zone of silence. There seemed nothing more to be said.

Then, quite suddenly, the apartment began to empty. The doctors Bloom were the first to go, followed by the women who had come alone, the ones who had been so distraught. Emily stood at the door thanking everyone for coming and receiving a murmur of condolence in reply. Behind me, two older men took a last sip of their drinks, put the glasses down, and shuffled from the room. They were the two who had been talking about Auschwitz and Ravensbrück and I wondered if they had settled their argument concerning tattoos. They seemed friendly with each other, so I supposed that they had. I had the German names in my mind so that I could look them up later and understand about the tattoos. Alone now in the dining room, I listened to the goodbye sounds at the door. I poured a scotch, my first of the afternoon, and stood sipping it, looking at the table with its remains, half-eaten sandwiches, crumpled napkins, dirty glasses, and stale cigarette smoke in the air. I stepped into the corridor and took a few steps down it. When I heard voices in Jack Brule's study, I ducked into the consulting room and closed the door. I could not avoid looking into the glassed-in bookcase and was surprised to see the skull on the top shelf. The bullet hole was conspicuous along with the gold-filled molar, and I wondered if the doctor had felt a premonition and had taken the skull out for a last look. Sudden noises in the corridor made me hold my breath; and then the voices receded and I relaxed and resumed my speculation about the origin of the skull. But it had yielded all it was going to yield. I sat on the edge of the couch and sipped my drink, thinking that a room like this one would encourage fantasy, the dark curtains and patterned carpet, the small window that admitted so little light, and Jack Brule silent in the ladder-back chair out of the patient's sight. I stood and stretched, glancing again at the skull in the bookcase, and exited into the corridor. The study door was open, the room empty.

Everyone seemed to have departed. I took my drink to the dining room window and looked out. The world was returning to normal, rush hour in Chicago, people moving across the street in the afternoon sunlight, everyone in a hurry as if they had urgent errands that needed attending to without delay. I stood at the window a few moments longer, watching the people in the park and thinking that I should call my parents and tell them what had happened. They had not met Aurora but that didn't mean they shouldn't know her father had died. I knew my father would have good advice; and my mother would know what to do. Below in the street, two gray-haired men stood talking, their heads close together. When the taller of the two turned to look up, I was startled to see Henry Laschbrook, Ed Hoskins at his elbow. Henry scribbled a note on the pad in his hand, and they both hurried away up the street, waving their arms for a taxi.

At a rustle behind me, I turned from the window.

Consuela said, Hello, Wils, in a voice so small it was almost a whisper.

11

WHEN I TOLD HER how sorry I was, Consuela gave a helpless shrug of her shoulders. She fell into the nearest chair and closed her eyes, her hands on her knees. She looked years older, her face swollen, her skin slack and without vitality. Consuela wore no makeup or jewelry and her black dress looked slept in. I wondered where she had been all this time.

I said, Can I make you something?

She said, Is there any Cinzano?

I said, They've cleaned us out. Except for scotch.

Scotch, then. I'll be in the living room.

I made the drink and followed her into the living room. Of course the Cinzano was on the drinks tray but when I moved to prepare her what she wanted, Consuela waved her hand. Never mind, she said. I don't care what I drink.

She lay back on the sofa, holding the drink with both hands on her stomach, staring into the middle distance, her lips moving soundlessly. It seemed to me then that Jack Brule's ghost was in the room with us. When I saw a drink untouched on the cocktail table I was certain of it. The apartment was silent and I wondered where the aunts had gone.

I said, Is Aurora all right?

Yes, she said. Aurora's fine. She'll be here shortly.

I've been worried—

She's dressing, Consuela said.

What a terrible shock, I said.

Yes, she said. Yes, it was. Consuela took a small sip from her drink and closed her eyes, grimacing as if the act of swallowing were painful.

I said, You were a long time with the men from the city.

Who? she said. Oh, them. Yes, they stayed quite a while.

Connie, I said. Can you tell me what happened?

She moved her head from side to side, her eyes still closed. She said, What did Aurora tell you?

Nothing, I said. I described the cab ride from the Art Institute, when she had been in shock, unable to say anything beyond the fact that her father was dead.

Jack shot himself, Consuela said. This morning. Two-twenty A.M., to be precise, in our bathroom.

I could not believe what I had heard. I turned away from her voice.

The noise, she said. The noise was terrible. I thought someone had thrown a bomb, yet I knew at once that it wasn't a bomb, that it was Jack and that he had shot himself not ten feet from our bed, the door closed, the tap water running. I knew all this because I was wide awake.

She took a long swallow of her drink, her eyes still closed.

The police came. They stayed for hours, it seemed to me. When they went away, they took Jack with them in an ambulance. There were three police cars and the ambulance, lights in the street. They were kind but they had questions and we had to answer the questions, about the ownership of the gun and the circumstances. The night's circumstances and Jack's state of mind. Who I was and what I was doing in the house. I had to give them my passport.

She took another swallow of her drink.

God, I loved him. We have been together more than one year.

She began to cry, choking, a kind of wail. I sat beside her on the couch and took her hand, stiff and cold as ice. Her fingers were curved like talons. She remained like that a moment, her face damp, her hands frigid. Then she leaned back with a long sigh.

Stay quiet, I said. You don't have to say anything more.

We had quarreled, she said. Gone to the theater and then to dinner, and at dinner we quarreled, something we did not do often but when we did, we kept at it until one of us declared victory and the other defeat. We quarreled in the cab home and quarreled when we got home and kept quarreling in the bedroom, and when we were exhausted the matter still wasn't settled. We didn't want to settle it. We wanted a quarrel that we could look back on later and remember as the worst quarrel we had ever had, a quarrel for the ages, neither of us giving one inch.

A quarrel of principle, she said.

Aurora heard us. Aurora liked it when we quarreled—

Connie, I said.

—and so I am certain she heard every word.

Fix me another drink, Wils. A big one.

I took her glass and refilled it from the bottle on the sideboard.

Thank you, Wils.

Connie? Would you like to rest awhile?

That's what she liked doing, listening at keyholes. Listening to her father and me quarrel, make love, make dinner, read aloud to each other—we did that, you know, in the evenings. So we had an audience. I think Jack knew it, too, knew Aurora was there and didn't care. Life in all its complexity overheard by a child with a vivid imagination. Consuela paused then, her eyes refocusing. She said, That which is overheard is never understood completely. She tapped a simple rhythm on the edge of her glass with her crimson fingernail. Around us the house was silent, and if I had not known better I would have said it was empty altogether except for us two in the living room.

But this quarrel was different, Consuela said. Jack was different. I suppose you'd say that we hit every note on the scale.

It was private, Wils. Private between Jack and me.

At one point, I think it was in the cab though it might have been later, Jack said I was not a suitable woman. He didn't like my manners, the way I talked, my character. He said I was Balkanized and he hated me for it. "A Balkanized personality" was the phrase he used. But he didn't mean it. I'm sure he didn't, it wasn't like him. I had said the same things to him, not in this quarrel but in another quarrel, and we agreed to forget it. I apologized right away and wrote him a note later. I was so ashamed. But he never apologized. So it's still there between us and it will always be between us, something unresolved.

You don't think he meant it, do you? One of those terrible statements that come out in the heat of a quarrel that's the truth. Straight from the heart.

Of course not, I said.

I don't either.

He wasn't himself, I'm sure.

No, she said.

People say things, I said.

Yes, they do.

Say whatever comes into their heads—

I wonder how often they say things and then shoot themselves.

Connie, I said.

Not often, I'll bet.

Somewhere in the apartment I heard a telephone, one ring and another, but whoever it was rang off after nine rings. I remembered the interminable sound of the telephone that night at dinner with my parents, the signal for the brick through the window. I stared at my drink and tried not to think of the nature of the quarrel and Jack Brule later in the bathroom.

And Aurora heard all of it, every word, Consuela said. I'm sure she enjoyed it. Otherwise, why listen? Why make the effort? So there were actually three of us in the quarrel, Jack, me, and Aurora, though only Jack and I had speaking parts. Aurora was the walk-on in the corner. We'd quarreled before, as I told you. But this was different. Jack was different, playing for keeps in a way he never had before. And he made no effort to apologize. Consuela looked at me, her eyes pleading, her hands beginning to tremble.

Why did he do it? she asked.

Not because of a quarrel, I said.

I want to believe that, she said.

Believe it, I said.

But I can't, quite, she said, her voice breaking. I want to but I can't.

You must not—

Blame myself? No, I won't blame myself. And I won't blame Jack, either. I'll pretend we're both blameless. Isn't that the best way? she said in a tone of voice that discouraged any answer from me.

I knew nothing of suicide, except that no family wanted to admit to one. I could not imagine the despair that would cause someone to take his own life, even a terrible illness or a prisoner under torture; and then I thought probably that was what it was with any suicide, a way to stop the torture. So you hanged yourself in your cell or swallowed the bottle of pills or put a gun to your head, knowing that each day would be worse than the last and the only release would be death. I supposed that once you were tortured you stayed tortured. There was no end to the memory of it. Yet it was hard for me to understand how a memory could stay fresh year after year; surely it would fade and the wind become wolves and the wolves become wind and in time the event would become an illusion, a kind of fable. Surely a simple quarrel would not be enough for a man to end his life. I leaned close to Consuela and told her my guess about Jack Brule at Bataan but she did not respond. I don't know if she was listening or, if she was listening, she understood. She seemed to diminish as I looked at her, sinking into the cushions of the sofa, her drink cold in her hands.

She said, Thank you, Wils.

Do you want to tell me about the quarrel?

No, I don't. You can ask Aurora. Aurora can give you chapter and verse. No doubt she will anyway.

I won't ask Aurora, I said.

She'll tell you, Consuela said.

I'll close my ears, I said.

No, you won't. No one ever does.

The afternoon light was beginning to fail. Far away on the Outer Drive I heard the rush-hour traffic, all those cars bound for the North Shore and the last weekend in August. I remembered that there was a dance tonight, an end-of-summer black-tie affair at one of the Lake Forest country clubs. Aurora and I had declined, planning instead—and now I couldn't remember what it was we had planned. My scheme to spend a night together in Quarterday had fallen apart. The ten days flew by and my parents were suddenly home from Havana. I had hardly seen them since their return, though I had noticed an unusual cigarette box in the den. I took that as a sign that things had returned to normal. I looked at my watch. Six o'clock.

There'll be an inquest, Consuela said from the couch. That's what the people from the city were here about. The coroner's office.

The coroner's office? I heard myself say.

I wonder if you would mind going with me, Consuela said. With Aurora and me, to the coroner's office. I'd rather not go alone. Would you mind awfully?

Of course not, I said. Tell me about the men from the coroner's office.

They were agreeable men, she said. Their questions were upsetting but they had to ask them. They apologized for asking but they had their instructions, the law was clear, given the circumstances. Jack's death was "wrongful," they said. It was only a formality anyway.

I know some of the people at the coroner's office, I said, trying to keep my voice under control. Was one of them a little taller than I am, gray hat, wing-tipped shoes?

Why, yes, she said.

Was his name Laschbrook?

I didn't get their names, she said. Is something wrong?

I don't know, I said. Let me make a call.

I stepped into the corridor, located the phone, and dialed the newspaper. When Henry Laschbrook came on the line I asked him what he was doing at Dr. Jason Brule's apartment, and when he replied curtly, My job, I said I was a friend of the family and would do everything in my power to see that he was fired. I knew the publisher. I would talk to Ozias Tilleman. I said the coroner's office would hear about his impersonation, a violation of the law. He would be prosecuted. Blacklisted from the newspaper business. I talked at him for five minutes, growing angrier by the minute and knowing at the same time that nothing whatever would happen to Henry. That was not the way Chicago worked. Lapse of judgment would be the explanation, competitive pressures leading to unseemly zeal and, by the way, were there inaccuracies in the reporting? When I finished, he said, Sorry, boyo, the piece is in the early edition of the newspaper. You'll find it on the newsstand. So fuck off.

I hung up the phone but I did not move. Aurora and Consuela were about to become news, their pictures and a picture of Jack Brule, "prominent society psychiatrist," a description of the apartment and of the death, the caliber of the handgun, the nature of the wound, who found the body and the probable cause, inevitably "despondency" following an argument with— "his mistress"? "a female friend"? I hoped to God the headline did not read LOVE NEST SUICIDE, but I knew as I mouthed the words that that was exactly how it would read. For the late edition they would have the doctor's war record and comments from his professional colleagues, if they could get the doctors to speak for the record. The story would run for two, perhaps three days, starting on page one and progressively receding inside the paper; and then it would disappear, leaving only the echoes that would follow Consuela and Aurora whenever they made news, including their own obituaries. I wondered how much Aurora and Consuela had told them, and how vivid they had been. Henry Laschbrook would have played them beautifully, radiating compassion, wanting only to understand the circumstances, inquiring only because the law obliged him to do so, in order that his report be as complete and factual as possible. All of it in confidence, of course.

I returned to the living room, now in near darkness. I switched on the lamps and turned to face Consuela.

I said, They weren't from the coroner's office. They were newspapermen.

Consuela stirred, her eyelids fluttering. She looked at her fingernails and said, I don't understand.

They were newspaper reporters, not from the coroner's office. That was a lie. They lied to you.

They lied?

Yes, for their story. It's one of the tricks they have. Usually they lie over the telephone but this time they decided it was better face to face. That way, they could describe the apartment. The bedroom. Where Jack died.

They asked to see the bedroom and I showed it to them.

It's not your fault, Connie. You couldn't have known.

Will they print what we told them?

Yes, they will.

Can you fix it?

No, I can't.

I thought anything could be fixed in Chicago. What do they call it? Pulling a string. When you pulled a string, things could be made to go away.

Most anything, I said. But not this. It's already in the paper.

In the paper? They seemed so nice.

Yes, I said. They have a way about them.

Consuela took a sip of her drink, made a face, and put it down. She said, I don't want to think about it. I have so much to think about and I don't want to think about this.

It's only a newspaper, I said hopefully.

Jack hated them, she said. Buzzards, he called them. Scavengers.

I feel awful about it, I said.

I had no idea, she said. They sounded so—official.

I'm going to blow the whistle on Laschbrook, I said. Speak to his boss, get him fired if I can . . . I imagined the conversation with Ozias Tilleman, a short walk down a dead-end street.

Consuela offered a thin smile, and for a moment a hint of her old asperity returned. What good will that do now, Wils?

Just then we heard a commotion at the door, the aunts evidently saying goodbye in whispers. Aurora said something I could not hear and then the door closed and in a moment she was standing in the doorway, dressed, like Consuela, in a black shift, choker pearls at her throat. Unlike Consuela, she looked lovely, her hair damp at the edges, freshly washed and combed. She stood indecisively in the doorway, steadying herself with one hand, her eyes focused on the untouched cocktail glass on the table near the window. I rose slowly and went to her, holding her face in my hands, believing that we were over the worst of it.

Get out, she said.

I took a startled step backward but saw at once that she was not talking to me but to Consuela, who seemed to withdraw further into the cushions of the couch.

Get out now, she said.

Consuela moved her head languidly back and forth, neither yes nor no but an involuntary movement that signaled deep fatigue.

I want you out of my house, Aurora said.

Consuela did not look up or give any sign of having heard. She might have been alone in the room. She looked to be way inside herself, not existing in the present moment but somewhere in the distant past. Aurora's voice was ugly, a timbre I had never heard. She advanced from the doorway and now stood over Consuela, her fists clenched at her sides. Aurora was breathing deeply, looming over Consuela like a prizefighter at a knockdown.

Take your things and get out, Aurora said.

Darling, I said. Wait a minute.

She said, Stay out of this.

I won't, I said.

You don't know what it's about, so stay out of it.

My heart was with Consuela, defenseless against Aurora's fury. She still had not spoken, having retreated somewhere into her memory, perhaps the moment she had seen Jack Brule disappear into the bathroom, the door slammed shut; and a minute later heard the shot that sounded to her like an explosion and in the appalling silence saying, Jack? in a voice not her own, waiting for the reply she knew would not come. How long did she wait before opening the door, or did they open it together, she and Aurora? Aurora was correct, I did not know what it was about, though obviously the mysterious argument figured in it somewhere. But this was the struggle of the strong against the weak, Aurora speaking with the remorseless clamor of the schoolyard bully. Consuela looked to me defeated, unwilling to defend herself or even to speak. Now Aurora was tugging at Consuela's hand as one would with a stubborn drunk.

I said, Stop it, Aurora.

She said, Help me get her out of here.

I said, We're all upset.

Are you going to help me or stand there?

Leave the poor woman alone.

Then you get out, too, Aurora said.

Don't do this, I said.

Whose side are you on, Wils? My side or her side? Look at her. She's disgusting.

Consuela had sagged back into the cushions. She still had not spoken and I could not swear she even knew where she was. But her abject manner inspired pity in me, and I thought that whatever she had said in the argument with Aurora's father—or he to her—she did not deserve this treatment. She did not deserve to be called disgusting. Aurora was so young, there was something indecent in her belligerence and contempt. Brutalizing Consuela would not bring Jack Brule back to life. And so I stepped between them, pinning Aurora's wrists to her sides and moving her away from the couch as I spoke softly in a low, reasonable voice, saying that we had to look to the future. We had to think about tomorrow and the day after. We had to decide about the funeral, where it would be and who would speak, the minister, the pallbearers, the music. I was remembering Squire's service in Connecticut, my mother and grandmother carefully reviewing the details. I said there were people to be notified and I would do that if she gave me the names and telephone numbers. I thought that by enumerating the mundane details we could allay grief, if only for an hour. We had to be practical. We had to stick together—and before I knew it, the word "teamwork" had tumbled out and I heard my father's voice merged with my own: no one ever won a strike. But Aurora was not listening. She had gone rigid, glaring over my shoulder at Consuela, who had curled up on the sofa, her eyes closed, her face slack. The glass of scotch had fallen from her hand, leaving a sloppy wet spot on her black dress. Aurora pushed against me but I held fast.

Let me go, she said.

Not yet, I said. Listen to me.

You are not on my side.

Of course I am, I said.

Then why are you on her side? What does she mean to you?

I'm not on anybody's side, I said.

I knew it. You're like the rest of them, Aurora said, beginning to struggle again.

At that moment I saw myself as a referee, the one who steps in to stop the bar fight in the name of good order. I suppose I saw myself as acting in behalf of Jack Brule, a decent respect for the memory of the dead man, loved by both women. I was appalled by Aurora's bullying and discouraged by Consuela's passivity, yet at the same time I knew there was something between them that I would never fathom, a kind of complicit rivalry. They each loved Jack Brule in a way the other could not. They each owned a piece of him but the pieces overlapped, and to claim one was to claim part of the other. The dead man had no say in the matter. I had never heard one woman speak to another as Aurora had spoken to Consuela. Of course I had heard the usual snide remarks made by one woman against another, and from them I had deduced that female friendships were complicated affairs, with much hidden from view; and now it seemed that I was like the rest of them, meaning men. I knew that at some fundamental level I was being disloyal to Aurora, my girl, the one I had promised to look after. But I thought her attack on Consuela was unworthy of her, malevolent almost, and it was my duty to put a stop to it. I had always believed that loyalty was the greatest of virtues and betrayal a vice, but it could not be as simple as that because justice was present somewhere; and just then I realized that I could not help Aurora. She had drawn a line I could not cross.

Go away, Aurora said wearily. You don't belong here.

I belong to you, I said. We belong to each other.

Not now, she said.

Yes, now, I insisted.

Then get her out of here, Aurora said.

What was the argument about? Why are you behaving this way?

Aurora frowned, then made a curt dismissive gesture with

her hands. I did not know what the gesture meant, and I wondered if she did. It was not natural to her. It seemed the sullen motion of an older woman, a woman of the world who had heard every quarrel under God's sun and was exhausted by them, fruitless, enervating quarrels in which there were no winners or losers, only frustrated combatants. Her hands fluttered, then came to rest, a gesture at once eloquent and enigmatic. I had an idea the flutter was involuntary, a family tic, handed down like blue eyes or a dimple. Like an ideogram, the stroke began as one thing and ended as another—from defiance to resignation in a fraction of a second; and still her expression did not change. I saw one of her Dutch ancestors look up from her dressing table at something her oafish husband had said, frown, and flutter her hands—and the husband was as nonplused as I was, staring dumbly at this pantomime. I plunged on with a sudden understanding that I no longer knew the girl I called Aurora.

I said, Isn't that what's behind this?

Go back to Quarterday, she said.

I'm trying to help—

This was all a mistake.

No, I said.

Then *help*, she said. Stop talking and help.

Tell me about the quarrel.

It's none of his business, Consuela said from the couch. We both turned to her, startled, as if a corpse had spoken. She uncoiled her legs and sat upright, staring hard at Aurora. Consuela's face was set, gaining strength as we watched her. She removed the empty glass from her lap and put it on the table with a smart click. The silence gathered, lengthening until it filled the room, muffling even the tick of the clock in the bookcase.

She's right, Aurora said finally.

Aurora doesn't know what it was about, Consuela said.

Aurora nodded slowly, still glaring at Consuela. I didn't hear it all, she said. The time was so late, after midnight. I was in bed. I had been reading and fell asleep over my book. I only heard voices. And then, much later, I heard the explosion. I don't remember the other things.

It was not an ordinary quarrel, Consuela conceded. One thing led to another. I would call it a soul quarrel. It was unfinished. But it was the sort of quarrel that people who love each other have. You cannot have a soul quarrel with someone you do not love deeply.

Aurora did not reply to that.

In any case, the quarrel would not translate, Consuela said. To repeat only the words would not be accurate because the words had specific private meanings. People who love each other have their own language, that's well known. The language is for them alone, not meant to be shared. At a sudden movement from Aurora, she added, Much as you would like to share it.

Not always, Aurora said dully.

Rarely, Consuela agreed. The quarrels are always about the same thing anyhow. The words change, the subject remains the same.

Do you want to say what the subject is? I said, and waited for Consuela's answer, certain that it would come in euphemism. The quarrel surely was about sex or money, perhaps some unfathomable combination of the two, a quarrel that would go to the deep structure of both subjects. Pride would be there somewhere, too, the organizing principle. And the quarrel would be savage, nothing withheld or glossed over, tigers' claws straining for the vulnerable point—

Consuela said, Virtue.

I did not know what to say to that.

We had different definitions of virtue, Consuela added.

How a life is lived, I said.

On what basis, she said.

Loyalties, for example, I said.

Loyalty comes into it.

And betrayal, I went on.

That also, Consuela said.

And you and Jack disagreed—

That night we did. It was only last night, wasn't it?

Yes, I said.

Well, that was what our argument was about. We could not

agree. The quarrel was bitter and got worse. But that was only because we could not find the words. I'm sure we agreed in our hearts. But our hearts could not speak. And Jack shot himself.

Aurora uttered a little broken cry, moving away from me and pouring a glass of water from the carafe on the table, spilling a little. She stood with her back to Consuela and me and I knew without being told that my presence was no longer welcome. Aurora and I had gone from lovers to enemies to strangers in minutes. We no longer knew each other. We had gotten crosswise to each other, and I am bound to say that this involved her pride and my ignorance. I was the mariner who knew the surface of the sea but had no understanding of the life beneath it. She was hurt greviously in a place I could not reach. Her father had turned his hand against her; and so her world was suddenly upside down. Her intuition was no good to her now, and neither was mine. There we were. I put my hands on Aurora's shoulders, feeling her tremble. She seemed unaware that I was touching her. I said that I would leave now, that if there was anything she wanted or needed, anything at all, she had only to call. I would be at home, Quarterday. I kissed her but her lips were stiff as cardboard. I said goodbye to Consuela and hurriedly left the apartment in Lincoln Park, as crowded now as when I had entered it. It did seem to me that ghosts were present, and that ghosts were life's defining characteristic.

12

I TOOK A CAB back to the Loop to fetch my car from the
parking lot across the street from the newspaper. Traffic
was light except around the movie theaters. Traffic was
light on the Outer Drive but slow because a fishy mist had
drifted in from the lake. The lights of the apartment buildings
back of Lincoln Park were blurred. I was well north of Aurora's
place before I knew it, gliding into the sweeping curve before
the Edgewater Beach Hotel. Then the Outer Drive ended and
the city ended with it, the buildings low and dimly lit and the
sidewalks vacant, a modest indoor Chicago diminishing to the
city limits and strait-laced Evanston. Ahead was the Bryn Mawr
El station and the lights of the Eleven-Eleven Club. The time
was seven-thirty. The first set would not begin for another
ninety minutes, and suddenly there seemed no better place to
be on a Friday evening. I parked on the street and hurried inside, the club wonderfully cool, smelling of beer and heavy with
cigarette smoke even though there were only half a dozen men
at the bar and a middle-aged police officer talking earnestly to
the owner at a table in the corner, the cop worried about something and the owner listening intently, though not so intently
that he did not find time to nod cordially at me; the week before I had won the club a mention in the paper's gossip column. I took a seat at the end of the bar, lit a cigarette, and

waited for Earl. Back of the bar was the bandstand with a cabaret piano, a set of traps, and five ladder-back chairs arranged in a semicircle behind metal sheet-music stands, though Brunis's jazz band rarely used sheet music. What they played, they played by ear. I thought of a row of easels without artists, blank spaces waiting to be drawn to life in an atelier with a few friends invited to watch. With a sly nod to the cop at the table, Earl asked loudly for my proof of age and winked when I handed him my press card. I sat alone at the end of the bar, fully at ease for the first time that day; and then I remembered walking out of the newspaper building at noon, my pay packet bulky in my pocket, as reassuring as a rabbit's foot. I was fully at ease then and fully at ease in the Art Institute later. Earl brought me a drink and said I looked terrible. What happened, did you get run over by a mother-in-law? When I told him I was finished at the paper he made a face and said, Stop the presses. Then he retreated to serve the cop another bourbon and ginger ale, bending close to listen to something the owner said.

When he came back, Earl said, Sorry about the job.

It was only a summer job. Thirty-five a week.

Shit job, Earl said.

Shit job, I agreed. Except for the glamour.

Right, he said, and laughed.

You meet such interesting people when you're working in news. Newspaper reporters and bartenders, one excitement after another all day long. How's it with you?

Can't complain. You staying for the set?

No. I have to drive north.

Putting on your monkey suit?

I shook my head, no monkey suit. I realized then that I was starving. I had had no breakfast and nothing to eat at the apartment. I said, Any chance for a sandwich?

I can send out, Earl said.

Chicken sandwich?

Sure. Be a minute. He moved to go, then reached behind him and slid a copy of the newspaper across the bar.

Here, he said. While you're waiting, have a laugh.

And another of these, I said, tapping my glass.

They're on the house, Earl said.

Thank you, I replied, and turned to nod at the owner, who smiled in return.

I sat alone, avoiding the newspaper. I did not read the headlines. I was avoiding the day altogether, looking at the empty bandstand and remembering the times I had been at the club late in the evening, listening to Georg Brunis and his sidemen with the solemnity of a communicant at Mass, some old blues played adagio and then, to wake us all up, he and the band would fly into "Muskrat Ramble" or "South Rampart Street Parade," the faces of the musicians gleaming with sweat. Brunis, looking like a portly small-town accountant with his barbered hair and tidy mustache, led the ensemble with theatrical sweeps of his trombone, and then gave way so that the sidemen could take their solos. How many evenings had I sat and listened to this antique music—thirty? forty? Since the age of fifteen, with a doctored draft card and a composed manner to make my act plausible, careful in the beginning not to drink too much and never, ever to smoke more than one cigarette at a time. The Eleven-Eleven Club was so far away from Quarterday and the North Shore that it might have been in another country, in another century, the time always midnight—

I love to see
The evening sun go down.

The last time had been some Saturday night in July, after a party that had ended early. I had yet to meet Aurora. Six of us had raced in from Winnetka for the last few sets. The rude Englishman was with us, out of pocket as usual. He didn't care for the music, "dingo music" he called it. So he drank five or six scotches, not listening to the band but talking to Earl or whoever was in earshot—baiting them, asking impertinent questions and receiving puzzled answers. I was waiting for Earl to smack him but Earl never did, setting up drink after drink, a few of them on the house. Earl said later that he was tickled by the English accent. He had never heard one before, and then someone told him the limey was a lord, and he had never met a lord. Lord-in-waiting, I said. Earl said he had never met a lord or a lord-in-waiting; and so Sutcliffe or Wycliffe or whatever his name was got away with murder that night as he did most nights, towering over the people at the bar, his huge head thrown back, asking question after question, a kind of interrogatory monologue accompanied by his bray-laugh. He had begun his American tour in Boston and made his way to Long Island and then to Baltimore and Grosse Pointe before showing up in Chicago. He had introductions to people in each city and indicated he would be moving on soon to St. Louis and Louisville, where he had "connections." The rude Englishman traveled without money, though you would never guess that because he was beautifully groomed and tailored with all the correct accessories, MacGregor golf sticks in a St. Andrews bag, a Fabergé cigarette case, bench-made shoes, a gold signet ring, and a silver whiskey flask that looked as if it had seen service at Waterloo. He borrowed money as he traveled and there were stories that he had gotten a girl into trouble in Ipswich and brawled with an older man in Larchmont and was no longer welcome in either locality or on the North Shore of Long Island. Still, allowances were made because—God, he was amusing, with his stories of Harrow and dimwitted royals and their dogs and horses and losses at the baccarat table and swimming pool debaucheries in the wee hours of the morning. Also, he brought an unfamiliar vocabulary. Two of his favorite epithets were "swine" and "bounder," and soon we were all using them, even the debs and their fathers. Of course he never got anyone's name straight and that, too, was seen as an amusing eccentricity, typical of the English, so delightfully vague. That night I left the jazz club early because I did not want to chauffeur the rude Englishman back to wherever he was staying and being hit up for a tenner in the process.

Thanks awfully, Willy.

Left m' pocketbook at the links.

I ran out of distracting memories. My sandwich arrived along with another drink and I began to eat. The club was filling up and I moved to the last stool at the bar, resolved to leave when I had eaten my sandwich. Someone was pressing me from behind and I looked up, irritated, to discover Georg Brunis himself, signaling to Earl. I wished him a good evening and made room for him but as soon as the drink was safely in his hand he disappeared through a side door, his trombone case under his arm. The great jazzman was pink-cheeked and redolent of after-shave. It looked to me as if Brunis was prepared for a long and productive evening, hoping to God he didn't have to play "When the Saints Go Marching In" more than seven or eight times. I took my time finishing the sandwich and then, unable to find more excuses, I pulled the paper toward me, the club's cheerful ambiance falling away as if I had entered a tunnel. There was nothing on page one and nothing on page two or three, and when I found the headline on page five I almost read over it, beginning to turn the page before the words registered—

BATAAN

HERO DOC

A SUICIDE

—over eight terse paragraphs that began with name, age, address, cause of death, location of the body, and probable motive, "despondency." Paragraphs two and three had to do with the Bataan Death March, the number of dead overall and the number said to have been saved by the heroic Dr. Brule. Paragraphs four and five listed his civic activities and various commendations from medical and charitable groups and the Silver Star from the army. Paragraph six described where the body was found but not who found it. Paragraph seven noted that the doctor was divorced and lived with his daughter, Aurora, eighteen, his only survivor. Paragraph eight: "Chicago authorities said a note was found, but refused to disclose its contents. Funeral services are pending." I turned from the paper, grateful that Consuela's name was nowhere mentioned but startled by the reference to a note. Aurora had said nothing about a note and I tried now to imagine its form, written hurriedly in the minutes before the gun was cocked and fired—or perhaps not written hurriedly at all but at leisure, Jack wanting to be certain of the wording because there would be no rewrites in the last effort to explain himself. Probably he had had the words in mind for years and now they would be distilled, as concentrated as haiku. I wondered if he had brought a notepad into the bathroom with him along with the gun, an army-issue Colt .45, according to Henry Laschbrook. That seemed unlikely, but what, in these circumstances, constituted likely or unlikely? I wanted to know the contents of the note but doubted now that I ever would. Perhaps, someday, from Consuela.

No need now for the abusive, if futile, telephone call to Ozias Tilleman. Henry Laschbrook's piece was nestled between three paragraphs on an oil spill off New Jersey and an ad for auto parts, below the fold. Readers would likely pass it by as I almost had. I closed and folded the paper but Jack Brule did not go away. I glanced up at the vacant bandstand, the piano and set of traps, the five chairs, the metal stands and the chrome microphone, horn-high. A jazz club was no place to be in the hour before the first set. It was no place to be alone, trying not to think about Aurora back in Lincoln Park. I pushed off from the bar, time to go. The room was filling up rapidly; the cop was gone. I laid a five-dollar bill next to my empty glass and began to move through the crowd, two-deep now. Someone jostled me and I wheeled, prepared to jostle back, and stared into the chilly half-lidded eyes of the rude Englishman. He had the season's prettiest deb on his arm, and I guessed she had been warned what to expect because she had her purse open and her hand on her wallet. I thought the lord-in-waiting had left for St. Louis and Louisville, but apparently his "connections" had failed to materialize, for here he was, back again, full of brio and an attractive girl to pay his way. He stared at me without recognition. I smiled at her and said hello, disappointed to see a faint blush as she turned away, averting her eyes as she fussed with the wallet. Antoinette was not a worldly girl and was only now discovering how truly attractive and desirable she was. I was certain her very rich and adoring parents did not know where she was or who she was with, a source of dismay because she was not the sort of girl who would enjoy deception. They hurried past, the Englishman waving his arms and shouldering people aside to clear a space at the bar below the bandstand. I went on out the door into Bryn Mawr Avenue, a sultry early evening. I lit a cigarette and waited. When I heard wild applause in the club and the first soaring notes of "Lover Come Back to Me," I strolled away to my car down the street, though the song's melody stayed with me for quite some time along with Antoinette's blush.

I drove slowly, the windows down to clear my head. The traffic was sparse. There was a detour at Western Avenue but I did not need to pay close attention because I knew the route by heart, Chicago's great sprawl, a clutter of gas stations, steak houses, insurance agencies, and the stone spires of churches on the horizon. The Eleven-Eleven Club was an interlude, almost forgotten now except for the song, not Brunis's version but Mildred Bailey's version repeating itself in my head. The song was an old favorite, one I requested often at parties. Aurora and I had danced to it once, Antoinette watching us with a dreamy expression from the sidelines, and she wasn't the only one. I tapped the steering wheel to the music inside my head. I knew that wherever I went in the world I would associate the song with this day. I imagined a café in some unlikely city, Cairo or Singapore or Los Angeles, sitting with someone and hearing Mildred Bailey on the radio and remembering a summer in Chicago and north of Chicago, my father's troubles, Squire's death, the debutante parties, and Jack Brule and Consuela and beautiful Aurora and everything that surrounded them, including the photographs in the study and the untouched drink on the sideboard; and pausing in the conversation, my memory tumbling, suddenly nineteen years old once again and discovering how disturbed life could be and how unexpected its events and how unsettled and discouraging, all in the space of a summer when you left your own family for another's family believing that, in time, you would have your own life with the girl you loved. All these summer fragments lay around me and I knew there was coherence to them but I could not fit them together now.

Aurora and I were finished. I thought of a city destroyed in wartime, the inhabitants looking at the sky at the moment the bombs fell, dead silence before the catastrophe. In minutes there was no physical trace of what had been. Everything familiar was swept away and replaced by a wasteland. We did not know where we were. All that remained to us were our memories and these rested on rubble, untrustworthy memories. We would remember different things and the same things in different ways; and the city we knew so well had vanished utterly. We were no longer for each other but displaced persons trying to find our own way, and governed by opposing regimes. The distance was too great to be bridged. It was a chasm and when I looked across it I saw her turn her back and walk away. Aurora and I had existed in a tremendous zone of privacy and that had been violated, not only by the circumstances of her father's appalling death but by its epilogue in Lincoln Park when she had made her involuntary gesture, the one that seemed to come from another place entirely, centuries old and as immutable as a fossil. Aurora and I had failed in our understanding of each other. She had needed my help and I had not given it, or given the wrong kind and only added to her helplessness and fury. I was suddenly on the outside and so was she. God damn Jack Brule. God damn him to hell. And my sense of what had happened between us stopped there.

Now I waited impatiently for a traffic light, tapping my fingers on the steering wheel. I accelerated on the yellow, faster than I intended, the car barely under control. I was trying to remember how many drinks I had had at the Eleven-Eleven, three certainly, maybe four. Earl always poured with a heavy hand when it was on the house, giving good weight like an honest butcher, a bartender you could count on, damn right you could. There were no other cars on the road and as I looked left and right I realized the surroundings were unfamiliar. I had no idea where I was except that I was much farther south and west than I wanted to be, now in one of Chicago's many anonymous outlying neighborhoods. I was on a narrow brick street, three-decker houses either side, people sitting on their front steps listening to the radio. The street lights were weak, woodsmoke was in the air, and scrawny elms arched over the bricks, the whole of it giving the aspect of a rural village. The dull lights of a tavern were visible down the street and next to the tavern the remains of a house consumed by fire. Someone was poking about in the debris while a companion lit the way with a flashlight. They were moving with caution, lifting a charred board and looking under it and replacing the board. The fire looked to be days old and it was hard to imagine anything of value surviving. I saw now that they were wearing masks, handkerchiefs tied over noses and mouths like bandits in western movies, except these handkerchiefs were white and gave a funereal air to whatever it was they were doing in the ruins. The people on the steps leaned forward, their eyes following my car as I drove slowly to the corner, where I stopped and waited, trying to find my bearings. The tavern's façade was shingled, windowless, a place where men went to drink in privacy. Over the tick-tick of the car's engine I heard violin music, an unfamiliar European melody of high emotion, deeply melancholy and rhapsodic at the same time, the words in a language I could not identify. I listened a moment, trying and failing to translate the words, which seemed a long lament, a hard life of struggle and betrayal except for the vivacity of the treble notes. The two men in the ruins had stopped digging and were watching me.

What do you want? said a voice at my elbow.

The voice, guttural, heavily accented, startled me. Polish, I thought, but I could not be certain. I said, I'm lost. I want Foster Avenue.

This is not Foster, he said.

I know that, I said.

He shook his head. Foster. Long way.

Yes, I said. I'm lost.

Where do you go? he said, looking into the car, back seat and front. His huge hands gripped the car door as if to prevent premature flight. His voice was filled with old-world suspicion of outsiders. His breath smelled sourly of garlic and beer.

North, I said. The North Shore, I added, wondering if he knew where the North Shore was. He continued to grip the door and I wondered if this was the usual welcome for strangers in the neighborhood. Whatever it was, I didn't like it. Two friends joined him and they spoke for a moment in the unfamiliar language.

Go back the way you came, one of the friends said. Turn right.

Thanks, I said. I moved to put the car in gear, looking at the

215

hands gripping the door. The entire street was watching us now, including the two in the fire-ruined house, and three more standing in the open door of the tavern, beer glasses in their hands.

He pointed up the street. That way.

What's the name of the song? I asked.

They looked at me blankly.

The song on the radio, I said.

You go now, he said, tapping the hood of my car. The three in front of the tavern advanced unsteadily into the street holding their glasses of beer. They looked like workingmen who had been off shift awhile.

Gypsy music, isn't it?

The one with the garlic breath leaned on the door, the car gently rocking.

Get away from the car, I said. I didn't like being crowded and his sour breath and the car's motion made me queasy. I motioned in the direction of the ruined house. What are they doing in there? What happened?

Fire, he said.

Anyone hurt?

He took his hands off the door and looked at me in the way you look at anyone who has trespassed. He said, Drive careful. He sniffed the air and shook his head in disgust. I was no longer worth bothering about.

He said, You drunk.

Go away now.

Plenty cops here—

The fire, I said.

Not your business, he said. You don't belong here.

Thanks for the advice, I said. They stepped back. The three men stood watching me as I put the car in gear and drove slowly back the way I had come, nodding at the two with handkerchiefs over their faces and the beer drinkers, all this time the music rising in the street. All the radios were tuned to the same station. It sounded to me like Gypsy music but Gypsies were not a feature of Polish life, even Polish life in Chicago. Gypsies lived in Romania, unless the Reds had thrown them out. They lived also in the Balkans. Probably there were a few in Poland and in Germany. I didn't know about the Low Countries or Scandinavia. Of course Gypsies moved around, so they might be anywhere. The old people on the steps did not look like Gypsies but maybe they were trying to fit into the neighborhood, become good Americans like the first-generation Eastern Europeans who worked for my father. But this neighborhood was not as anonymous as I thought. It seemed to have an unhappiness all its own. I had behaved like a fool but that had had no effect on the unhappiness. I was counting again and discovering that I had had not three or four drinks at the Eleven-Eleven but five drinks, one drink too many in the space of a little more than an hour, and on an empty stomach, except for the chicken sandwich. Maybe it was only four drinks but I had had a drink at Aurora's also, making five in all. Quarterday was forty miles distant, and when I found the Skokie peat bogs later on, I was still worrying the Gypsy problem and where it fit in the Polish scheme of things and whether the great composer Chopin had borrowed melodies from them as he went about his piano business. Probably he did. The Gypsy gift to the world was music, along with fortunetelling. Also, they stole things. They did not recognize the sanctity of private property and in that way they resembled the Communists. Still, there was much to admire in Gypsy culture. They did not leave traces as they moved from place to place in their caravans, keeping to themselves, desiring only freedom of movement while they lived off the land.

13

I PULLED INTO the driveway of the house in Quarterday and turned off the engine. I sat in the sudden silence, not moving, so happy to be home that I wanted to applaud. Quarterday was a small corner of the world but it was mine, unlike Chicago, which was for anyone who wanted it badly enough. The effects of the scotch had mostly worn off, leaving me with a dull headache and a flannel mouth from too many cigarettes and a belief also that I had pushed things to the limit in the not-so-anonymous unhappy neighborhood. I had behaved like a fool, worse even than the rude Englishman, but it had worked out all right. I was still in one piece and so was the neighborhood, except for the vacant place where the house had been. I knew then that the men in the masks had been looking for valuables left behind, or even bodies, as neighbors would do after any conflagration. But I would never forget the smoky smell in the air; woodsmoke, all right, but it did not issue from a fireplace or a cooking stove. All the houses were made of wood and I supposed it was only a matter of time before the same thing happened again, a spark from somewhere, a fire spreading along the floors and walls, the inhabitants in a panic. I had seen nothing about it in the newspaper but there were fires all the time in Chicago, and the newspaper's writ did not run in that neighborhood.

The dog next door was barking. I saw the sycamore trees and beyond them the sixth fairway and the raised green, its flag limp. The golf course was brilliantly moonlit. The house was dark save for a sliver of light from the den and a glow from behind the closed curtains of my parents' bedroom. The time was ten o'clock but I felt I had been awake for a week and had lived a lifetime in one day. Now time came to a halt. The earth ceased to turn. It was there in these familiar surroundings, the trimmed hedges, the silhouette of the eaves of the house against the night sky, the shade trees and the lawn and my mother's slumbering garden beside the front door, that I broke down.

After a while I opened the car door and got out and stood in the moonlight, stretching my arms, the night so warm it felt like the tropics. I walked around the house to the grove of sycamores and the pond where my father skated before his knees gave way. I stood with my hands in my pockets remembering my father's circuits around the pond, his stick hitting the branches of the trees. There was something of feng shui in the arrangement of things that caused me to wonder if my mother had applied Oriental principles to the outdoors; and then I noticed the skeletal outline of a backhoe next to the pond and knew that more changes were planned. I walked across the lawn to the terrace and looked in through the French doors. My father was sitting in his usual chair reading a book in an attitude of complete contentment, knees crossed, the book in his lap. He was alone. I could hear Gershwin on the phonograph, my father's foot moving in time to the music. A Havana cigar in its silver tube rested next to the glass ashtray, the remains of a drink nearby. He looked up suddenly and smiled and I thought for a moment that he had seen me, but he was only reacting to a passage in the book. How I envied him at that moment. I watched him for a minute more, then backed away into the shadows and returned to the driveway and came in through the front door.

It's me, I called, and went at once to the downstairs bathroom. I washed my face and hands, combed my hair, and looked in the mirror. The mirror disclosed no more or less than usual, so I straightened my tie, made a face, and walked out the door.

My father put his book down when I walked in but I knew he was still at a country club somewhere in Pennsylvania. He was reading one of John O'Hara's novels, holding the place with his finger as he remarked dryly that it was good of me to come home before midnight, he wasn't certain that I hadn't decided to leave home for good, put in with my new Chicago friends . . . And then he focused and stopped talking. He put his book aside and waited.

We stared at each other. Finally he said, Something at the office?

I shook my head.

He said, I'll get us a drink. What do you want?

I said, Scotch.

While my father rummaged for ice, I picked up the new cigarette box from Havana. The silver had the feel of satin and the hallmarks were English. It was perfectly plain, no decoration of any kind, no indication it had been owned by anyone else. I wished I had a souvenir from Aurora, something I could put on a table somewhere; and I wished she had something from me. I replaced the cigarette box when my father returned with the drinks, put one beside me, and sank heavily into his own chair.

He said, I like O'Hara. But God, his people get into trouble. The women are always in heat and the men can't keep their trousers buttoned and someone's always broke or going broke and borrowing money from the wrong sort of man. What kind of trouble are you in?

Not the kind you're thinking of.

And what kind is that? What kind of trouble am I thinking you're in?

Police trouble, I said. Am I right?

It had crossed my mind, he said. Your mother and I, we don't know where you've been, what you've been up to. All I know is, you haven't been home. And now you show up on a Friday night looking like something the cat dragged in—

Drunken driving, something like that?

I hadn't gotten that far in my thinking, he said.

Homicide? I said.

Don't get fresh with me, he said.

It isn't police trouble, I said wearily. It's personal. It's more in the nature of O'Hara trouble.

My father looked at the ceiling, then back at me, his expression stern and infinitely sad at the same time. Who's the girl?

Aurora Brule, I said.

The doctor's daughter? The headshrinker, lives in Chicago? Jesus, Wils. He sighed heavily and took a long pull of his drink, staring into the glass before he put it down. His mouth moved as if he were saying something to himself, trying it out before he spoke aloud. He said, Do you love her?

Of course, I said.

Well, that's something.

She's a wonderful girl, I said.

I remember her, he said. Pretty girl.

Very pretty, I said.

So you've been with her these past weeks. And I suppose longer than that.

She's changed my life. And now—

I'm sure she has, my father said.

—it's just gone to hell, I said brokenly.

Does her family know? my father asked gently.

About us? Well, yes.

How far along is she?

It took me a moment to understand what he was asking, and I had to compose myself before answering. I said, She's not pregnant, Dad. It's not that kind of O'Hara trouble. O'Hara trouble comes in all colors of the rainbow and this is another color altogether.

Thank God, he said. Then he paused before adding, I'm sorry. I sort of jumped to conclusions, I guess. The stuff you read in the papers—

I wish to God she was pregnant.

No, my father said. You don't.

How do you know what I wish or don't wish?

Maybe you could tell me what it's about. Because as it is now, I'm pretty much in the dark.

Just then we heard my mother's voice at the top of the stairs. Teddy? Who's down there? Who are you talking to? My father forced a laugh and said, It's Wils, come to pay us a visit. We're just having a nightcap, then I'll be up.

Wils? my mother said. Are you all right? I knew she had heard the timbre of our voices and intuited that something was amiss.

I cleared my throat and replied heartily that all was well, that my father and I were having a nightcap and we would be up shortly. I'm celebrating, I said. This was my last day on the job!

She did not say anything for a very long time and then I heard, That's nice, dear. Her voice was full of sleep and she didn't believe a word.

Good night, then, she said.

With my great gift of narrative, I began in the middle of the day and went back to the end of last month and stayed there awhile, my father's expression growing more puzzled with each halting sentence, describing Jack Brule and the Lincoln Park apartment. Finally I simply began when I walked into the newspaper office to receive my last assignment from Ozias Tilleman. I replayed the conversation with Henry Laschbrook and the long walk to the Art Institute, Aurora not at her class. I asked my father if he had ever visited the Impressionist and Post-Impressionist rooms at the Art Institute, the barmaid, the postman, the clown, and the others, but I didn't wait for an answer. I was so eager to get on to Edward Hopper and the woman in the motel bedroom, the telephone just outside the frame, the door prepared for a single knock. Wonderful rooms, I said. You should go if you haven't.

I have been, my father said.

You can go again.

It's the greatest art museum in America, I went on. Chicago's crown jewel.

Then I was outside on the steps, watching Aurora stumble from the cab and put her arms around the lion's plinth. We were in the cab heading for Lincoln Park, the cab driver a perfect prick, Aurora unable to finish a sentence. And then I was alone in a room full of people, making certain the ice bucket was full and the bar stocked, meeting Aunt This and Aunt That and a few of the others, Jack's patients, medical colleagues, friends of the family. The names flew by. People were in shock and many of the women were weeping openly, while others behaved as if this were a normal Friday afternoon in Chicago. I ducked out for a minute alone in Jack's consulting room and saw the skull once again. Aurora was somewhere else in the apartment, talking to the men from the coroner's office. Or that was who they said they were; actually it was Henry Laschbrook and Ed Hoskins from the newspaper. The ruse was often used by Henry to gather the news.

They're bastards, newspaper people.

Buzzards, Dad. They have no respect for anything.

I paused there, uncertain what came next. I was lost inside this story, a blind man blundering into a familiar room, bearings lost. I believed I should explain about Consuela, so I asked my father if he had ever heard of Famagusta. No, he had not. Wasn't it in Paraguay? No, I said, not Paraguay. Famagusta was a port city on the island of Cyprus, eastern Mediterranean, Cyprus was an island well known in antiquity. Aphrodite rose from the sea at Paphos. Consuela was from Cyprus; or that was one of the places she was from, the others being Greece and Hungary. Consuela was writing a memoir of her summers in Famagusta, where she lived in a house by the sea. I paused again, trying to get the events straight in my mind. Also, I said, she was Jack Brule's mistress. She lived in the apartment. They shared a bedroom. Jack was divorced from Aurora's mother. The mother lived in Michigan with her new husband and their child. Aurora was not at all close to her mother. The divorce was bitter and she took her father's part. She chose him over her mother. They knew a judge who fixed the custody agreement.

Consuela's very nice, I said.

The first time I met her, I liked her right away.

She's very attractive, a nonconformist.

I never met anyone like her.

My father nodded at that, offering a sympathetic smile.

Can you imagine, Famagusta?

My father excused himself and went to the kitchen. I heard ice clink in his glass. When he came back, he had a fresh drink and settled himself as before in his usual chair.

Jack Brule committed suicide, I said, after a terrible argument with Consuela. I never learned what it was about. But the argument was bad enough so that Aurora woke up and heard some of it. I don't know how much. They were arguing in their bedroom. Jack went into the bathroom and shot himself. That's it. He left a note but I have no idea what was in it. After everyone had cleared out of the apartment, Aurora and Consuela had a battle. Aurora wanted to throw her out of the house but she wouldn't move. Consuela was destroyed by what had happened. She lay on the couch with her eyes closed while Aurora went at her. It was awful to watch. Awful to listen to. I tried to intervene but that did no good. Aurora turned against me, and then Consuela roused herself and spoke to Aurora and they seemed to make it up. And in the blink of an eye I was on the outside of things. There was nothing I could say and I had no idea what to do. When I approached Aurora, she turned her back. It was between the two of them. And they seemed united against me, the outsider, the boy from out of town. They were a family after all and I was a new arrival. My grief could not equal theirs.

Do you suppose that was it?

An unequal weight of grief?

My father sipped his drink and did not reply.

When I tried to mediate between them I stepped over the line and they took offense, Aurora especially. She may have thought I was disloyal, not on her side, opposed to her. I tried to put myself in her skin but could not. Was it my inexperience? But I had no authority to speak in that room. I suppose you could say I was not entitled to speak. What do you think is the more terrible loss for a woman, a lover or a father? I waited for my father to say something but he seemed lost in thought.

Wouldn't it depend on the individual? I said.

My father raised his eyebrows and said softly, It usually does.

Also, I said, the nature of the death. An unnatural death.

Yes, my father said.

Have you ever known a suicide?

He moved his shoulders doubtfully, neither yes nor no.

I was just wondering, I said.

Tom Felsen's brother, my father said slowly. Younger brother, two years behind us in high school. He had a rough time of it. Tom's father was a difficult man, humorless, angry most of the time. He was a farmer who hated farming. Tom's brother was very quiet, not a popular boy, not good at sports, not good at much of anything. He was bullied at school and bullied at home. Tom did his best to protect him but after Tom graduated the brother was left on his own. His name was Roy, named for his father. Everyone called him Little Roy except for his mother. I think she was bullied, too, by Roy Senior. My father sipped his drink and was silent, his expression formal, as if he were testifying in court. He said, Little Roy hanged himself. In the barn, from a rafter. I was away at Dartmouth. By the time I got the letter from home the funeral was over and done with. The family put out some story about an accident. Everyone knew the truth but no one spoke it. I wrote Tom a letter but never got a reply, and when I saw him at Christmastime he thanked me for my letter but said he didn't want to talk about his brother. He let me know he was no longer on speaking terms with his father, but they had been on the outs for years so I didn't think much about it. Tom was on his own by then, a deputy sheriff, making plans. Years later I learned that Little Roy had committed suicide and the cause was still considered a mystery, and not a subject for conversation. Of course he had been bullied. But there had to be something more. Or something else, and I don't know what that was. I don't think anyone knows to this day. I suppose only Little Roy knew the whole story.

I think Tom's been trying to get even ever since, my father said.

Jack Brule was in the war, I said.

Lots of men in the war, my father said.

The Bataan Death March, I said. He spoke to me about it. And I saw some of his photographs, Jack and his comrades in the Philippines. He said what disturbed him most was not the hatred of the Japanese for him but his hatred of them. He couldn't get over it. The hatred was still there. I think hatred was his constant companion. Hatred was the brother who wouldn't go away.

A terrible episode, my father said.

Aurora didn't know anything about it. Her father wouldn't say. Maybe Consuela knew something. But she never told Aurora.

Shame, probably.

Despair, I said.

At something he did or something he didn't do, my father said, completing his own sentence. I wasn't in the war. I don't know how they got on from day to day and the combatants weren't interested in reliving those days. They still aren't. It's nobody's business but theirs, so they put it away like an old love letter they can't bear to read but don't want to destroy, either. I think with suicides there's also an element of revenge. But I don't know anything about it, really.

My father paused there, rising, stepping to the terrace doors. He stood, rocking on his heels, then turned to the phonograph, silent these many minutes. He carefully set the needle on the record and turned the volume low, so that when Gershwin's music began again it was barely audible. He said, There will be some things in your life that you'll never speak about. Not to your wife and not to your children, not to your closest friend. Not on your deathbed. Most often this will involve an episode that you'll want to forget, something shameful or dishonorable. Maybe only something cheap, a failure of nerve or a failure to comprehend; a failure of character, in other words. But if you lead any sort of real life, you'll have the other thing, too. Something magnanimous, a large-hearted act committed when no one was looking and you won't want to say anything about that, either, because the words will stick in your throat. You'll know what they are but there's no reason for anyone else to know. Try to avoid being sloppy about things, Wils. Sometimes I think the only memories worth having are the ones that are private.

I said, You can't mean that.

But I do, he said.

Can you tell me, I began.

No, I cannot, my father said, smiling one of his thin smiles. I tried to see behind it. Something to do with his business, I thought, the strike or its aftermath; or his life with my mother, some indiscretion, or more than indiscretion, betrayal or an act of dishonesty. He was looking at me evenly and I was listening hard but I knew I had all I was going to get. At that moment my father was impenetrable. He was fifty years old and as I looked at him, his heavy shoulders and head, his wrestler's build, I knew I would make a different sort of life for myself. Mine would be a twentieth-century life, the modern world, where spillage was inevitable, even necessary. Some disorder was welcome, was it not—and then I remembered Jack Brule.

My father smiled suddenly and said, in conscious parody of his gruff voice, Be a god damned adult, Wils. Then he turned and limped back to his chair, easing himself onto the cushion.

You win, I said.

Winning doesn't come into it, he said.

Your way, I went on, sounds lonely.

Can be, he admitted. He extracted his Havana from its silver tube and rolled it between his thumb and forefinger, testing density. But he did not light it. He said, Butch Greenslat had an interest in suicide. He'd had a client or two over the years, took that way out. We often talked about it over a drink at the end of the day. Butch had a philosophical turn of mind, when he wasn't chasing women or putting the fix in at the Hall. He had a theory that suicide, like any affair of pride, required equilibrium, the perfect harmony of emotion and will. A kind of sublime handshake was how Butch put it. Think of a musician at the height of his powers, the pure note of a horn, the note held to the limits of breath. My father hesitated, listening to Benny Goodman play the opening notes of *Rhapsody in Blue*.

I listened to Goodman's run, the notes rising and dispersing, ending in silence.

You can't arrest it any more than you can arrest a puff of smoke, my father said. Its course is inevitable unless something interferes with the equilibrium, changing the field of force, and in Jack Brule's case, nothing did.

That would be Butch's explanation, I think.

I hope you can make it up with your girl, my father added.

I shook my head. I think she's dispersed, like your black smoke.

She'll be having a bad time of it, he said.

I think so, I said.

It'll work out, my father said.

For me or for her? I asked.

For her, he said.

I hope so, I said with a confidence I did not feel. I think, with Aurora, it's an affair of pride.

I'm very sure it's more than pride, my mother said from the doorway. I had no idea how long she had been standing there in the shadows listening to my father and me. Her face was set in a frown, her arms crossed, her manner distant. I'm sure she only needs to find her own way. *Only,* my mother repeated with a cold smile. Not that she'll have much help.

You didn't used to listen at keyholes, my father said.

Come to bed, Teddy, my mother said. You, too, Wils.

In a minute, my father said.

It's late, she said.

We haven't finished, my father said.

It's never finished, my mother said as she turned her back and walked out of the room.

14

THE DAY WAS overcast when I left Quarterday but brightened when I reached the city. I had trouble finding the Lutheran church, a few streets west of Lincoln Park, stuck between low-slung apartment buildings in a residential neighborhood. The church was constructed of red brick, and if it weren't for the steeple and the clerestory windows you could mistake it for a school or a warehouse. I was a few minutes late and most of the mourners were already inside. The hearse and three black Cadillacs were waiting at the curb but the chauffeurs were across the street fanning themselves with their billed hats; the day was warm. A few older men were finishing cigarettes on the church steps. I recognized them from the parties earlier in the summer, only now they were in business suits, looking impatient at eleven o'clock in the morning. They were staring at their shoes and shaking their heads when I passed by. I heard one of them say, Jesus, what must Jack have been thinking to do such a thing, and one of the others replying that he didn't know but it certainly wasn't anything good, but Jack was always a queer duck, even for a head doctor. I nodded and they nodded back, trying and failing to place me as they flipped their cigarettes on the gritty patch of lawn and consulted their wristwatches once again. Inside, I recognized the doctors who had been arguing about German tattoos, and a few of the

women who had been in the apartment on Friday. All the
women wore white gloves and hats. I looked for Marlon Brando
but he was not in sight. I did identify what looked like Adlai
Stevenson's bald head but I could not be sure, the church was
ill lit and crowded. Charlie Smithers and his wife were seated
near the front, son Al wedged uncomfortably between them. I
was surprised to see only a few friends of Aurora's, Dana and
Antoinette and one other girl whose name I could not recall,
sitting together in the middle of the church. I wondered what
had happened to her schoolmates and the boys she had dated
over the years, but perhaps she had discouraged them from
coming; and then Oscar Palshaw walked by. Probably Aurora
wanted only to get the service over with, do what was necessary
without the chore of greeting friends and listening to their so-
sorrys and what-can-I-dos, everyone nervous and on the edge
of tears. I had tried to call Aurora half a dozen times but the
phone was busy; twice it went unanswered, even when I let it
ring a minute or more, imagining Aurora sitting alone in her
room and listening to the monotonous interruption, unwilling
or unable to move. I had no idea what had become of Consuela. I had written a note also but had heard nothing in reply.
Now I noticed the aunts in the front pew, facing the closed casket and its spray of white roses. Aunt That's son Oliver was next
to her and on the other side a pretty girl in a wide-brimmed hat,
and I knew without asking that she was the cheerleader, Aurora's Texas cousin. The older man on her right was as weatherbeaten as a fence rail but turned out in banker's gray for the
occasion, and two rows behind them, inconspicuous in the
shadows of the far end, was a grieving woman with her head
on the heavy arm of her blank-faced husband, surely Aurora's
mother and the piano-playing stepfather, the Elliotts. He was
staring intently at the casket, covered by an American flag. On
the flag was a decoration, no doubt the dead man's Silver Star,
and I wondered if he would approve of such a dramatic memento—and then I remembered Aurora and me discussing
when the future began, with graduation or a job or marriage or
children and never imagining that it would begin with a funeral. The church was appointed in a plain style. Behind the

casket was a lectern where the minister would stand and beyond that risers for the choir, except the risers were empty. The light inside was wan and seemed to evaporate as I looked at it, drawn upward to the vault of the nave. A somber attendant in a black suit handed me a program as I slipped into an empty pew at the rear of the chamber and bent my head to say a brief prayer, wishing Jack Brule Godspeed and some measure of grace and consolation for his daughter and for Consuela. Whatever ill will I had toward the dead man was gone, and it was not my place to judge. The program proposed a hymn, a reading from Scripture, another hymn, another reading, remarks by the Reverend William Chasewell, and a final hymn. We all sat uneasily in the half-light listening to the organist play scales. Under the music was a hushed sibilant rustle, people whispering mouth to ear. The woman in front of me remarked to her neighbor that she had refused her daughter permission to attend the funeral, too depressing for a young girl, not at all appropriate given the unwholesome circumstances. She'll discover that side of things soon enough. Poor Aurora. I closed my eyes and thought about affairs of pride and the marriage of emotion and will; and you would have to add imagination to reach the perfect equilibrium when, I supposed, anything was possible. Perhaps when they said emotion, they meant imagination. This plain church discouraged the expression of either. Submission was recommended. We all sat dumbly listening to the organist practice his scales. The Reverend Chasewell was standing behind the lectern now, a Bible in his hands. He was as tall as Jack Brule but older and seemed to regard his congregation with mild distrust, his eyes narrowed and his mouth a thin suspicious line. He had the superior bearing of a Victorian gentleman. At his perfunctory signal everyone rose and the organ sounded the notes of the first hymn. At a movement behind me in the center aisle, I turned to discover Aurora and Consuela, dressed identically in black, unveiled, advancing a step at a time. They walked side by side, both bent slightly at the waist and moving so slowly they might have been struggling through water. They looked like sisters, only a few years separating them, their heads almost touching, walking in soldierly uni-

231

son; and then I saw they were holding hands. The congregation, singing, turned to watch them, and time itself stopped in a sudden gulp of held breath. Some of the women turned away in distress, though Olivia Elliott never moved, her eyes resolutely forward. Aurora paused, her hand resting lightly on the pew rail not two feet from where I sat. She was wearing her father's wristwatch, her left hand made into a fist so that it would not slip off. I smiled at her but she stared straight ahead, pausing as if to gather strength for the march down the center aisle to the casket with its draped flag, white roses either side, the Reverend Chasewell standing motionless, waiting. My hand clasped hers until she looked sharply at me, her eyes alienated and unfocused; and then she smiled crookedly, a look of studied resolve. I am not certain she knew who I was. Her hand was under mine and then it was gone. Aurora and Consuela went on up the aisle, laboring against the current that threatened to overwhelm them. They were holding hands so tightly, wrists touching, that they resembled—not lovers, not sisters, but prisoners shackled by fate and circumstance, the vultures in the trees; and they would not give in. Their heels clicked on the stone floor, a tempo at odds with the hymn but consistent somehow with the frank curiosity on the faces of the congregation. The Reverend Chasewell's frown was commentary on the disgraceful irregularity, daughter and mistress marching down the center aisle as if they were members of a wedding. Robert Elliott raised his head and gave a cross look, but it went unseen. Aurora and Consuela were unaware, their eyes set on a point in the middle distance. At last they reached the front of the church and took their places beside the aunts, still holding hands. They began to sing. I sang, too, and listened to the Reverend Chasewell read from John, and sang again and listened to the Reverend Chasewell read from Ecclesiastes, and then listened to the Reverend Chasewell read his appalling lesson until I could listen no longer and quietly slipped out of the pew and stepped into the indifferent light of midday Chicago. The hearse and the three black Cadillacs were waiting at the curb, their chauffeurs looking listlessly at me, alone on the porch. Two motorcycle patrolmen, ominous in white helmets and black leather leggings, waited to conduct the cortege to the cemetery. I did not know in which of Chicago's many graveyards Jack Brule would be interred. I wondered what words, if any, would be etched on his tombstone; and finally I wondered why his remains were not bound for Arlington, where the war dead were. But I thought I knew the answer to that. I stood on the front steps listening to the final hymn, the one about God's mighty fortress. The congregation was not in good voice and the music was pale. I strained to hear the words but what I heard instead was a kind of groan, voices under the organ, an indistinct murmur. I listened for Aurora's alto but it was lost somewhere in the interior and I suspected she was not singing but listening, as I was, for one clear note, evidence of the heartbeat beneath the skin. Then the hymn concluded. The patrolmen fired up their engines, the chauffeurs returned to their cars, and Aurora and Consuela were walking down the porch steps, followed by the aunts, the Texas cousin and her father, the Elliotts, and other family members I did not recognize. There was a moment of confusion after Aurora and Consuela disappeared into the lead limousine, the one behind the hearse. Mourners gathered on the church steps watching the departure, the funeral party debating which car to enter as the chauffeurs stood at attention beside open doors. I saw Aurora's arm fall from her open window, that gesture again. She caressed the skin of the limousine as if it were a cat's fur, her father's wristwatch limp around her wrist. At last the cars pulled away from the curb and moved slowly up the street, the hearse so long and black it seemed to go on forever. Aurora's arm disappeared from the window of the limousine behind it. I walked away among strangers, searching for my car. Nothing in this neighborhood was familiar. The hearse turned the corner and disappeared. I was nineteen years old.

FAMAGUSTA

15

THAT'S WHAT I know of that long-ago summer under the high-topped tents, an unfinished season sure enough. By the end of the decade my parents had given up the Midwest and moved to Florida, where my mother gave lessons in feng shui and my father practiced coming out of a fairway sand trap with a five iron; and a decade later they were both gone. When they moved south, I had no reason to visit Chicago and never did again. Still, wherever I went in the world I was careful to check the papers for a Chicago dateline, and over the years understood that the city was having something like a renaissance. It was in the *Herald Tribune* that I found a two-line obit of Ozias Tilleman and, a little later, two paragraphs on Georg Brunis. One of the Cordes girls married a tennis professional and I always checked the tournament summaries to see how he had done; but by the early 1960s he had slipped in the rankings, and disappeared from the sports pages. In the last year of the Eisenhower administration, Charlie Smithers got an ambassadorship, one of the Caribbean nations. Much later, my old day school hired a new headmaster, a Melville scholar from Hotchkiss or St. Paul's, one of those two.

Quarterday, the North Shore, Lincoln Park—that world is lost to me now. It began to diminish when I went away to college and acquired an adult life—the University of Chicago was good at that—and continued to diminish over the years. It's a fact, as I predicted, that from time to time Aurora dances in from the wings of my memory and I recall the mysterious gesture she made that afternoon in her apartment and, weeks earlier, the soft sound of her bears tumbling from the bed, Benny Goodman's clarinet rising from a car radio in the park. Whenever I see one of Brando's pictures I remember his grave expression as he listened to the doctors Bloom describe the manner of Jack Brule's death. Each presidential election is cause for reflection on the accidental encounter with Adlai Stevenson on Astor Street, a middle-aged man in a suit one size too small, bound for a rendezvous with a woman in Libertyville—or so I hoped. These recollections last no more than a few seconds, a snapshot as opposed to a film, and then I return to the here and now. Mysteries have an allure for me and I have always been reluctant to delve too deeply into Aurora's, a reporter "digging" into the "story" for the "truth." Searching in a dark room for a black hat that isn't there, as a cynical colleague of mine once put it. Sometimes you make too much of things, Aurora said to me more than once, and she wasn't the only one, exasperated by my lack of intuition and, all too often, by my excess. When you are trying to understand the way the world works and have so little to go on, you make what you can from the materials at hand, and so it's natural to infer quite a lot from almost nothing. Intuition is the subtitle for experience. You believe you have found someone to trust who will trust you in return, no small hope. And when you give away a piece of your heart, you'd like to believe it's being safely kept, since you can never get it back. I have never had the slightest illusion that I could bend the world to my will, and I refused to bend to the world's, and so I have lived a kind of shadow life.

Then, many years later, my work brought me to Cyprus.

I finished my business in Nicosia by early afternoon and decided to take a roundabout route to Famagusta, visiting some of the places I had seen decades before. The day was fine, the sky a Mediterranean blue, warm enough so that I could put down the top of my rented Alfa. I drove north over the mountains to

Kyrenia, St. Hilarion Castle gloomy on a mountaintop miles away. I made the journey in no time at all, had a snack at the port, and hiked up to Bellapais, Lawrence Durrell's village of earthly delights. In the old days I often took tea with a poet who lived there and in time came to depend on him for political intelligence, the endless back-and-forth of the Greeks and the Turks on the divided island. The poet described conditions on Cyprus in language so richly ambiguous that I regularly quoted him in my reports to the Secretary-General, himself a man of no little subtlety, who used to say that at the United Nations ambiguity was a sacrament and its graceful expression a virtue of the highest order, and if the poet ever got to New York he wanted to give him lunch. But the poet was disinclined to leave Bellapais for any reason, though mightily tempted by the Sec-Gen's invitation. Do you happen to know His Excellency's sign, Wils? When I said Virgo, the poet raised his eyebrows and laughed and laughed. He was long dead now but I found his house with no difficulty. It was owned by an Israeli expatriate who kindly invited me in and was very pleased to learn that his retirement villa had once been a poet's workshop. The garden was filled with butterflies coasting among the lemon trees, just as I remembered it.

I motored east to Famagusta, driving slowly because I was searching for a village I knew well in the early 1960s. It was my coming-of-age village, the place where I found my métier. I was awakened early one morning by the concierge of my hotel. Please, Mr. Ravan, can you go at once and try to stop them from killing each other? He gave me directions to the village and I did go at once, arriving just before dawn. It was a Turkish village and the Mukhtar was dead, lying under a tree with a bullet hole in his chest. Rigor mortis had already set in and I remember that his hands were rigid, raised one inch above the ground where he lay, as if he were levitating. The villagers gave me an account of the battle, an atrocity. They showed me pictures of other atrocities in the Turkish community over the years, one picture after another of dead women and children and an occasional adult man, all the corpses mutilated. They kept the pictures in a scrapbook. The Greek marauders had come from over the hill; they lived in the adjoining village. So for the better part of a week I shuttled between the two communities, trying to get a sense of what had actually transpired. The Greeks asserted that the Turks had struck first, and they had the corpse of a Greek woman to prove it. They, too, had photograph albums of past atrocities and insisted that I inspect each one, and learn the names and ages of the dead. The wrong was never-ending. It would take centuries to settle the scores that needed settling and the island would know no peace until the accounts were squared and the Turks back in Turkey where they belonged; and the Turks said the same of the Greeks. They were an impossible people, their victimhood inspiring a kind of grandiose self-love. No people had ever suffered so greatly, endured so much, while an indifferent world looked on. Can no one aid us in our mortification? The aroma of burning charcoal hung over both villages, a pall I came to identify as the smell of poverty. So my heart went to them and I promised to help.

I had a contingency fund and spent all of it. I arranged for a squad of our blue helmets to conduct periodic patrols and eventually I secured a cease-fire and a protocol of the sort of behavior each community expected of the other. Trust and the perception of trust; and I swore them to secrecy. This was my first assignment outside the building in New York. I had only a watching brief from the Secretary-General's office and by inserting myself into this local dispute I had violated my instructions. If one of our peacekeepers had been injured or killed or if the operation had become controversial, I would have been fired and deserved to have been fired. The press never got wind of the cease-fire, and if the Greek and Turkish authorities in Nicosia knew of it, they never said anything. When I returned to New York a month later, the cease-fire was still holding but there was so much violence elsewhere on the island, no one noticed. I never explained myself, then or later—not to the poet, not to the Sec-Gen, not to Ambassador Stevenson, not even to my family—and so it was that I came to understand what my father had meant when he said that a magnanimous act needed no amplification. I had all these thoughts in mind when I went searching for the village, in vain as it turned out. The island had changed, and the village was very small in any case. But the aroma of burning charcoal was everywhere.

I drifted through the Kyrenia Mountains and to the plain that led to Famagusta, the medieval city that lay like a mouth under the Pinocchio's nose of the Karpas Peninsula. The poet said that the tourist officials liked to compare Famagusta favorably to Carcassonne and Dubrovnik, but that was because they had never been to Carcassonne or Dubrovnik. Famagusta's golden age was the fourteenth century and the years since had not been kind, the usual capitalist mischief. Still, I had found it pleasant enough with its ruined churches and bustling markets, reminders of the various foreign marauders, Egyptians, Venetians, Genoese, Ottomans, and British. The city had taken a terrible pounding during the war. The poet spoke of Famagusta the way my father spoke of Quarterday when he was a boy, God's own acre until it was transformed into a sprawling suburb glued together by shopping malls, auto dealerships, restaurants, and bulbous office buildings designed by the three blind mice. I came over a rise and saw Famagusta Bay in the distance, sultry in the gray light of late afternoon, freighters on the horizon, barely visible through the smoke that lay over the city. Aleppo was little more than two hundred miles to the northeast.

The first few times I was in Cyprus I tried to reach Consuela but she was never at home. The phone went unanswered. My last visit was many years ago but I was busy and never made the call. We had not seen each other since Jack Brule's funeral and it's fair to say she slipped from my mind. Cyprus itself moved to the world's back burner, a perennial problem that was hopeless but not serious; and now here I was again with yet another fresh approach to the never-ending wrong. This time I was determined to see her, and when I called she picked up at once. We did not recognize each other's voice and spent a few confusing minutes making recognition noises. When that was done, I asked her to dinner. No, she said. You come here.

It's time we caught up with each other.

It's been forty years, I said.

She said, Come at seven.

Then she added, Why are you here?

I work for the UN, I said. I'm here on business.

Dirty business, she said, and laughed. You really work for the United Nations?

Have done for as long as I can remember. I walked out of the University of Chicago with a law degree and an introduction to Adlai Stevenson.

Did he help?

He did, I said. Chicago boys stick together.

The UN, she said. I can hardly believe it.

It suits me, I said. I'm a sort of referee. They call it conflict resolution but you and I would call it mediation. Referee. Her laughter began back in her throat, a husky chuckle. I said, I've tried to call but you're never at home.

When was that?

Years ago, I admitted.

I lived in Athens for a while. And New York for a while. I lived in one place and another. Here and there.

But you're back now, I said.

I'm home, she agreed.

I'm happy to hear your voice, Consuela.

And I'm happy to hear yours, Wils.

Her villa sat atop a hill overlooking the water. The westerly wind had blown away most of the smog. She was some distance from Famagusta, only the glare of the lights of the busy port a reminder of its industrial presence. I had brought some wine and a bottle of Cinzano, surprising myself that I had remembered the Cinzano. I parked the car and walked up the path to a low iron gate, opened the gate, and followed the path around a whitewashed bungalow. There were other villas round and about, some dark, others occupied. It did not seem a fashionable district. The night was warm and the sea air damp, insects active around the windows of the house. From the interior I heard recorded music, and unless I badly missed my guess, Consuela was playing the *Goldberg Variations*. I turned the corner, the sea suddenly in view. The moon was rising somewhere over Syria, its golden light playing on the surface of the Mediterranean, most ancient of seas. Consuela was sitting in a canvas chair, smoking a cigarette and looking out over the water, wearing a bright red caftan and sandals. She was deeply tanned. Her white hair was freshly coifed, her perfume the vaguest addition to the salty climate. She had added weight but she was instantly recognizable, her profile and the way she held her cigarette, and her theatrical air, even when sitting quietly alone and smiling at something private. My failure to find the Turkish village had discouraged me, but now I was glad that I had come. I hesitated a moment, looking at Consuela serene in the moonlight and wondering if she, too, was apprehensive.

I said, Connie.

She did not stir except to tap the ash of her cigarette into a saucer.

I said again, Connie, and touched her on the shoulder.

Oh, Wils, she said, rising with difficulty. When she tilted her head to one side I saw the button in her ear, a hearing aid. You're here at last, she said, and we kissed on both cheeks. When I handed her the wine and the bottle of Cinzano, she laughed and said, You remembered.

Of course, I said.

You look the same, she said after a moment of appraisal.

And so do you, I replied.

Well, that's out of the way, she said.

Consuela led me inside and pointed to the ice bucket. I set about filling glasses with ice, and for now those were the only sounds in the room. It was evident that we had only one subject but the time had not arrived for its exploration. When I handed her a Cinzano and soda, my eyes strayed to a side table and a framed photograph of a handsome middle-aged man in a bathing suit, a towel around his neck and a child's pail in his hand. My husband, Consuela said, following my eyes.

Max and I live in Athens, she went on. Famagusta is not to his taste. He prefers Rhodes. So when I come here he goes to Rhodes and we rendezvous again in Athens. Max is an art dealer and we have been married now almost fifteen years. There was one other husband before him but that husband left me and I do not care to talk about him. Consuela's tone reminded me of Aunt That from so many years ago, her disappeared husband, Worm, Welch, some eponymous name; and I wondered how many disappeared husbands there were in the world, millions probably, scattered on every continent.

Those are Max's children when they were young, she said, pointing to a framed snapshot of two toddlers at play. I myself have no children.

And you, Wils, she went on. Are you married?

We live in New York, I said. But I am often abroad. So we are often apart.

And children?

We have two boys, both still in school. I was forty-one when the twins were born. That's too old to be a father for the first time.

I used to regret not having children, Consuela said. Now I regret nothing.

I said, Tell me, Connie. Did you ever publish your memoir?

My God, she said. What a memory. No, I never did. I'm still working on it.

That means you have more to say, I said.

I think it will be finished when I am, Consuela said.

We were standing on the deck now with our drinks. Two freighters moved on the horizon and we were both silent, watching their slow progress. I thought about Consuela's memoir, knowing now that it was a life's work and not intended for publication. She lit a cigarette and blew a smoke ring, watching it fall and rise again before collapsing. Something moved against my ankle and I quickly stepped back; but it was only a cat.

Yours? I said.

The neighbor's, Consuela replied. Filthy animal.

She said, Your twins would be about the age you were when we met.

Just about, I said.

God, I loved that age. All that heat.

I said nothing to that.

But I didn't think to ask, Consuela said. What is your wife's name?

Margot, I said.

From New York?

Margot's a Chicago girl, I said.

An old flame? Consuela asked with a smile.

An economist, I answered. We met in New York.

Ah, Consuela said. The Chicago diaspora.

We found enough to talk about during dinner, the wretched political situation on the island, the new Democratic administration in Washington, movies we had seen, movies we hadn't. Consuela slowly cleared the dishes, brusquely refusing any help from me, and returned with cups of Turkish coffee and a tray of liqueurs in thimble-sized glasses. When the coffee was poured and we each had a thimble of cognac, Consuela cleared her throat and spoke without preamble.

Aurora went away to Barnard and I never saw her again. There was some business with Jack's estate but that was handled through lawyers. I stayed on in the apartment for six months or so, not in very good shape, I'm afraid. I didn't have many friends in Chicago. Jack was my friend and we spent most of our time alone. So I moved to London, then Athens. But I always had my house here when things got tedious. When the estate was finally settled, Aurora and I lost contact completely. Jack left me money and some books and his Brancusi and Aurora resented that, but there was nothing she could do about it. Jack's will was quite specific. I have no idea where she lives or with whom. I have no idea what she does. So I'm afraid I can't be much help to you, Wils.

That's not why I'm here, I said.

Why are you here, then?

She lives in Key West, I said.

You've kept up?

No. But every few years she writes a novel and I read it. The author's note on the last one said she lived in Key West. Before that she lived in Rome. Also Iowa City, Nantucket, Cambridge, and Greenwich Village. There were other cities but I've forgotten them. She moves around a lot.

Is she married?

The note doesn't say. Only the cities.

Why am I not surprised, Consuela said.

I smiled at that.

So Aurora writes novels. It makes sense. She was always writing things down, scraps of conversation, descriptions of things. People, too. She kept a kind of diary, called it her archives. She was forever asking about my early life and about Famagusta, its history, who lived there, the pace of life, what we did. Her questions were quite impertinent. She seemed to think Famagusta was fabulous, a golden city of magic and dreams, a city of the imagination, whereas actually it's an island city like any other island city. It has a lighthouse, a foghorn, and a fishing fleet. Cathouses near the docks. Hospitable to refugees. I don't know what she was after. I told her to read *Othello,* her father's favorite play. You couldn't forget for one second that Othello was a *general,* Jack said. And the play is set in Famagusta.

And did she?

I suppose she did. She read everything else.

I said, A few years back she wrote a novel called *The Goldberg Variations* that I bought at once, thinking that it might reveal—I don't know what I thought. I imagine I thought it might have something in it about us. What happened to her father. The situation generally. But it didn't. *The Goldberg Variations* was another midlife-crisis novel. And from it I deduced that she was married and that the marriage was not succeeding.

It's a mistake to infer the author's life from the author's fiction, Consuela said.

Do you think so?

Yes, she said. I'm quite sure.

I thought of it when I heard the recording on your stereo.

My little joke, she said.

Mischievous, I said. Aurora told me once that "the Goldberg variations" was a private joke between her and her father.

I think it was, Consuela said. Jack had a patient named Goldberg. The variations referred to her. Something sexual no doubt.

Sounds like it, I said.

We sat in silence drinking coffee. I looked at my watch, calculating the time it would take to drive to my hotel in Nicosia. I was leaving on the morning plane to Athens and then to Vienna before returning to New York. I was suddenly sorry that I had come. It was a mistake to try to bridge forty years in a single evening. We had not known each other well then, and the years had not improved matters. We were truly strangers to each other. That afternoon in Lincoln Park was a loose end that would stay loose, a detail of personal history. Still, I had come a long way to see Consuela.

She said, Wils, why are you here? You didn't answer my question.

I knew where you lived, I said. I wanted to say hello.

Nonsense, she said.

All right, I said. Do you know what happened between me and Aurora?

She said, Ask her. Write her a letter.

I said, I never saw her again. I wrote but she didn't answer.

She left almost immediately for Barnard, Consuela said. The day after the funeral.

When you walked down the aisle together, I reminded her.

Her idea, Consuela said. Aurora said we'd been through a shipwreck. We were together in the lifeboat whether we wanted to be or not. And after that, we wouldn't ever see each other again.

I thought it was heroic, the two of you together, facing them down.

You would, she said with a ghost of a smile.

I wish I could have been of some help.

Yes, she said, her ghost smile still in place. I know. But that conflict was not ready for resolution.

Did she think I betrayed her?

I don't know what she thought. Betrayed would not be the word, though. I think she drew a line between things, and you were on the Before side of the line. What she thought came After is anyone's guess. But it wasn't going to be you, Wils. Chicago was not in her future. Chicago was yesterday. Aurora was a very strong-willed girl. She had a broken heart. Her father was dead. She was alone. She knew she would have to make her own way.

What a shame, I said.

Give it a rest, Wils, Consuela said in a voice approximating Aurora's. The candles began to gutter so that we were sitting in near darkness. She refilled the thimbles and lit a cigarette, the flare of the match illuminating tears in the corners of her eyes. After the shipwreck, Consuela said, Aurora told me she would always be alone. That was her fate. It was written.

Foreordained, I said.

That was what she believed, Consuela said. So she went away.

I'm sorry, Connie.

She shrugged, tobacco smoke spilling from her mouth, a failed smoke ring.

I have no right to ask these questions, and now I've upset you.

You have every right, she said. We all have rights. Isn't that what you believe in America? Consuela's words were slurred around the edges and I realized that she was tight.

I said, Why did Jack kill himself?

She shook her head. Her hand went to the button in her ear.

I said again, louder, Can you tell me why—

I heard what you said. I don't like the question and I don't know the answer.

You must have a guess. Was it something that happened in the war?

I'm an old woman, she said. I've had too much to drink. I'm out of guesses. It was a long, long, long time ago. Certainly the war was in him and all around him but I don't know what was in his heart. Maybe Jack got tired. People do.

The argument, I said. What was that about?

She gave me a baffled look. Why, we were arguing about Aurora, of course.

You were arguing about Aurora?

I thought she was too involved with you. And Jack was too involved with her, always applauding the decisions she was making for herself. He disagreed. He didn't want Aurora to miss out on things. His words, "miss out." And so he was always talking about her life at school and after hours and I didn't like it. Also, I wanted a child of my own and Jack didn't want to give me one. Those were the two main lines of the argument. Went

248

on for hours, so as you might imagine there were other elements. I don't choose to remember them. I did most of the talking because Jack preferred silence to talk. Except when he was talking about Aurora. He got his knocks in but there were fewer of them. It was Jack who insisted that the argument was actually about virtue. I was selfish. He wasn't selfish. Jack insisted I had no idea what sort of man he was, nor the sort of girl Aurora was. I lacked American insight. But Jack knew nothing of women, not the smallest thing. And beyond that I will not go. And all this time Aurora was listening, writing in that wretched little book she carried around. Satisfied now?

No, I said.

I didn't think you would be.

Satisfaction doesn't come into it, I said.

Whatever you want to call it, Consuela said.

I don't want to call it satisfaction.

It's late, she said. I'm tired.

There was a note, I said.

Consuela sighed. Yes, Wils, there was a note. She drained her thimble of cognac and followed it with a sip of coffee, the cup rattling in the saucer. I thought she was going to make me ask her directly what the note said and I was determined not to do that. All my life I have trained myself to ask the awkward question, the one that went to the heart of the matter. You pulled on your bully's face and waited until the answer came, as eventually it always did. But on this occasion I said nothing more, the silence between us lengthening until it seemed to surround the known world. Even the insects paused. Consuela rose, fussing with her earpiece. She hesitated a moment, then looked away from me and said softly, "Farewell the tranquil mind. Put out the light."

It's on his gravestone, she said.

Aurora's decision. I didn't approve.

They're lines from *Othello,* I said.

Yes, she said. I suppose they are.

The time was near midnight. I drove to a café on the quay at Famagusta. I knew it from previous visits. I remembered men playing backgammon and a cheerful ambiance generally. I sat at a table on the sidewalk and watched the boats rock at anchor. I was thinking about memories, memories told, memories kept, memories that meant one thing to you and something else to another. They were incomplete, reduced or enhanced, worn smooth from frequent handling, like a lucky coin in your pocket. Famagusta was a city of memory, one civilization laid atop another; and I suddenly thought of Prince Chigi's many-storied palazzo in Rome. In Famagusta there were remains of Egyptians, Greeks, Macedonians, Venetians, Genoese, Ottomans, and British. Probably there were others, nationalities long vanished. I imagined that within a short distance of where I sat there were reminders of all the visitors, a fallen column, a cobbled street or a ruined bathhouse, a stable or a square, and of course the lost ships at sea. Substitute memory for architecture and human beings resembled cities. People came into your life without warning, stayed awhile, and went away, always leaving something of themselves behind, a look, a word or a phrase, a gesture. They left their mark and remembering them was a way of remembering yourself at a certain age, nineteen, say, or forty-one, and how you played the hand you were dealt, how attentive you were to the fall of the cards, the bets, and the stakes. How receptive you were to refugees. An oily breeze came off the water, an exhausted whisper of a breeze from the east. The weather was changing. Famagusta was exhausted, overrun again and again, crowded with memories. The poet had insisted to me that its people had no loyalty toward Cyprus. They had lost confidence in it. Whatever affection they had for Cypriot soil or Cypriot history or Cypriot culture had been exhausted and so they lived by myth, in order to successfully account for themselves. On the divided island they had no language of their own, only the imports from Greece and Turkey. They did not have the means to express themselves *au fond*. Of course the poet was eccentric. He may have been mistaken. Poets always made too much of things. I wondered what sort of life Aurora had found for herself in her nomadic travels and in her work, and if she was still alone or had found someone. Probably a novelist was never alone because she would have all those characters inside her head, a self-created repertory company to keep her occupied — and wouldn't that be sufficient until night fell? I watched light play upon the surface of the water, the light fracturing as the water moved, slack tide. Inside the café, men were shouting at one another, some backgammon argument. And then the shouts subsided and once again I heard the rattle of the dice cup. In a little while the lights went out one by one and I was alone in the silence of the port at Famagusta.

The American Ambassador

"A splendid book...thoughtful and fast-moving." — *New York Times*

This riveting tale of suspense also serves as a meditation on the fragility of Western values in an age of terrorism.

ISBN 0-618-34078-5

The Congressman Who Loved Flaubert: 21 Stories and Novellas

"Masterpieces of balance, focus, and hidden order." — *Chicago Tribune*

Some of Ward Just's best short fiction, these accounts of life behind the scenes in places of power have the ring of flawless authenticity. ISBN 0-395-90137-5

A Dangerous Friend

A New York Times Notable Book, selected as a Best Book of the Year by *Time* and the *Los Angeles Times*

Set in Indochina in 1965, Just's twelfth novel is the story of an American civilian caught in a political and spiritual crossfire. ISBN 0-618-05670-x

Echo House

Finalist for the National Book Award

Echo House is an epic chronicle of three generations of Washington power brokers and the women who love them.

ISBN 0-395-90138-3

Jack Gance

"Just has earned a space on the shelf just below Edith Wharton and Henry James." — *Newsweek*

This passionate tale of Washington politics reveals the hard price one man pays on the route to becoming a U.S. senator. ISBN 0-395-85602-7

The Translator

"Intelligent, allusive [and] richly, persuasively textured." — *Washington Post Book World*

At the breakup of the European cold war order, the hopes, dreams, and life of an expatriate in Paris are forever changed.

ISBN 0-395-95766-4

An Unfinished Season

A New York Times Notable Book
Winner of the Heartland Prize

Set in Eisenhower-era Chicago, this brilliant work evokes a city, an epoch, and a shift in ideals through the closely observed story of a nineteen-year-old reporter. ISBN 0-618-56828-x

The Weather in Berlin

A New York Times Notable Book and a Los Angeles Times Best Book of the Year

In this atmospheric novel, a famous American director travels to post-Wall Germany to rekindle his lost genius.

ISBN 0-618-34079-3